KILLER

BY

NUMBER

OTHER BOOKS BY
JEFF VANOUDENHOVE

THE DARK SERIES:

** *Book 1 - DARK PLACE*

** *Book 2 - DARK LANE*

** *Book 3 - DARK QUEEN*

** *Book 4 - DARK CHILD*

** *Book 5 - THE FINAL DARK*

SCREAMS IN THE DARK AND OTHER TWISTED TALES

THE ALPHABET KILLER

JUST LISTEN

THE LETTER MAN

EMMA

For signed copies of the author's books, please visit:
javo-publication.square.site

KILLER BY NUMBER

JEFF VANOUDENHOVE

Javo PUBLICATION

Westfield, MA

JAVO Publication
Westfield, Massachusetts 01085

ISBN
979-8-9918888-3-7

Library of Congress Control Number:
2025908453

Cover design by Jeff VanOudenhove

*For Brittany
Who has always shown such unwavering support for my
writing*

Immerse yourself in the series!

Book 1
The Alphabet Killer

Book 2
The Letter Man

Better in the Dark

They had to have known it would come to this. It was destiny. It was *MY* destiny. They created this monster in that lab of steel bars and concrete, hiding me away from the world that despised me for what I'd done. Couldn't they see I did it all for them? I was the good guy - the hero taking out the trash. I was cleaning the shit stains from the streets – making the city a better place. They didn't want that. They didn't understand. Now, they'd have to live with the consequences. They wanted me to be the bad guy? I'll give them the bad guy. I'll give them the *worst* guy they've ever seen.

The Alphabet Killer was another life, a forgotten relic whose time was cut short before his final masterpiece could be realized. But he lived by a code, killing only those who'd given up on themselves, those wretches who lingered on the edge, stealing the precious oxygen from those who deserved to live. They *wanted* to die but weren't strong enough to do it themselves. The Alphabet Killer helped them along. But I've now put him behind me like I've done with so many things - just as I have done with my so-called successor.

The very idea that The Alphabet Killer had spawned such a crazed lunatic as The Letter Man disgusts me. His twisted ways distorted and tainted everything I had achieved. His warped sense of killing, continuing on the path I had begun, was distasteful. The legacy of The Alphabet Killer was, at that moment, set ablaze, his ashes scattered to the wind, his existence wiped clean from the city's collective thoughts. It was fitting that The Letter Man met his end at the hands of an honorable officer of the Southbridge PD.

Like my father before him, Mick was a dedicated detective on the force, striving to keep his city from crumbling to the ground under the heavy heel of the criminals that infested the streets like cockroaches. I'm sure he never imagined he'd have been thrown into the fire as quickly as he had. I thought he'd have burned faster than flash paper. Mick surprised me. He took the wannabe copycat down, though I had to do some hand-holding along the way. It's too bad my dad didn't survive to see Mick rise into his new role as successfully as he has. He would have been proud of ol' "Uncle Mick." Maybe he would have been proud of me, too.

None of that matters now. It's in the past. I don't need my father's pride, nor do I need his pity. The system kept me in the dark for too long. Perhaps that was their saving grace. I'll make them wish I was still there.

I bet *she* wishes the same.

I stare at the pitiful thing across from me, her lips quivering, even with the gag in place, bound tightly around her head. Her tears have long since dried, the blindfold soaked with salty regret. Regret that she found herself a victim, with me as her host. She has played her role well, and I will continue to play mine.

I watch as she dips her chin to her chest, her spirit broken, her struggle at an end. She has nothing left. Her shoulders drop in agony, having spent the last hour wrestling with the cord rope that has kept her arms bound behind the chair. She has no idea I've shared her company the entire time, watching her every move, listening to every whimper. I sat in silence, the worn oak table between us, allowing myself the pleasure to take it all in – the sound of her cries, the taste of the fear that lingers in the air around her. It was only a matter of time before she gave up hope - before she relinquished the idea that someone would come to her rescue. It isn't in the cards. She knows that now; she's given up. She has succumbed to her destiny.

Round one was to soften her – to see if I would break her. She is more resilient than I gave her credit for. That's more fun for me. I exhale heavily from my mouth, no longer trying to conceal my presence. The pretty, young blonde lifts her head in curiosity and fear, perhaps wondering if she had just heard the breath of her savior or captor. I'm almost sorry I have to break the news to her. Almost.

"I'm sorry you had to be the first," I say, building upon the fear. "It's nothing personal."

She wriggles and tugs at her restraints, a final surge of energy. She's good. She is just how I want her to be. Her screams exit her lips as barely audible mumbles through the ball of cloth wedged in her mouth. Her nostrils flare as snot oozes from her nose. I stand and lean forward, swiping my thumb above her upper lip to remove the undesirable mucus. She flinches and shakes her head at my touch. Her body begins trembling again as it had when she first awoke. I hear her legs rubbing together, straining against the bonds that hold her ankles and knees in place - a wasted effort. She's not going anywhere.

I slide my thumb along the top of the table, smearing the nasal fluid across its surface. What little amount remains on my skin finds its way to my tongue as I lick away the residual snot. That is what I have become. That is what they have made me. Though I have freed myself – not only from the physical cage they had locked me in but from the prison in my head that had kept me from recognizing my full potential - it is they, the ones who would rather I rot in the dark, who have unleashed me upon the world. I won't squander the opportunity.

"There's no use in struggling," I say gently to her. "You should save your strength. It's going to be a long night."

Here, in the bowels of the apartment building, the boiler roars, sending heat out in waves. Sweat drips down the side of my neck and mingles with the hem of my shirt. It's a comfort to me - not so much for my guest.

Though I can't see them fall from her eyes, I know the tears have begun anew, the blindfold absorbing them before they can escape from under the fabric. The scared young woman mutters something unintelligible into the cloth. I know it was a question. I'd been asked it before when I was my other self. *"Why are you doing this?"* It's a nice touch. I could lie and tell her I'm ridding the streets of evil, cleansing the city of those undeserving of life, but this one.., this sweet, innocent, trusting girl, has done no wrong. She was just a lone body, a lonely soul in the wrong place at the wrong time. Or, for me, the right place at the right time. Every killer needs a victim; she would do.

This isn't about cleaning the streets of filthy scum or trying to impress my dad. I've taken a different path. I have darker intentions. I am reborn. I am set on my mission. This is purely for fun.

I grasp the knife that rests on the table, and I walk to her side. I grip the blindfold and slide it from her eyes, resting it atop her head. It was only a formality. She already knows her tormentor. She knows who I am. She squints, turning away from the fire's light while her eyes adjust. When she is able, she turns her stare to me and gazes into my eyes – into the eyes of a monster. I show no emotion. How can I? She is one of them – those who have created me. But she serves a deeper purpose. She is but the first, the catalyst in my game. She has done well thus far, though I am not finished with her yet. I do hope she can keep pace with me. She will deliver my message, and the hunt will be on.

The woman's terrified look tells me she thinks I'd be better in the dark. I think she's wrong. I offer her a smile, though she takes no comfort in it. Yes, this one will deliver my message. Of that, I have no doubt. I flash my knife to her so she understands my intentions.

"Shall we begin again?"

Chapter 1

The Hardest Hit

I pressed my hand to my left cheekbone, my body bent over from the shock. Marion placed her hand on my back, keeping me from falling from the concrete step. I'd pretend she was checking on my condition, but she wasn't that type of woman. I was fine, by the way. It's nothing that hasn't been dealt to me before. I had to hand it to Mick; he had one hell of a right cross. I deserved it.

"You son of a bitch!" Mick yelled. "How could you? You had us all believing you were dead."

It served me right for showing up on his doorstep unexpectedly after having been "dead" for nearly three years.

"I know, kid. I know." I stood and raised my hands in front of my chest. "Take it easy; I'm unarmed."

"You.., you..," he stumbled for the words, then charged at me.

I stiffened, expecting the worst. Instead, Mick wrapped his arms around me, squeezing the ever-loving hell out of me.

"This doesn't change anything," he said, holding me tight. "You're still an asshole."

"I tell him that every other day," Marion quipped.

Mick released me and stepped back. He glanced at Marion and then back at me, shaking his head.

"I think I'm going to be sick."

He bent over, supporting himself by clutching his knees.

"Yeah, well, not on my shoes, huh," I said, trying to keep things light.

"Mick," Marion began, "can we take this inside?"

Mick pushed himself upright, still looking piqued. "Fuck! Fuck!" He turned and walked back through the door, leaving it open. I think that meant we were welcome, even if we weren't.

I followed Marion inside and closed the door behind me. Mick was still facing away, his hands cupped over his face.

Marion started. "Mick..,"

"Don't, Agent Hayes," Mick cut her off. He dropped his hands and turned, a look of disgust and confusion plastered on his face. "What the fuck?" his eyes shifted to mine. "You're alive? I was at your funeral, Jimmy. We buried you. What the fuck is going on?"

"I'm sorry I couldn't tell you, kid."

"Enough with the goddamn 'kid' stuff," Mick roared. "You faked your death? Is this some sick joke? Who knew about this? Lieutenant Garrett? The Chief?"

"Nobody knew about it," I replied. "They couldn't. Only Marion, Karen, and the funeral director. And now you."

His eyes widened. "Karen knew?" he questioned.

"She arranged for the closed casket," I answered.

"She never said…" He fell silent, backed up, and sat on the couch, bringing his hands to his forehead. "I can't believe this. Why?" He dropped his hands and looked up at me and Marion. "Why?"

I never thought I'd have to tell the story. It was supposed to remain dead and buried – like me. But that was before this started up again. Before Ben..,

I couldn't let him continue. He needed to be stopped. He's *my* kid, and I needed to be the one to stop him. But I couldn't do it alone. Mick had visited with him in prison. He had conversations with him. And judging by the letter I spotted on the table when I walked in, Ben had also been in contact with Mick.

"I'm glad you're sitting," I said. "I'll give you the abridged version."

I sat in the cushioned chair to the left of the couch. Marion sat beside Mick on his left. Perhaps it was to comfort him, or maybe it was to keep him at bay should he decide to lash out at me. If that were the case, I didn't like his odds; I'd seen how fierce that woman could be.

I laid it all out for Mick, starting with that day on the rooftop when I realized my life had been shit. I died that day, though I had already been dead inside long before. I had nothing. I lost the one person I cared about. No.., the one person I was *supposed to* care about. Ben should have been my life. Instead, it was the damn job. It had always been the job. I needed to get out. Death was an easy solution. I could have stayed there. Marion brought me back from the brink. Without her, my life meant nothing. I couldn't go back. I couldn't go back to being the uncaring son of a bitch whose work consumed everything. That's what would have happened if I didn't stay "dead." I wasn't proud of my decision. Or maybe.., maybe I was.

"And that's all there is to it," I finished. "I wanted.., no, I *needed* to get out. It was either my life or my soul."

Silence gripped the moment. Mick sat motionless, his eyes glossed over. I wasn't sure if he'd heard a word I'd said. I glanced at Marion and then back at Mick. I hoped he'd say something. I'd be damned if I was starting over again.

"I.., I can't believe I'm looking at you right now," Mick responded. "You're in front of me. Alive! I don't know what to do with this. My hands are fucking shaking."

Marion reached over and grabbed one of those shaking hands and squeezed.

"We know it's a lot to take in, Mick."

Mick ripped his hand from hers and stood.

"A lot to take in?" he shouted. "Jesus Christ - if that's not the understatement of the year." He took a few steps away and then turned, continuing his rant. "Three years! It's been three years, Jimmy! You were dead! What the hell am I supposed to do with this? Why didn't you stay dead? Why are you here? Why now?"

I reached forward and snatched the letter from the table, holding it up for him.

"I think you know why."

"Ben?" he questioned. "I just received that this morning. How could you have known?"

"I didn't. I only know of the victim who showed up at the FBI's field office."

"What? What victim?"

Marion took it from there while I read the letter.

"Two days ago, our offices received a call from a woman who claimed she'd been held captive by The Alphabet Killer. We thought she was someone from three years ago who had gotten away and was finally ready to tell her story. She said we misunderstood. He took her only five days ago."

"Five days ago?" Mick questioned.

"That's right. Ben took this woman, tied her up, and tortured her for six hours."

"How do you know it was Ben?"

I dropped the letter I'd been reading onto the table and answered, "Because he didn't attempt to hide his identity. Ben let her see him. He let her watch everything he did to her. He wanted her to see the monster he'd become. She recognized him right away as The Alphabet Killer. She knew she was as good as dead."

"But she got away?" Mick asked.

"No," Marion replied. "Ben let her go."

"He let her go? Why would he do that? He must have known she'd go to the authorities."

"He wanted her to," I responded.

Mick flashed a confused look.

"He told her he was letting her live because he wanted her to contact the FBI," Marion said. "This woman has a younger brother and sister she cares for. Ben told her that if she went to the police instead, one of her siblings would be next. When she called, she asked to speak with me specifically. She said she had a message for me. I sent a car to pick her up."

"What was the message?" Mick asked.

Marion reached into her jacket pocket and pulled out a folded envelope. It had her name scribbled on it. She looked at me as if questioning whether she should share the information. I nodded. It was my idea to involve Mick in the first place. She didn't like the idea, but Ben is *my* son. I'd be damned if I didn't get some say in the matter. She handed Mick the envelope. He opened the flap and pulled out the letter, his eyes widening with each sentence.

This rests on your shoulders now, Special Agent Hayes. I will no longer carry the burden of my father's death. It is you who got him killed. You distracted him from his duty. He couldn't focus on his responsibility as the city's finest detective. And now, the people of Southbridge will pay for your mistake. You took their hero. Now, no one can save them – not even you.

Consider this a warning. Vivian is alive because I let her live. Call her "Victim Ø." The rest will not be as fortunate. You've awakened the monster within me, and I will do what I must to live up to that expectation. The days, dear Hayes, are numbered. And numbers are what I'm all about. Don't get in my way.

Mick looked up from the paper, wide-eyed and fear-stricken. "He's completely lost it."

"We don't think he has," Marion said, stripping the letter and envelope from Mick's hands. "He knows exactly what he's doing. He stated that he didn't want me getting in the way, yet he sent the woman he tortured to deliver the message to me. Seems counter-productive, wouldn't you say?"

"What are you suggesting?" Mick asked. "That he wants you to catch him?"

"I'm suggesting that he..," she stumbled with her words.

"He wants Special Agent Hayes dead," I spoke up. "He wants revenge. It's that simple."

"Fuck!" Mick gasped. "You really think he's that messed up as to try to kill an FBI agent?"

"He's got nothing left to lose," Marion replied. "He's lost his father, his mother, his uncle. If he gets caught, he's already serving multiple life sentences. His life is meaningless. But something that would give it meaning is to kill the one person he believes responsible for his father's.., for his *hero's* death. Me."

"And I'm sure as shit not going to let that happen," I added.

"And what about this Vivian woman?" Mick asked. "The one he called 'Victim Ø'?"

"She's being held for observation at a medical facility near our field office," Marion replied. "And, quite frankly, she's afraid to leave. That son of a bitch did a number on her." She turned her stare to me. "Sorry, Jim. I can't pretend just because he's your son."

I felt my chin dip as I averted my eyes. "Yeah."

"So, if he wants you dead," Mick stated, pointing at Marion, "why all the threats about killing other people? Why not just go after you?"

"Don't you get it, ki.., Mick?" I almost slipped out of habit. "This is a game to him. It's always been a game." I nodded to Marion. "Show him."

Marion reached back into her pocket and pulled out three keyboard keys. She rolled them around her palm with her fingers before handing them to Mick. Mick studied them for a moment before commenting.

"The numbers 1, 3 and 4. What are they supposed to mean?"

"That's what we don't know," Marion answered. "They were in the envelope with the letter. No explanation. He wrote in his message that numbers are what he's all about. He's playing a game with us to which only he knows the rules."

"It's gotta be an area code," Mick jumped in. "413 – Western Mass. Makes sense."

"We thought that," I responded, "but we can't be sure. That doesn't tell us anything. There's gotta be something more to it."

"Well, how the hell am I supposed to know?" Mick raised his voice. "I didn't even know *you* were alive. How am I supposed to figure out some numbers game? And what does this mean now – you being here? Are you planning on showing up at the station as if nothing ever happened?"

"Nobody can know about me, Mick."

"So, what? I'm supposed to bury this - pretend I never saw you? Jesus, Jimmy! How the hell am I supposed to do that?"

"You'll figure it out," I said.

"Then why even come here at all? Why me?"

"Because you were the last person in contact with Ben. You interviewed him on multiple occasions. You got to see how he thinks – how his mind works."

"If Special Agent Hayes told you all that," Mick responded, "then she must have also told you he only offered up what he wanted us to know. He's smart, Jimmy. Smarter than me."

"He's smarter than me, too, Mick. But maybe if we work together..,"

"Fuck you!" Mick blurted. "You were like a brother to me. Then you go and pull this shit. You couldn't confide in me, Jimmy? You make me believe my best friend was dead for three years, and then you show up thinking I would want to work a case with you. Fuck you! Why don't you tell me what you're *really* here for?"

He was upset with me. He had every right. He was like a kid brother to me, and I held him at arm's length. I could have told him. Maybe I *should* have told him. Shit. Maybe Marion was right. She said this was a mistake – that I'd only be compromising my situation. But here's the thing.., that's my kid out there. He's my responsibility. I couldn't end all of this while I was alive - maybe I could do it while I was dead. And Mick, well, he was the closest thing to family Ben had left. I had to let him know.

"I came here to warn you, Mick."

"Warn me?"

"This doesn't play out well. The letter you received confirms it. Ben doesn't care who he hurts anymore. He won't hesitate to kill even those closest to him. I thought you should know. The people in this city aren't safe. I can feel it. It's going to get bad, Mick. *Really* bad. I need you to keep sharp. For Gina and your little girl."

Just then, Mick's phone blared. He pulled it from his front pocket and put it to his ear.

"It's Mick," he began. "What? Shit! When? Okay. I'll be right there."

He hung up, his face telling the story.

"What is it?" Marion asked, already knowing the answer.

"A body. A woman was found dead in Bentley's Bakery."

"You think Ben had something to do with it?" I asked.

Mick's eyes shifted between me and Marion. "She had the number 7 carved into her stomach."

Chapter 2

The Sweet Smell of Death

How was I supposed to keep focused on my job? The friend I thought was dead shows up on my doorstep like it's an average, everyday occurrence. And I'm somehow supposed to keep my mouth shut about it. Don't get me wrong, I was glad he was alive, but Fuck. How could he do that to me?

I pulled up behind Lieutenant Garrett's vehicle in front of the bakery. I could see Barry, the medical examiner, through the front window. He was discussing something with Vera and her sidekick, Danny. Lieu was near the front door, barking orders to the two uniformed officers out front. There weren't any news crews around yet, which was good. They only ever got in the way.

I stepped from my car and nodded to the two officers. They stood at either side of the door, their posture rigid as if they were medieval knights standing guard for their king outside the entrance to a castle. I entered the bakery, the smell of fresh cakes, tarts, and pies overpowered by the stark smell of death. Lieutenant Garrett pinched the hair of his graying mustache between his index finger and thumb, glaring at the bloody body of the woman on the floor in front of the pastry display. Seeing her appearance, I wondered how I would ever look at another danish again.

"Hey, Lieu," I began. "When you called me, I didn't realize you'd be on scene."

"I've got one good detective, one mediocre detective, and two lousy detectives. There is no punchline to that joke. My mediocre detective is on vacation, and I don't trust the lousy detectives enough to give them this assignment. That leaves you and me."

If I understood that right, the lieutenant just paid me a compliment. Like I need that kind of pressure after what I've been through already today. And it's still early.

"So, what's the story with this one?" I asked, pointing to the deceased, though I knew more than I let on. "Who called it in?"

"A sixteen-year-old kid reporting for work this morning found the body. The girl ran back outside to her mother, who then called 911. The poor kid will probably never recover after seeing this shit. I'll let Barry fill you in on the rest of it. I've gotta get some air."

He stepped away, and I looked to Barry for answers.

"We've got an interesting one here, Detective," Barry stated.

"And how is that?" I questioned.

"No blood anywhere other than what you see on the victim. She wasn't killed here."

"You're telling me her killer took the time to bring her body here and dump it where we could find it?"

"That's my initial thought, yes."

"Why do you suppose they'd go through all that effort?"

Just then, a voice chimed in behind me in the doorway.

"He's sending a message."

We all turned and saw Special Agent Hayes standing firm, her arms crossed about her chest. She was looking as confident as could be. Lieutenant Garrett appeared over her shoulder, his eyes narrowed with skepticism.

"What the shit?" he expressed. "You goddamn feds sure know how to make an entrance."

Special Agent Hayes shifted sideways to let the lieutenant squeeze by, smiling at him as she did.

"Lieutenant Garrett," she greeted, nodding her head.

"Hayes," he replied in his gruff voice. "What the hell is the FBI doing here? Wait. Here's a better question; how the hell did you hear about this shit so fast?"

Vera jumped at the chance. "I told you before, Frank. Big Brother watches our every move. They've got eyes and ears everywhere."

"Enough with the conspiracy theory bullshit, Vera. And how many times do I have to tell you – it's *Lieutenant*, for Christ's sake."

"Yeah, yeah," she responded, flopping her hand forward, brushing off his comment.

The lieutenant turned his attention back to Hayes. "So, how about it? Not that I'm against seeing something a little more attractive than a dead woman at a crime scene, but would you mind filling me in on what you're doing here?"

"I was coming to see you on another matter," Hayes replied. "Then I heard about this over the scanner and thought I'd check it out myself. Now, it seems the two matters may be related."

"Well, doesn't that just brighten my day," Lieutenant Garrett responded sarcastically. "What's the other matter?"

Hayes pulled out the familiar letter she'd shown me and handed it to the lieutenant. While he read through it, I leaned into her and whispered, "Where's Jimmy?"

She whispered back, "I dropped him off at our hotel."

Lieutenant Garrett looked up from the paper just as we separated. "What the fuck is this?"

"I figured you'd have questions," Hayes replied.

"Oh, I've got some questions, all right. Ben Haddick sent you this?"

"Not exactly. It was delivered to us by the woman mentioned in the letter. Vivian."

"And who is this Vivian woman?"

"She's an anesthesiologist at St. Regis Children's Hospital, and right now.., someone who was very lucky. Ben held her captive and tortured her. When he let her go, he told her to deliver that letter to me. He wanted me to know it's not over, that it's starting again. Vivian is lucky to be alive. We believe her to be his first victim since his escape from prison, used as a pawn to gain our attention. It looks like we've now got ourselves a second victim; this one, not so lucky. He's got our attention now."

"In case you hadn't noticed, Agent Hayes," the lieutenant said, pointing toward the dead woman, "that's not a letter on the woman's stomach; it's a goddamn number."

I had to jump in.

"I received a letter from Ben, too."

"What the Christ, Dooley?" Lieutenant Garrett roared.

"It was just this morning before you called. It said something about letters being finite, but numbers going on forever, or some shit."

"Goddammit!" the lieutenant yelled. "When is this shit going to end?"

Vera tapped Barry on the arm to get his attention.

"Hey, gingerbread," she said, referring to his red hair, "got any popcorn? This is getting juicy."

I shot her a stern look and shook my head to let her know this wasn't the best time for her inappropriate humor. Actually, there was never a good time for Vera's brand of humor.

"These were in the envelope along with the letter," Hayes added, pulling her hand from her pocket. She handed the three keyboard keys to Lieutenant Garrett. He studied them and then shook his head.

"1, 4, and 3? What's that supposed to mean? I'm no Einstein, but the numbers add up to eight. This woman has a 7 cut into her stomach."

"That's what we're trying to figure out, Lieutenant," she replied. "Mr. Hinkman," she continued, turning to the medical examiner, "what can you tell us about the victim?"

"Well..," he began, "not to sound insensitive, but.., she's dead. According to her driver's license, her name is Judith Bentley. She's thirty-six years old. Looking at the inspection report on the wall," he pointed to a framed document behind the counter, "I'd say she's the proprietor of this fine establishment. Hence the name - Bentley's Bakery. She has multiple contusions along her arms where she was forcefully grabbed and held. There are ligature marks around her wrists and ankles, suggesting she was tied up. There's some bruising and swelling around her face, along with some gash marks on her lips and gums. She was struck several times by her captor."

"Jesus," I let out.

"Yeah," Barry responded. "If it *was* Ben..,"

"It *was*," Hayes blurted.

"Right," Barry continued. "Well.., I'd say he's gained a bit of a mean streak."

"You mean his previous kills didn't already tell you that?" the lieutenant barked.

"You know what I mean, Lieutenant. Anyway, continuing.., Judith here has three stab wounds to her back and rear shoulders and one in her left upper thigh. The kill shot, if you will. The weapon, most likely a knife by the look of the wounds, pierced her femoral artery. She would have bled out in minutes. But, as you can see from our surroundings, there's no blood on the floor or walls. The blood on her clothes has been dry for some time. She died elsewhere, and then, she was brought here."

"What about the 7?" I asked.

"Yeah, the 7," Barry answered, sounding perplexed. "That actually wasn't cut into her as the lieutenant suspected; it was seared into her flesh, perhaps, from a branding iron or similar tool from the look of it."

"She was burned?" Lieutenant Garrett questioned, rubbing his forehead.

"Yes. The black you see isn't old, dried blood. It's burnt flesh. Liquid pustules had formed in the wound and burst, giving the appearance of plasma expulsion."

"Fuck!" I let out. "Tied up, beaten, stabbed, burned. The son of a bitch who did this is sick."

"What about you, Vera?" Agent Hayes inquired. "Have you found anything that could link Ben to the murder? Hair, fingerprints, sweat.., anything?"

"Danny pulled a couple of prints off the door, but I'm not expecting anything conclusive from those. The vic did have some skin under her nails that I scraped out. It looks like she put up a fight, however short-lived it may have been. Good for her. I won't know anything for sure until I get the sample back to the lab for processing. Oh, and based on the tan line on her left ring finger, it looks like she's missing a ring. Perhaps an engagement ring or wedding ring. It could have fallen off during a struggle, or it could have been stolen. Other than that, everything's clean. I mean, except for her blood-stained clothes."

"Did anybody find a note or something?" the lieutenant asked. "Ben, the little prick, always left a note after each of his kills."

I watched Vera and Barry look at each other and shrug their shoulders. That meant no note.

"Um, guys," a voice said from behind the counter. We all looked over to see Danny curiously staring at the register. "What about this?"

Special Agent Hayes was closest to the counter's entryway. She walked to the register, glanced at the touchscreen, and shook her head.

"Well, what is it?" Lieu bellowed.

"The numbers 2 and 1. And what looks to be a partial print."

"Just great," he griped. "More fucking numbers. We don't even know what the first three meant."

"Actually," I stated confidently, "I think I just figured it out."

"Care to enlighten us?" Hayes requested.

"Ben was leading us here. The numbers 1, 3, and 4. Or, 3.14. That's Pi. Look where we're standing. We're in a bakery. Pies. He was giving us a clue to his kill."

"So then, the numbers on the register could be a clue to his next target," Vera yelled. "I love this puzzle shit."

"Vera!" Lieutenant Garrett shouted.

"Sorry, Lieu."

Hayes patted Danny on his upper arm, "I'm going to need you to pull that print from the register screen."

Danny nodded.

"I *know* you're not thinking about taking over this investigation, Hayes," Lieutenant Garrett began, "but we're going to have ourselves a little discussion. I want you and Mick in my office in an hour. Barry, Vera," he pointed his finger sternly at them, "I want both of your finished reports on my desk by tomorrow morning. Everything you get from the victim."

"You got it, boss man," Vera replied.

Barry remained silent and nodded.

"Jesus fucking Christ!" Lieu continued. "When will these lunatic, mother-fucking, serial killer scumbags give me a fucking break?"

Chapter 3

Warning Signs

Hayes was punctual; I had to give her that. She came striding through the bureau door a few minutes before we were to meet with Lieutenant Garrett. I was glad she showed up when she did. I had no intention of going into Lieu's office alone. I was still struggling with the idea of Jimmy being alive. I know they told me I had to keep that to myself, it being an FBI matter, but shit. How could I keep something like that under wraps? Why did they have to involve me at all? It's not like I had a poker face.

Hayes glanced over at me sitting behind my desk and nodded her head toward Lieu's closed door as if she were already calling the shots. Same old Hayes, I guess. I could see through Lieu's semi-opened blinds that he was at his desk writing something. That didn't stop Agent Hayes, however. She barged right in without knocking. Sure, go ahead, stick your head in the lion's mouth before I even have a chance to get up from my seat. Maybe he'll no longer be hungry by the time I get there.

I heard Lieu bark, "Knocking would be a better idea." On my way over, I watched Hayes cross her arms about her chest, unfazed by his remark. How could I have forgotten? Lieu might act like he's king of the jungle to the rest of us, but he was of little significance to a big-game hunter like her.

I stepped to the open door, but unlike Hayes, I knocked on the metal frame to announce my arrival.

"Get in here, Dooley, and shut the door," he said curtly, waving me in.

It figured. Hayes poked the beast, but I was the helpless gazelle about to be eaten. Wasn't that always the way? I closed the door and maneuvered myself to the vacant chair on my left. I didn't bother trying to be gentlemanly to Hayes by asking if she'd like the seat. She never took me up on my offer before. I was beginning to think she never sat on the job.

"I want to know what you know," the lieutenant snapped, pointing at Agent Hayes.

That was a loaded question. I was glad he didn't ask *me*. I might not have been able to contain myself.

"You show up at my crime scene," he continued, "flashing me some numbers and handing me a letter by Ben Haddick. For Christ's sake, the kid escaped from prison six months ago. Nobody's heard a peep from him since. Your people were supposed to be all over that. Suddenly, he's sending Christmas cards to you both? I want to know what the fuck is going on here."

"What's going on," Special Agent Hayes answered, "is that Ben is back to his old ways, and his mind is even further gone than when he began. If we don't stop him, things are going to get far worse than what we saw in that bakery."

"We don't even know for sure if that *was* Ben," Lieu said.

"What's it going to take to convince you, Lieutenant?" she responded. "Ben is out there, and he's planning his next kill. Those women – Vivian, Judith – they're only the beginning."

"I think she's right, Lieu," I added. "It's not a coincidence we both received letters from Ben. And then two victims turn up? It's gotta be him."

"All right," Lieutenant Garret conceded. "Let's say I believe you. That letter you received, Hayes.., it reads as if Ben blames *you* for his father's death. Do you have any idea why he would think that?"

I wondered that same thing, so I'm glad the lieutenant asked. Agent Hayes brought her hand to her chin and gazed down at the floor. She took a deep breath and let it out. She turned her head to me and then shifted her eyes to the lieutenant.

"Jim and I.., became intimate during The Alphabet Killer case."

My eyes widened at her comment as Lieu let out an exasperated gasp. What the hell did I just hear? Jimmy and Hayes were having an affair? When Jimmy told me he was giving me the abridged version, I now understood why. Were they still together? Is that why they showed up at my door together?

"It was only one night," Hayes continued. "I knew it was a mistake to get involved during the investigation. I went to his place and told him we needed to keep things professional. Ben showed up just as I was leaving. He's a smart kid; I'm sure he picked up on the sexual tension between his father and me. That's why he blames me for 'distracting' his father."

"Well, shit!" the lieutenant said. "That explains more than I wanted to know. Fuck! So, you think the kid might be out to get you?"

"Oh, I know he's out to get me," Hayes replied.

"Then you also know you can't be anywhere around this case."

"The hell I can't. If Ben wants revenge for his father's death, I'm not lying down on this."

"I can report this to your superiors, you know."

"You won't do that," Hayes replied confidently.

"And why the hell not?"

"Because, like it or not, Ben wants me on this case." She looked at me. "He wants us *both* on this case. That's why we received his letters. And that's why we'll be working together on this."

"You'd better watch yourself, Hayes," Lieu said. "The FBI is..,"

"I'm not here in any official FBI capacity," Hayes interjected. "Not yet, anyway. But you should know that it's coming."

Since they both seemed to be ignoring me, I jumped in. "Does anyone care what I have to say about this?"

"No!" Lieu barked.

That was fast, but I wasn't letting it deter me.

"What if I don't want to be involved in this case? I *can't* be. I've been through this once already; it nearly broke me. I've got a young daughter. I don't want anything to do with this heavy shit."

"Are you a cop, Dooley?" the lieutenant questioned.

"Yes."

"Then it's too damn bad. You can't just pick and choose what you want to do. You signed up for this. We've all got a job to do, and that's to protect the citizens of this city. And need I remind you, that includes your wife and kid."

"But Lieu..,"

"I don't want to hear another word, Dooley; this is your case. Deal with it."

I sat back in my chair, crossed my arms, and pouted like a little school kid. Once I realized what I was doing, I quickly sat back up and asked, "So, what do we make of the numbers?"

Lieutenant Garrett looked up at Special Agent Hayes.

"You got anything?"

"I think we need to determine whether the number on the victim's body is in any way related to the numbers that were on the register."

"7, 2, 1," I mumbled. "2, 1, 7. It could be any combination. Or maybe it's nothing. Do those numbers mean anything to either of you?"

"Not that I can think of," Hayes answered. "But I haven't had time to process all of this yet. I need to see all the possible combinations.., maybe cross-reference them with addresses."

"We can't even be sure the numbers mean anything," Lieu spoke. "Maybe those numbers on the register were there before Ben dumped the body."

"We'll know soon enough when we get the report back from the lab," Hayes offered.

"Or when another body turns up," I added.

"That's not going to happen," Lieu said. "We need to figure out those numbers. If Ben *is* leaving us cryptic clues, then he wants us to know where he's going to be. We just need to figure it out before he kills someone else."

"If he hasn't already," I jumped in.

"You're a real fountain of positivity, ain't ya, Dooley?" Lieu said. Then he looked at Hayes. "What about this Vivian woman? Does she have any more information about Ben? Maybe he said something to her about the numbers."

"I'm going back tonight to question her," Hayes responded. "She's been pretty out of it since she arrived. I'm hoping I can squeeze something out of her. No guarantees. She's been through a lot."

"Understood. In the meantime..," he pointed his finger at me, "I hate to do this to you, Mick, but I want you to take a uniformed officer with you to deliver the bad news to Judith Bentley's family. They should hear it from you before it's plastered all over the six o'clock news. Why don't you take Carpenter."

"Let me take the new kid, Riley," I suggested.

"Why would you want the rookie?"

"Because he hasn't had to do that shit job yet. And if Hayes is right about what's coming, and we can't stop Ben, then I have a feeling Riley's going to need all the practice he can get."

Chapter 4

Compassion and Pain

The best part is watching you squirm. It's not the squirming itself that excites me, but the idea that you think you might somehow free yourself. Do you think I would allow that? You are here for a reason. I won't be denied my pleasure. You twist, you turn, but still, your bonds hold. I've had practice perfecting them over the years. There's no escape. Just as there is no escaping my wrath. But please, for my pleasure, keep trying.

You need to understand; I wasn't supposed to be like this. I was meant to be good – to DO good. When I tried to be that person, they locked me away. They had no idea. So now, I do what I want. Uncaged. My own good work. You'll get to experience it firsthand. Just as all the others have - as all those to come shall.

I watch the sweat dribble down your forehead and mingle with the cloth of your blindfold. Your cheeks are red, your lips chapped. I apologize for the heat; it's a necessary inconvenience. It's only temporary. You'll be cold soon. Very cold.

Can you sense it? Do you feel it in the air – that your end draws near? Do you know your reaper sits before you, cherishing these quiet moments before the pain begins? It won't be long now. Your death will serve a purpose. If you play nice, I might even fill you in on it.

The brunette twists her upper body, pulling her right arm with all her might, a last-ditch effort to free herself. She screams into the gag, the sound muffled and distorted, buried beneath the rumble of the furnace. The woman is unsuccessful in her attempt to break free and slouches forward, her muscles drained, her will broken. It is time.

"If it makes you feel any better," I begin. The woman snaps her head up and rapidly shakes it from side to side as if unaware of the direction from which my voice came. I enjoy it. It means she still has some fight left in her. It's not as exciting when they give up. "You aren't the first. You won't be the last."

I slide my chair out from under the table, the scraping sound of the legs against the concrete floor forcing the woman's attention forward. She knows where I am now.

"We all have a job to do," I state, rapping my knuckles on the tabletop in quick succession as I stand. "Mine is to play the role of the monster everyone wants me to be. As such, I will do things to you that you will not like. Painful things. Your job is that of the messenger. You will deliver a message to those who think they can stop me. I wish it didn't have to be like this, but there is no other way. They won't catch me, but sadly, you won't be able to tell them that."

The brunette's struggle renews, her arms and legs tugging in vain. The knots tighten with every labored movement. I slide my first two fingers along the table's surface as I slowly walk toward her. Stray tears manage to escape from under her drenched blindfold. They run for dear life down her darkened cheeks. I stand behind her and place my hands on her shoulders. I feel every tremble of her body. I lean forward, bringing my lips beside her left ear. I smell the fear emanating from her every pore. It excites me. I softly whisper to her. For the briefest of moments, her trembling stops. She understands.

I stand back upright and grab the knife that rests before her on the table. She knows something is about to happen and begins to shake again. Her whimpers go unrecognized as I slide the flat of the blade down her arm, the warm steel against her skin offering her insight into what is to come. She drops her head in despair and cries tears the world will never see.

"Shall we begin?" Adrenaline surges through me.

There is no smile on my face as I plunge the knife into her left thigh. I show no joy in what I must do. It just is. The cut is what will end her life; I've sliced the femoral artery. She will bleed out, but not before I inflict more pain upon her. A quick death will not send a strong enough message. They must learn how ruthless I can be. They will learn how right they were about the monster. They have no idea what's coming for them - but they will.

The woman convulses in pain. I squat beside her chair, watching the blood trickle from the gash in her leg as the red stain in her pants grows. Removing the knife would cause her to perish too quickly. I want her to last – to feel what I do to her. The knife stays.

"Try not to struggle too much," I tell her. "Trust me; you wouldn't want the knife to dislodge. It's keeping the bleeding to a minimum."

She immediately stops her wriggling, realizing I speak the truth. Her muscles tense as she lets out a muffled scream. If I had feelings, I'd almost feel for her.

"What say we play a game to pass the time?" I tilt my head sideways, expecting an answer that never comes. A simple head nod would have been polite. And they say *I'm* the monster?

"It's a simple game," I continue. "I will ask you a series of questions. For every answer you get right, the longer you live. For every wrong answer.., well.., you won't like the results. Now, I'd like to remove your gag, but frankly, I don't trust you not to scream. So, I'll make it easy for you. The answers are all numbers. Just nod your head the number of times you believe the answer to be. Do you understand?"

The woman keeps her head slumped to her chest, unresponsive to my question.

"I see we've gotten off to a shaky start," I tell her. I grab a clump of her hair and yank her head back. "It's not difficult; you simply nod like this." I force her head back and forth to make her understand the rules. "Now.., do you understand me?" I ask again, letting her go. She quickly bobs her head.

"Good. I knew you'd come around. Now, let's start with a simple one. What is one plus two?"

She hesitates for a moment, twisting her head to the side as if uncertain whether that was the real question, then slowly bounces her head three times.

"There. That wasn't so hard, was it?"

That one was rhetorical; I'll forgive her for the lack of a response.

"Question number two: how many stooges were there?"

The scared woman quickly nods three times. I wait. I truly hoped she'd change her mind. She doesn't.

"I'm sorry," I begin, "but the correct answer is four."

I watch as her head pops up intently. She begins shaking it from side to side, knowing what is coming. She knew the rules. Pain was the punishment.

"I'm willing to bet you thought of Larry, Moe, and Curly. Poor Shemp gets little respect, though arguably, the funniest of the bunch."

Visions of my time watching reruns of the classic show with other inmates settle upon my brain. Those were the only good times prison afforded me. The rest was pure hell, which I now deliver upon my prey.

I force her chair sideways so I can stand in front of her. I look down at my right hand, the scars of past harsh encounters displaying heavily on my knuckles. I form a fist, not out of anger but out of compassion. This woman knows what it is to feel, to hurt. The pain is a reminder she is still alive. I envy her. We are opposites, this woman and I. She is alive but will soon be dead, whereas I am dead inside and can only feel alive when others suffer by my hands.

"I'm sorry," I tell her. My words are a lie. I feel nothing as my fist slams into her left cheekbone – not once, but four times - one for each stooge. The bruise forms immediately on her face as her head flops back and to her right before dropping down to her chest. Her quiet moans tell me she is still conscious. Good. There is still more work to do.

I place my hand under her chin and slightly lift her head. I glance at the table on my left to remind myself of the various tools I have at my disposal. I feel a grin touch my lips. I look back at the woman whose head – no, whose life I hold in my hands and try my best to comfort her.

"That was a minor setback," I assure her. "You're doing great. Shall we continue?"

Chapter 5

The Wreckage

Officer Riley stared at me while I tapped my fingers on the steering wheel. I hadn't yet opened my door since we'd arrived at Judith Bentley's residence, my uncomfortable gaze through the windshield telling him all he needed to know. Whatever his expectations were when he put on that badge, this wasn't a situation for which a rookie could prepare. Riley wasn't going to enjoy the experience; none of us did. It never got any easier, no matter how much time you had on the force. And Riley, he wouldn't dare make the first move. We sat and waited until I was ready.

"I see you staring at me," I said, not subverting my gaze. "You're wondering why we're still in the car. Trust me, you'll understand in a moment. You'll want to put on your big boy pants for this." I thought I heard the rook gulp. "Let's go. Let's get this over with."

I opened my door and stepped out, waiting for Officer Riley to do the same before heading up the walkway. The silver Honda Fit in the driveway was a promising yet bittersweet sight that someone might be home to receive the horrible news. The car, the imperfect lawn with clumps of brown spots scattered throughout, the small ranch house looking in need of repair – all indications that the victim was of modest means, an average woman with an average family, like my own, whose world had just been devastated in the blink of an eye. It wasn't fair. Why did things like this have to happen?

On our way to the front door, a man peered out the window from behind tan-colored curtains draped in front of them. He looked distraught. Judith's husband? Before we even made it to the top step, the door flew open.

"Oh God! Don't tell me..,"

It hit me before I could open my mouth. My heart sank.

"Are you Judith Bentley's husband?" I asked, hating myself for what would come next.

"Yes, I am."

"I'm very sorry, sir..,"

I didn't get the rest of the words out before the man doubled over, supporting himself with his hands against his knees.

"Oh my God! Oh my God!" he cried. "What happened? She didn't come home last night."

"Sir, perhaps we can step inside?"

"Tell me!" he yelled. "Was it an accident? Was she hurt?"

"I think it's best if you sit down," I offered, though the man looked as if he was about to *fall* down instead.

"No, I'm okay," he replied, pushing himself upright and wiping away tears that had run down his cheeks. His eyes were bloodshot, and his lower lip was quivering. I glanced at Riley, his head down, his eyes glued to his shoes for fear of breaking down himself. It's the same reaction I used to have. I could handle a woman crying - as if something inside my brain somehow accepted that women were the more sensitive ones. When a man showed that kind of emotion, something I wasn't used to seeing, it gutted me. Men were supposed to be the strong ones. They didn't cry. Gina *(I love that woman)* taught me otherwise. Men.., women.., we were all the same. But as a cop, the job did a number on you. You learned to curb those emotions fast, or you wouldn't last long. As painful as the experience was, in the end, it was necessary. It would make Riley a better officer.

"May we come in?" I asked, pointing inside. The objective was not only to deliver the awful news about his wife's death but to eliminate him as a suspect in case Ben wasn't the killer. I didn't think it was the husband, but we had to cover our bases. So far, he was only the mournful spouse. If it was an act, he deserved an Academy Award.

"Yes, sorry," the man said, stepping aside. "Come in."

The rook and I walked into the living room. I took a quick glance around to see if anything stood out to me as being suspiciously unusual. I'd seen some weird shit in my time, such as a kitchen table with two place settings where there should only have been one, indicating the husband had company. A man was hiding in another room with whom the husband had been having an affair. And only a day after his wife's death.

One woman had life insurance paperwork scattered all over the coffee table. She'd been frantically filling them out, hoping to submit them before the body of her dead husband turned up.

There were all kinds. And as much as I believed Judith's killer to be Ben, for all we knew, her husband could be a sick individual who wanted her dead. These visits were always multi-faceted. Even when a suspect was in custody with no doubt of guilt, it was surprising to learn how many spouses had a hand in their partner's death.

"Sir.., your name?" I questioned.

"Jeremy," he replied. "Jeremy Bentley."

He didn't offer a hand, nor did I expect it.

"Mr. Bentley, I'm sorry to inform you that your wife's body was found in the bakery this morning."

Jeremy immediately covered his eyes as he broke down in an uncontrollable sob. Saliva dripped from the corner of his mouth and mingled with the hairs of his goatee.

"How?" He managed to squeak out. "What happened?"

I sighed heavily. "Sir, we have reason to believe someone killed your wife."

He slid his hand down from his eyes to cover his mouth.

"Killed?" he mumbled almost incoherently through his palm. "Who? Why?"

"That's what we're going to find out."

"Can I see her?"

"I'm afraid that's not possible at the moment. After the medical examiner has finished his assessment, you'll be allowed to see her."

"His assessment?"

He wasn't making this easy for me; he wasn't getting it. I had to spell it out for him.

"The autopsy."

"Oh God!" the man yelled, almost falling over. "She's being cut open."

Riley jumped to the wobbly man's aid, grabbing his forearm and shoulder and leading him to the couch. Jeremy Bentley sat and closed his eyes. He brought his shaky hands together into a praying position and pressed them against his lips. While he gathered himself, I continued.

"Mr. Bentley, I know this is difficult for you, but I have some questions that I must ask."

He opened his eyes and nodded his approval.

"You mentioned your wife hadn't come home last night. Do you happen to know where she might have been?"

"What do you mean?" he questioned. "Didn't you say Judith was at the bakery? I assumed she was there getting things ready for the morning. That place was her dream. It's all she talked about. If she wasn't here, she was there. When I went to bed, she hadn't come home yet."

"And what time was that?"

"A little before 9:00."

"And when was the last time you spoke with her or had any communication?"

"Um..," he rubbed his forehead, trying to recall. "Oh, she texted me." He pulled his cell phone from his pocket and pulled up the text. He handed me the phone. The last message from Judith was at 5:17 p.m. yesterday. It read:

```
Go ahead and warm up some leftovers for dinner.
I'll be a few more hours.
```

It was followed by two texts sent by her husband this morning:

At 6:46 a.m.
```
Did I miss you this morning, babe?
```

And then again at 8:22 a.m.
```
Honey, did you even come home last night?
```

Both went unanswered. Sometime between 5:17 last night and 6:46 this morning, Judith Bentley was taken, beaten, killed, and dumped at her bakery. How many hours of torture did she have to endure? I felt rage boiling up inside me.

"Mr. Bentley, do the numbers 2, 1, and 7 mean anything to you? Possibly in another order?"

"What? 2, 1, and 7? No. Should they?"

"I can't say," I replied. "But since they didn't immediately sound familiar to you, I'm guessing the answer is 'no.'"

"Why? What is that about?" he questioned.

"Sorry, it's something we're looking into."

"When can I see my wife?" he pleaded, indicating he'd had enough of my questioning.

I quickly typed his contact information into my phone and handed his phone back to him.

"I've got your information, Mr. Bentley. I'll have someone from the morgue call you when it's time. I'm very sorry about your wife. I promise you, we'll do everything we can to catch your wife's murderer."

The man remained silent, nodding, renewed tears streaming from his eyes. I looked at Officer Riley and nudged my head toward the door. Delivering the unfortunate news was *almost* the worst part. Walking away, knowing the wreckage we were leaving behind..,

That was the worst.

Chapter 6

Countdown

Looking at Vivian's battered face was a reminder of how far gone Ben's mind had become. He was no longer just a killer; he was brutal, violent, uncaring.., a true psychopath in every sense of the word. How did he end up like that? Not that it mattered. We needed to stop him before there were any more senseless deaths. If this woman could shed any light on what Ben was planning, we needed to get it from her. Marion was with whom Vivian was most comfortable speaking, which worked in our favor since she was also the only person among the FBI's rank who had the most experience dealing with The Alphabet Killer. If anyone could win over Vivian's trust, it was Marion.

I didn't like that I was stuck on the outside, watching the investigation unfold without being able to get my hands dirty. Relegated to only observing the questioning from behind the two-way mirror instead of being in the room with her felt like a punishment, but my situation dictated that it had to be that way. I was just thankful

Marion's superiors let me sit in on this. Even they were smart enough to know she would share the information with me anyway. Why not let me witness it for myself in case I could offer insight? Good boys.

The woman sat motionless, her arms in front of her on the table, her fingers intertwined. The bottom of a gauze bandage was visible on her right arm just below the sleeve of her short-sleeved shirt. The dressing was fresh, changed each morning to cover the blistered flesh, the wound still oozing where Ben had branded her with the number Ø. It was one of two he'd marked her with, the other on her right side just below her ribs. The thought of Ben delighting in her screams as he burned her sickened me. I could only hope she passed out from the pain and didn't give him the satisfaction.

The door to the interrogation room opened, and Special Agent Hayes walked in. She carried with her a simple notepad and pen. She pulled out the chair across from Vivian and sat down, flashing the distraught woman a comforting smile – the same smile I fell in love with.

"Hello, Miss Yarrows.., Vivian," Hayes began. "Thank you for agreeing to speak with me again. I know your time here hasn't been the most pleasant. Can I get you something to drink?"

The woman looked apprehensive, biting her lower lip nervously as she turned her head to stare at the large mirror on the wall.

"I apologize for the uncomfortable setting," Hayes continued. "And yes, we are being observed right now. It's necessary. We want to make sure we don't miss anything. You do understand, don't you?"

Vivian turned her head back forward, her eyes lowered to the table. She slowly nodded.

"Good. That drink?"

The woman subtly shook her head, declining.

"Okay then. I know you've been through a lot these past couple of days, but I'd like to ask you some more questions. Will that be all right with you?"

The woman nodded again.

"Okay, good. Now, Vivian, you said..,"

"Viv," the woman interjected.

"I'm sorry, what was that?" Hayes asked.

The woman turned her eyes up to look at Hayes. "Everyone calls me Viv."

Hayes smiled. "Very well. Viv. You stated your captor removed your blindfold so you could see his face."

"Yes."

"And you're sure it was Ben Haddick? The Alphabet Killer?"

"Yes. I recognized him from the news coverage."

"Did you happen to look around you? Could you describe where you were?"

The woman closed her eyes and scrunched her face to concentrate.

"It was dark. It was very dark - except for the orange glow from the fire. The heat.., so much heat. It was so hot. And sticky. There was an echo. But the heat. It was unbearable. And the flames and the metal and..,"

Her eyes flew open, and her body jolted as she reached for her branded arm in terror.

"It's okay; you're safe!" Hayes reminded Vivian, patting the air above the table to calm the woman's nerves. "He's not going to hurt you anymore."

Vivian squeezed her arm just below the bandage before finally relaxing her shoulders. She brought her hands back to a clasped position in front of her, her heavy breathing beginning to calm.

Hayes stared at the bandage for a moment. She then shifted her eyes to meet Vivian's.

"Is the pain manageable? We can get you a..,"

"It's fine!"

Hayes pressed her lips together, frustrated. I'd seen that expression before, that look in her eyes when she wanted answers but wasn't getting the ones she wanted. She was fine, though; she knew what she was doing.

"Let's talk about that for a moment," Hayes responded. "He burned a number into your skin. Do you know why?"

"He said I was the first," Viv replied. "He said there would be others."

"Did he say how many others? Did he give you any indication as to who those others might be?"

"No," she answered, her eyes watering.

"Did he mention anything about a timeline?"

Marion's questions were becoming short, quick. She was losing her patience. I thought warning her agent-friend, who was in the booth with me, would be a good idea.

"You should probably get her out of there before she loses it. She can be quite.., fiery."

The stiff jackhole standing next to me let out a slight chuckle. "Relax, buddy. Hayes has it under control."

Did that whipplestick call me *"buddy"*? He'd better watch it; the last guy who called me that lost some teeth. I still have the scars on my knuckles to prove it. Anyway, we watched on, listening to the interview.

"Timeline?" Vivian questioned. "No, nothing like that."

"Did he tell you anything? Anything at all?"

"No."

"A location, maybe?"

"No."

"Why he's doing this?"

The woman hesitated, drawing in a breath.

"No."

"Come on, Viv; give me something. I know there's something you're forgetting. Think. Help us help you."

The woman woefully shook her head. "I'm sorry."

"Dammit!" Hayes yelled, slapping her palm on the table.

Vivian stiffened and reeled back. The smug fed beside me quickly burst out of the booth on his way to retrieve Marion. I shook my head. *I tried to warn you, dipshit.* What's wrong with you, Marion? Why are you letting this case get to you? I watched the interrogation room door creak open.

"Special Agent Hayes. A word?"

Hayes put on a fake smile, stood, and adjusted her outfit.

"I apologize, Miss Yarrows. I'll only be a moment."

As Hayes walked to the door, Vivian lifted her chin and spoke.

"Countdown!" she said enthusiastically.

Hayes stopped in her tracks, looking back at the woman. She then gestured to her compatriot in the doorway by sticking up her index finger, suggesting to give her a minute. Personally, I would have used a different finger. She closed the door and walked back to her seat.

"Countdown?" Hayes questioned.

Vivian nodded. "He said he'd started the countdown. When it gets to zero, it would all be over."

"What would be over?" Hayes asked. "The killing?"

"I don't know."

"Do you remember anything else?"

"No, that's it. Just that it would end with zero."

Even from my vantage point behind the glass, I could tell the wheels were spinning in Marion's head. There was something she didn't like. She let out a heavy breath.

"Thank you, Viv," Hayes nodded, standing once again. "You are, of course, free to go. You don't have to stay here."

The woman's face became flush with fear. "Could I please stay a little longer?"

Marion let out a sympathetic sigh. "Of course," she nodded. "For a little while, but then we'll have to get you back to the hospital."

She opened the door. Her dark-suited associate was still there, his nose pressed to the door frame.

"Miss Yarrows will be staying here awhile longer. Please get her anything she'd like."

She walked past him unapologetically. A few moments later, the door to the observation room opened.

"I don't like it," she blurted before the door had even closed.

"Well," I responded, "I don't like that you lost your cool in there, but it happens. What was that about?"

"That?" she replied, pointing to the two-way glass. "Nothing."

"Really?" I questioned. "Nothing?"

She gave me a disgruntled glare. "That was me doing my job, Jim. I needed her to see how upset I was about not getting answers. I needed to jog her memory."

"You had me fooled," I said with a tilted grin. "So tell me – what is it you don't like?"

"The countdown. *'When it gets to zero, it would all be over.'* That's what he told her."

"That's kinda how countdowns work, babe," I responded facetiously. It was a good thing Marion understood my inappropriate humor.

"You don't get it," Marion said harshly. "*Vivian* is number Ø. She was his first victim, but it sounds like she'll also be his last. He'll be coming for her. We have to keep her protected."

"Why would he do that?" I questioned. "He already had her. He could have killed her then. Why let her go?"

"I don't know. But the body that turned up this morning - Judith Bentley; she had the number 7 burned into her. He must be counting down from there. If I'm right, Ben will be looking for six more victims before turning his sights back to Vivian again."

"There's already been too much death," I expressed. "If that's what you think this is, we can't let that happen. We have to stop him. *You and Mick* have to stop him. Whatever it takes."

"You know as well as I do what that could mean."

I stared at her stone-faced, my mind reeling. I *did* know what that meant. We needed to put an end to Ben's killing spree, but sometimes, in our line of work, when the situation demanded it, things didn't always end well for the killer. As much as it ate me up inside, I could no longer think of Ben as my son. He was a cold-blooded killer. That was that.

"Whatever it takes," I reiterated.

Chapter 7

Juggling Act

Pulling into the driveway, it occurred to me I'd been gone all day without letting Gina know where I'd gone off to. When she came home to an empty house, she must have assumed I'd gotten dragged off to work, but still, I should have been more mindful to at least have sent her a text. The whole matter of Jimmy not being dead had thrown me for a loop. Add to that the letter I'd received from Ben and the murder victim we were already attributing to him, even though there wasn't enough evidence to support that. It was already a difficult task, juggling work and family life. Now this shit? Could I handle another serial killer - or spree killer - whatever the hell they were calling these maniacs? And what was I to tell Gina?

I stepped from my car, my mind racing. I couldn't tell her about Jimmy; that was drilled into me by Special Agent Hayes, and I didn't want to say anything about the latest homicidal nut job on the street. That would cause her to worry before we even knew anything. That didn't leave me with much to talk about.

I opened the side door into the kitchen, expecting Gina to be in the other room with Stella Mae. Instead, they were both at the kitchen table; Gina was feeding our little peanut.

"There he is!" Gina said in a high-pitched voice, smiling at Stella. "Can you say 'Hi Daddy'?" She held Stella's wrist and bobbed the poor girl's hand up and down in a forced wave. Stella smiled and made a giggling noise, baby food spilling down her chin and landing on her bib.

"Hello, baby girl," I said excitedly, running to the side of her highchair and kissing her forehead. "I missed you." I then leaned over and kissed Gina on the cheek. "I guess I missed you too." I smiled and winked.

"I see how it is," Gina responded. "As soon as you get another little woman in your life, I'm chopped liver."

"You can't blame me; she doesn't talk back."

"Hey!" Gina exclaimed playfully, pulling the burp cloth from her shoulder and snapping it at my leg. "Not yet, anyway. Wait until she's a teenager."

I had to admit, I loved these little moments between us - which is why I dreaded what came next.

"Where've you been, babe?" Gina asked. "I thought you were going to take it easy today? Don't tell me Frank guilted you into picking out something for his wife for their anniversary next week. I swear, that man has got to start figuring out what his wife wants by himself. Or he's going to find himself on his own."

"It wasn't that," I answered. "I got called in on a case."

"It's Saturday, baby. What could be so important that couldn't wait until Monday?"

I pulled up a chair on the other side of her as she brought a spoonful of puréed carrots to Stella's open mouth.

"You know that new bakery over on Delano?" I asked, trying to ease into it.

"Yeah," she replied. "I heard good things about that place. Barbara, down at the nail shop, swears by their raspberry scones. Don't tell me somebody already broke in and vandalized the place."

"No, it's..," I paused and looked at Stella's innocent smile, wishing everything could be as beautiful. But it couldn't. The world was a dark and ugly place.

"What is it, Mick?" Gina questioned, turning her attention toward me.

"The owner was found dead inside the place this morning. Some kid employee found the body."

"Oh no; how awful."

"Yeah."

"Was she killed? Do you know who did it? Did you catch the person?"

I took in a deep breath, then let it out. I stared silently down at the table.

"Mick, what's wrong?" She reached over and tenderly grabbed my hand.

I should have known this would happen. Gina knew all of my facial expressions. I couldn't keep anything from her if I tried.

"Don't freak out," I warned her, "but we think it might have been Ben."

"Ben *Haddick?*" she questioned loudly, pulling her hand away from mine. "You're kidding me!"

"I wish I was."

"What makes you think it was Ben?"

Shit! I'm so stupid. Why did I always do that? I put myself in these impossible situations. I told myself I wasn't going to worry her. Idiot!

"Remember that letter I received from him that the post office had lost for a long time?"

She nodded her head.

"Well, I received another letter from him this morning."

"What? Here? What did it say? Where is it?"

"It doesn't matter," I said.

"Of course it does," she responded. "Let me see it."

"Hon, I really don't think..,"

"Mick!" she stopped me. "I love you to the moon, but you can't keep stuff like that from me. I get that you have to keep some police stuff under wraps, but if that letter was delivered to our home.., our *home*, Mick, I deserve to know. We're supposed to be a team. I want to see it."

Gina could be demanding, but she was level-headed. She kept me grounded. She was the glue in this relationship – always had been. I didn't know what I would do without her. And, as always, she was right. I couldn't keep something like that from her.

"Let me get it," I nodded.

I kept telling myself it was the right thing to do. I hated worrying Gina, but knowing about and reading the letter could help protect her and our little girl. Hopefully, she'd be more cautious when going out for any reason. As a cop, I was used to looking around, checking my surroundings, and being suspicious of people; it was that part of me I didn't appreciate. I wish I could be more trusting. The job turned me into that. But it had also saved my ass on more than one occasion. If it meant coming home safe to my wife and baby girl each night, I'd take the bad with the good.

I reached into my sock drawer and pulled out the letter I'd buried there before I left the house this morning. I should have taken it with me to submit as evidence. I wasn't thinking straight. Jimmy really messed me up. I quickly skimmed it one last time before huffing and walking back with it clenched tightly within my fingers. Gina was wiping orange mush from under Stella's lower lip while Stella's arms waved aimlessly in the air as if she were catching invisible fireflies. Gina looked at the paper in my hand, glanced up at my eyes, and then back to the paper. She pursed her lips, then snatched the letter from me, dropping the cloth she'd been using onto Stella's highchair tray. While Gina read, I pulled the now mush-covered cloth from the tray before Stella could use it as a weapon, sending orange projectiles in all directions. Though it might have been fun watching some splat against Gina's face, I wasn't going to tell her I thought that.

"What does this mean, Mick?" Gina asked after she finished reading, concern showing on her face. "He's back to his old ways?"

"We don't know yet," I answered. "All we have is a body."

"Then, what makes you think it was Ben?"

"Because he mentions something about numbers in there," I pointed to the letter she still held.

"Yeah, so?"

"The body.., the woman.., she had the number 7 burned into her."

"Oh my God! It's true, then."

"Hayes is convinced..,"

"Hayes?" Gina blurted. "As in, Special Agent Hayes? What does she have to do with this? The FBI is already involved?"

Shit again!

"Um.., yeah," I replied. "Ben's an escaped convict. A murderer at that. It's normal for state and federal law enforcement to be looking for him."

"On the same day that you receive a letter from Ben?" Gina questioned skeptically.

She was smart. What did I expect? She was the wife of a cop.

"Hayes received a letter, too. She was already on her way to Southbridge when word of the second victim..,"

I froze. I realized it as soon as the words left my lips.

Shit! Shit!

"*Second* victim?" Gina raised her voice.

Stella looked up, swiveling her head between us, and let out a laugh, unaware her daddy was about to get throat-punched by her mommy.

"Gina, I..,"

"You weren't going to tell me?"

"I can't tell you everything, Gina," I argued. "You know that. There's an ongoing investigation, and I can't discuss the details. I'm sorry."

"Just tell me this," she insisted. "The other victim.., did they have a number on them too?"

I dropped my chin to my chest and gave a slight nod.

"Holy sh..,"

"Shhh," I said, placing my index finger in front of my mouth to quiet her. "Stella." I pointed at our little girl.

Gina reached down and pulled Stella from the highchair. "Come here, baby girl." She held her against her chest, gently rubbing her back. "Your daddy's a poop head, and we're mad at him right now."

She shot me an evil eye and then squeezed by me and the table on her way to the living room.

"Gina..,"

"I'm not listening," she returned.

Double Shit! Shit!

Did I mention how difficult it was juggling work and family life? Was there even a chance we could catch Ben, or the lunatic, or whoever it was before the weekend was over? It would sure make my life a hell of a lot simpler.

Was there any chance at all?

Please?

Chapter 8

The Gamble

Gina was nice enough to pretend she was okay with me going to work on Sunday. It's not like it was a regular occurrence or anything, and this wasn't a typical case. It quite probably involved someone we knew. We'd both spent enough time with Ben when he was younger; he felt like part of our family. He took a liking to Gina from the moment they'd met, though he never came around to calling her aunt like he'd called me uncle. Gina wasn't offended by that. I'd been in his life since he was born; she was a late addition to the family. Still, they had mutual respect for one another, and Ben was always sweet and very kind to Gina. It broke her heart – all of our hearts - when we learned he was The Alphabet Killer. After that, she said she could never think of him as that sweet little boy anymore, and I know that bothered her more than she let on. If the latest victim *was* Ben's doing, she wanted him caught. And if that meant I had to spend the occasional Sunday in the office, she'd let it slide.

When I got to the station, I went straight to Vera's lab. I hoped to avoid Lieutenant Garrett as long as possible, and I gambled that Vera hadn't turned in her official report yet. If the look on her face as I descended the stairs into the dragon's layer was any indication, I gambled correctly.

"If you say one word about a report," she hollered through the glass, "I'm not letting you in."

I didn't say anything, choosing to shake my head instead. I watched as Vera looked toward her labmate, Danny, and nodded. To avoid upsetting the dragon, the assistant came bounding over as quickly as his feet could carry him. I didn't know why people felt the way they did about Vera. Deep down, she was a sweet woman.

"What the holy hell brings a dick like you to my lab this early in the morning?" she barked as the door opened. "And on a Sunday to boot."

As I said.., deep, *deep* down.

"And by 'dick,'" I replied, "I assume you mean detective?" I tried to maintain a positive attitude.

"Sure, let's go with that," she answered. "Why are you here?"

"I'm sorry to bother you, Vera. I was hoping to get confirmation, one way or another, on whether the killer was Ben or not."

"Well, you can stop your wondering," she replied. "Both the skin samples and the fingerprints are a match. It's Ben. He doesn't seem to be worried about covering his tracks this time. That son of a bitch." Vera looked skyward as if she were religious. "Sorry, Karen; you weren't a bitch," she added under her breath. "Can you believe that kid? Jim would be rolling in his grave right now if he knew his son was back on the street pulling this shit."

I displayed an awkward smile while nodding. How would Vera react if she knew Jimmy wasn't *in* his grave? I wasn't the best at putting up a front, so I turned away and glared at Danny as if I were interested in whatever the hell it was he was doing. I thought he'd feel uncomfortable if he saw me watching him, but when he looked up, the lab tech smiled and waved like an excited elementary school kid. Suddenly, *I* was the uncomfortable one. I decided to take my chances and turn back to face Vera. Maybe if I changed the subject, she wouldn't recognize the guilt on my face for knowing Jimmy was alive. Another gamble, but I..,

I caught myself in mid-thought. *Another gamble?* I tilted my head down and furrowed my brow. Could it be that simple?

"What's got you all dour?" Vera asked. "Didn't you hear me? We now know Ben is the killer."

"Yeah, I got that," I responded, brushing her comment off while I thought. I didn't mean to be rude, but my gut was churning. Was that the feeling Jimmy used to get all those times he'd tell me how a good detective relies on evidence, but a *great* detective relies on his gut? I'd be the first to admit I wasn't a great detective, but something hit me. I'd be making a mistake if I didn't follow up on that feeling.

"Vera, do you ever gamble?" I asked. "I mean, at the casino?"

"I've been known to hit the slots now and again. I do pretty well. Especially when the night ends with some young hunk coming home with me and hitting *my* slot – if you know what I mean."

"Um...," I glanced over at Vera's sidekick. "Do you think Danny wants to hear all that?" I laid it on Danny's shoulders when, really, it was I who didn't want to hear about that crap.

"Eh, I could give two shits," Vera replied. "Besides – what makes you think he hasn't dreamed about hitting this sweet package himself?" She looked over at her young tech. "Isn't that right, Danny-boy?" She puckered her lips and made two kissing sounds. Danny's eyes widened like he was a deer frozen in a car's headlights, and then he quickly sat down in his chair, hiding his blushed face behind a monitor. She might have scarred the poor guy for life.

"Why do you ask, anyway, Mick? Thinking about taking me out and getting lucky with me?" She winked.

"No!" I expressed quickly and probably a bit too loud. "I mean, that's not why I was asking. I was thinking about the numbers Ben has been leaving with the victims. I think you were right when you said he was giving us clues to his next victim."

"When are you knuckleheads gonna learn? I'm *always* right. It's called being a woman."

That was probably an accurate statement. When it came to these psychopaths and their twisted games, Vera knew her stuff.

"I'm thinking of the numbers he left with the latest victim," I said.

"1 and 2?" Vera questioned.

"Yeah. Only reverse them, and you've got..,"

"21!" she shouted. "Now I understand your casino reference. Blackjack, anyone?"

"I have no idea if that's what it means," I remarked, "but at this point, it's worth a shot."

"Let me know if you need a partner on that. Just give me enough time to stop at the ATM."

"Yeah, right," I chuckled. "I'm not sure if Lieutenant Garrett would even buy into my crazy idea."

"Well, I'll tell you what. I've got to drop this report off to him. Why don't we find out together?" Vera grabbed a folder from the corner of her desk and tapped the edge twice against her palm. "Hold the fort, would ya, Danny," she called out. "I'm going upstairs to play with the big boys."

Vera practically shoved me through the door on her way out. There wasn't much I could argue about. Once she got an idea in her head, there was no getting in her way. We climbed the stairs to the Detective Bureau, walking into an empty room, save for a light coming from Lieu's office. His door was open, and we could already hear him shouting obscenities. We didn't hear anyone else. Either the man enjoyed his alone time, practicing his bark for the coming Monday, or he was on the phone. Either way, it probably wasn't the best time for us to barge in, but, you know.., Vera.

That woman walked right in and stood at the front of his desk (I mean, his door *was* open, after all). I slunk in behind her, bending my knees and ducking my head slightly to use her as a shield should anything happen to fly our way. Lieutenant Garrett slapped an annoyed look across his face but continued his conversation. Or yelling.

"And I suppose your superiors are getting their jollies off that idea," he grumbled. "I know you're going to do what you think is best, but Jesus Christ, do you think he'd be stupid enough to try? Yeah. Okay. Listen, I've gotta let you go. I've got two trespassers in my office. Keep me posted. Yeah."

Lieu ended the call in his usual manner – hanging up without saying goodbye. Then he looked at us with his typical grim expression. "What?" he barked.

"Here's the report you wanted, Frank," Vera said, placing the folder on his desk.

Frank picked up the folder and handed it back to her.

"You want to try that again?" he griped.

Vera rolled her eyes and snatched the folder from him. She exaggerated a smile and placed it nicely back on his desk. Then, she said in a pleasant voice, "Here's the goddamn report you wanted, jackass!"

Lieu squinted and pointed at her. "I'm going to let that go because I like you. Would it kill you to call me Lieutenant?"

"Monday through Friday, I'll call you Lieutenant all you want," she answered. "When you make me come in on a Sunday to finish a report that could've waited until Monday, you get what you get."

"Fine," he acknowledged. "So what's the verdict?"

"I hate to say it, but it's true. It looks like Ben is our killer."

Frank closed his eyes and huffed. "That's it then. We gotta get a warrant out for his arrest. I've gotta call it in downstairs, too. Sergeant Hannidy and his men are going to have their hands full."

"They're not going to know where to look," I said. "Ben doesn't have any place to go. That means he could be anywhere."

"Then they're just going to have to look *everywhere*, aren't they? That goddamn kid," he murmured. "What the fuck is he up to? I've got the state police riding my ass. I just had Special Agent Hayes on the phone telling me she believes the killer.., *Ben*.., is going to go back after his first victim when he's through with his twisted-as-fuck objective."

"What makes her think that?" I asked.

"I don't know," he replied. "Something about counting down until he kills zero, or some shit."

"And Vivian is Victim Ø," I responded. "Makes sense."

"I'm glad it makes sense to *one* of us. Ben is playing some fucking numbers game, and none of us know what it's about."

"Speaking of a numbers game," I jumped in, figuring there wasn't a more appropriate time, "I have a theory about the numbers left at the bakery crime scene."

"All right, let's hear it."

"You're going to love this one, Frank," Vera blurted.

I shot Vera a look as if to say, *What the hell?*

"I'm waiting," the lieutenant said impatiently.

"If Ben is giving us clues to his next kill, such as I believe he did with the bakery..,"

"Right," Lieu interjected. "3.14. PI. Pies."

"Yeah, that's right. And I think the numbers left at the bakery – 2 and 1 – are supposed to represent 21. Or Blackjack. I think Ben is trying to lead us to the casino."

Lieutenant Garrett's eyes narrowed. "That's either the dumbest thing I've heard come out of your mouth, Mick, or the smartest. Are you planning on going to the casino to find out which?"

"There's something in my gut telling me I should check it out, Lieu."

"Your gut, huh?"

"If it turns out to be nothing, then it's nothing. I'd rather find out for sure and be wrong than to be right and be too late."

"All right," Lieu agreed, nodding. "Go check it out."

"He's not having *all* the fun," Vera chimed in. "I'm going with him."

"Wait, what?" I questioned.

"Oh, Christ!" Lieutenant Garrett let out.

Vera crossed her arms about her chest. "You got your report," she stated, looking at Frank, "and you," she added, looking at me, "need someone with you who knows what the hell they're doing. I'm officially off the clock; you might as well take me along. Someone's gotta keep you in line." She smiled and winked at me.

I smirked and shook my head. Something told me I wasn't winning this battle. I only hoped I wouldn't regret my decision.

"Okay, fine," I gave in. "But this isn't a date," I said jokingly.

"Yeah, right," Vera said, flashing a seductive grin and batting her eyes. "You wish, twinkle toes."

"What the fuck am I listening to right now?" the lieutenant grumbled. "Don't start that weird-ass shit in here. If you're going, you're going. Now get the hell out of my office."

I nodded. "Thanks, Lieutenant."

"Yeah. Thanks, Frank," Vera added as we exited.

"Goddammit!" Frank yelled. "It's Lieuten.., aw, never mind."

He took that better than I expected. More importantly, he trusted what I had to say. My gut had better be right. I'd feel like an idiot if it turned out to only be indigestion.

Chapter 9

High Stakes

The Meridian Paradiso Casino over on the east side had opened only a year before. It was a large-scale project funded by Ray "The Weasel" Wenzini, one-third of the city's scumbag crime bosses. Like a character straight out of The Godfather, Ray became head of the Italian crime syndicate when his father, Antonio, was killed during the turf war years back, which led to the division of the city's three crime districts. A truce was struck between the crime lords, giving them free rein within their own territories as long as they didn't interfere with another boss's turf. And though the police remained active during the power struggle, hauling in third-tier lowlifes and drug pushers, the crime lords were untouchable. Sadly, it was in the city's best interest if they continued their illicit activities and shady business dealings. There was less bloodshed on the streets and fewer civilian casualties.

While the rest of us working-class stiffs struggled to make ends meet, Ray got richer by lining the pockets of the Gaming Commissioner, who pulled enough strings to allow Ray to open the city's first casino. Such was the way of the world. The rich got richer while the poor..,

"Park here, you idiot!"

...got to spend their afternoon with Vera.

After listening to the woman bitch about my driving the entire ride, we managed to find a decent spot near the front entrance. Before we exited the car, I wanted to make something clear.

"Vera, as much as I appreciate the wonderful company and the valuable insight you might be able to provide about the psyche of a twisted killer like Ben, I'm still in charge of this investigation. Let me do the talking."

"What the fuck, Mick?" she responded. "You think I'm here to step on your itty-bitty toes? Check your manhood at the door. I'm here to find my next date. Now, let's get on with it."

I rolled my eyes and stepped out of the car. Vera charged forward, leading the way to the large glass entry doors. I hadn't been here before, but Vera looked right at home. The sounds and flashing lights of the slot machines hit me as soon as I walked in, disorienting me from where I needed to go. Vera kept me in line.

"This way, twinklenuts."

She marched straight to a series of Blackjack tables arranged in a semi-circle in the middle of the large gambling hall. There was no doubt – she was familiar with the casino's layout. She squeezed between two tables and leaned against a padded railing surrounding the pit area. She nodded to the nearest dealer on our right.

"What's going on, Federico?" she asked as if he was a close friend.

At first, I thought she read his nametag. I should have known better.

"Ah, Vera, my friend," the dealer replied, smiling while throwing cards toward disgruntled players. "How are you today?"

"I'm good. Listen, is Louis here? I need to talk with him."

"Louis has the day off today," Federico replied.

"On a Sunday? How did he manage that?"

"It's his kid's birthday."

One of the patrons at the table slammed his hand down. "Hey, you mind? We're trying to play here."

Vera turned her stare to the angry man.

"Shut the fuck up, numbsack; I'm a cop on official business."

I didn't know whether it was the cop comment or that Vera gave his attitude right back to him, but the man tightened his lips and went back to staring at his cards.

"Who's the pit boss today? And where are they?" Vera asked the dealer, looking around the enclosed area behind the tables.

"Ellen," he replied. "She's over at table six, handling a dispute."

"Aw, shit!" Vera exclaimed. "That bitch? Figures. Come on, fruit cup," she said, slapping my upper arm. "Thanks, Federico."

She led me past several tables to the far side of the Blackjack circle, where a tall woman with long black hair, down to the small of her back, stared aggravatingly at an unruly gambler being spoken to by security. Vera stopped before the table and pointed at the woman.

"That's Ellen. You said you wanted to do the talking. She's all yours. Good luck."

That didn't sound promising.

"Excuse me," I said, raising my hand to get the woman's attention.

Ellen turned and glared at me as if I had no right to call to her. Her eyes shifted to Vera, and they narrowed. I saw the woman's chest heave in and out with an almost disgusted breath. She faked a smile and walked over.

"Yes?"

"Hello. I'm Detective Dooley with the Southbridge Police Department. I was hoping to ask you a few questions."

"Haven't I been berated enough by you people?" she replied, sneering at Vera.

"Um..," I looked at Vera and signaled for her to walk away. She begrudgingly complied. With Vera gone, I continued. "This is about an ongoing investigation. Has there been any unusual activity around the Blackjack tables recently?"

"This is a casino, Officer Dooley. There's nothing *but* unusual activity that goes on here."

"Right, but I meant specifically in this area. Has anyone been acting strangely?"

"Again," Ellen replied. "This is a casino. People don't exactly act normal when they're here."

"I understand, but..,"

"Oh, for fuck's sake," Vera yelled out. She had obviously remained close enough to hear my awkward attempts at questioning. In my defense, I had no idea what questions I should be asking. I wasn't even sure if this was where I needed to be.

"What my partner is trying to ask," she stated, walking back our way, "is if you've had any missing dealers?"

Partner? But, yes, that was a good question.

"We have dealers call out all the time," Ellen replied. "They don't last long."

"Right. Of course," I said.

"Although..," the pit boss responded, tapping her finger on the cleft beneath her nose while glancing at a closed table. "Stepan has been with us since the beginning. He was a no-show today, and he didn't call in."

"And that's unusual?" I asked.

"It is for Stepan," she replied. "I don't think the man has missed a day since he started."

"I see. Can we get Stepan's address?"

"I'll have to call it into my boss."

"Please."

She got on a phone while I looked over at the empty table, hoping this was a rare instance where Stepan had contracted some rare virus that rendered him bedridden with no opportunity to call in sick. Could I convince myself of that? A moment later, Ellen hung up the phone.

"Someone will be down in a moment."

"Thank you," I said.

"Now, if you'll excuse me, I have a job to do."

"Of course."

The woman walked away to oversee the tables while I turned to Vera to express my concern.

"You thinking what I'm thinking?" I asked.

"Well, I don't think the man contracted some rare virus that's kept him in bed with no access to a phone," she answered.

Okay, that was scary. We literally just had the same thought. Please don't tell me I'm turning into Vera. My wife would kill me.

Just then, a voice sounded from behind me.

"You were looking for Stepan's address?"

I turned to see a serious-looking man dressed in a black, three-piece suit, red tie, and hair slicked back with gel.

"I am. We are," I corrected myself.

"May I ask what this is about?" the man questioned.

"Actually, no, you may not."

"We have a policy here at the Meridian Paradiso. We don't make a habit of giving out our employees' addresses. It's for safety reasons."

"I understand," I said. "This is concerning an investigation we're conducting." I opened my jacket and flashed the badge clipped to my belt.

"I'd like to help you, officer, but I'm afraid it's policy."

Vera jumped in. "Listen, slick, do you have the address or not?"

"I do. But as I said..,"

"How much do you think your bosses would like it if your stupidity caused a mass exodus of customers?" Vera continued. "I bet that revenue loss would come out of someone's paycheck. Maybe someone as dumb and ugly as you?"

I didn't know what was happening. I wasn't sure I wanted to know.

"Last I heard, Ray the Weasel wasn't too fond of employees costing him money," she continued.

The man turned and glanced at the phone.

"Go ahead," Vera goaded. "Let's see if security can get here before I announce," she began to raise her voice, "that the casino is owned by the city's largest drug syndicate. Don't you think the people should know that their hard-earned money is contributing to the addiction problem of today's youths?"

"Hey, hey, keep it down," the nicely dressed man begged, looking up at the cameras. "We all got a job to do, you know? There's no need to involve Mr. Wenzini in any of this."

"We're the police," I jumped in. "You do realize we can get Stepan's address easily enough? We were expecting a little cooperation. It would be a shame if certain government authorities began taking an interest in some of the casino's bookkeeping practices. I wonder what they'd find?"

"All right, all right. I get it. Take it easy." He leaned over the railing, "Listen, there's no need to involve anyone else. Do you understand what I'm saying? Mr. Wenzini wouldn't appreciate people up in his business."

"Well, that all depends on you now," I stated. "Doesn't it?"

The man shook his head and spoke quietly, "Mr. Greguric's address is 21 Plymouth Drive."

I pulled back and turned to Vera in surprise. If there was any doubt in my suspicions before, it had now faded.

"We've got to get out of here," I said, my eyes wide. "Now!"

"I had that same thought," Vera confirmed.

We didn't bother thanking the man; he didn't deserve it. We both high-tailed it to the front door, hoping we learned of Ben's clue before it was too late. 21. That led us to the casino. It was now leading us to Stepan Greguric's address, also 21. This fucking game the goddamn kid is playing. What's it gonna take for this to be over?

Chapter 10

Numbers Game

He's been asleep far too long. Perhaps I shouldn't have held the sevoflurane-drenched cloth over his nose and mouth for as long as I had. I'm still learning. Unfortunately, I'm on a tight schedule and must speed things along. He'll forgive me, I'm sure.

I grab the paper cup from the table, water spilling over the side of the rim, and toss my hand forward, splashing the contents onto his blindfolded face.

"Wakey, wakey."

The man jolts awake, shaking his head from side to side, disoriented and confused. He begins yelling what I imagine are obscenities into the cloth covering his mouth while he jerks his body back and forth, realizing he is bound to a chair. He is like the women, helpless and weak. He will try and pretend he is strong and unafraid. I will show him otherwise.

"Struggling will do you no good," I inform him. "This ends only one way. I'm sure you know what I mean."

He doesn't take kindly to my words and yanks harder against his bonds. He screams more indistinguishable swear words that become muffled behind the gag. Why don't they ever listen? I don't have time for this.

I stand from my side of the table and lean forward, sweat dripping from my forehead. I reach back and swing my right hand forward, slapping the loud man across the cheek to gain his attention. He stops his yelling for a moment. It's long enough for me to speak.

"You need to be a good boy and listen," I state, looking down at the back of my right hand as I feel the sting of sweat entering the still-open gashes. *Stupid bitch and her nails.* I shake my hand to relieve the pain. "How long you live is up to you. How painful your death is.., that's up to me. I suggest you be smart about things. Now, let's let you have a look so you can see how serious I am."

I step to the side of the table and reach for his blindfold. When he feels my fingers touch his skin, he reels to the side. I slap the top of his head, this time with my left hand, to keep my right from throbbing.

"Knock it off!" I tell him.

He brings his head back straight, his body beginning to shiver. It's not from the lukewarm water with which I awoke him. The extreme heat has already dried most of that. No, the shivers are from fear. Just the way I want it.

"Let's try this again." I grab the side of the blindfold near his temple and pull it upward onto his forehead. He scrunches his face and blinks several times to gather his vision. It only takes him a few seconds to register how dire his situation is as I witness his eyes widen at the sight. He mumbles something into the cloth that, in my head, translates to, "What the fuck?". It sounds appropriate, given his current situation. He tilts his head upward toward me. I watch his eyes widen even further. I smile.

"You recognize me?" I ask.

He nervously nods his head several times.

"Good. Then you know what's about to happen."

He shakes his head from side to side in denial. His eyes follow mine, looking at the items displayed on the table. He knows.

"Here's how this is going to play out," I begin, reaching for the knife, its blade stained with the blood of his predecessors. "I want to remove your gag." I point the tip of the knife an inch away from his eye. "I don't want you to scream. That would get messy."

He subtly nods.

I grab at the cloth in his mouth and yank it down until it dangles freely around his throat like a neckerchief. Another balled-up cloth remains stuffed in his mouth.

"No biting," I say, grinning.

I reach in, grab the saliva-soaked wad, and carefully work it free. The man breathes heavily from his mouth, catching his breath as if his nose hadn't been adequate. But no yelling. He knows his place.

"I'm afraid we don't have as much time as I would have liked...," I extend my left hand to the table and open the wallet I pulled from his pants. I glance at the man's license through the clear plastic window within. "...Stepan. Are you from the motherland?"

Stepan stares forward, tightening his lips.

"That's not being very polite," I say, gritting my teeth. "I asked you a question." I stab the knife into the front of the uncooperative man's shoulder. He lets out a scream through clenched teeth, trying to be strong. Or maybe, trying to save his eye because of my earlier threat. "I'll ask again; where are you from?"

"I am from Moldova," he answers through labored breathing, spit flying from his mouth.

"That wasn't so hard, was it?" I say, pulling the knife free. His body convulses sideways. Tears escape from his eyes. "Well, Stepan from Moldova, I'd like to play a game of numbers. Being a dealer, you must be pretty good with numbers."

He stares at me, seething. "I don't want to play a game," he responds in a thick accent.

"That's your choice," I respond. "But here's the thing - you're going to die today. It can be quick and painless, or I can make it slow and *very* painful. I'll let you work out the details in your head. So, shall we begin?"

Stepan turns his stare straight ahead, a scowl on his face. I begin the game.

"A girl walks into her bedroom with a chicken under her arm and her puppy following behind on a leash. On her bed is a sleeping cat. She throws the chicken onto the bed, which scares the cat. The cat jumps off the bed into the girl's arms, causing her to drop the leash. Now free, the puppy jumps onto the bed, sending the chicken to the floor. How many legs are currently standing on the floor?"

Stepan remains silent, his eyes unwavering.

"Make it easy on yourself and give me an answer."

"If you are going to kill me anyway," Stepan replies, "then make it hurt. I want to remember what it feels like to be alive."

I feel my shoulders drop as I let out a disappointed breath from my nose. "The answer was eight, by the way.

You probably thought four. Everyone forgets the bed has legs, too. Come on, Stepan; give it a try."

The stubborn dealer curls his upper lip in defiance, remaining silent and focused forward.

"You're really not going to play this game with me, huh?" I question, trying to sway his decision.

He shifts his eyes to me and then back to forward.

"Very well," I say, placing the knife on the table. Stepan's eyes follow my hand to the pliers. "Painful it is."

Chapter 11

...6

Everything seemed to be moving in slow motion. My legs were unsteady. I squatted just inside the door, feeling helpless as Barry walked by me, snapping the latex glove against his wrist as he forced his hand into it. I could hear every intake of breath as the oxygen filled my lungs – every beat of my heart. I turned my head to the right. Vera was standing outside the open door, relaying the events of the past twenty minutes to the uniformed officer, the red and blue lights swirling in the distance behind them, making me feel nauseous. I turned my head back, forcing my eyes to the floor. I sluggishly wiped my forehead of the clammy sweat that had formed almost instantaneously. We were too late.

My eyes shifted upward from the floor to see Barry leaning over Stepan Greguric's mutilated body. He turned to me and began speaking. I could see his lips moving, but there was no sound. I shook my head to loosen the cobwebs. Barry spoke again. Still, there was silence. I brought my hands to my eyes to clear them, thinking I was mistaken about what I saw, when..,

"Detective Dooley!"

Reality resumed, crashing full speed into my skull. The voice belonged to Lieutenant Garrett. He was standing in the doorway, a cigarette dangling from his lower lip.

"Are you going to answer the man, or what?" he barked.

I forced myself to my feet and looked over at the medical examiner.

"I'm sorry, Barry. What were you asking?"

"Has anybody moved or touched the body since you first arrived?"

"Ah.., no. No, nothing like that," I stammered. "Once we saw what we were dealing with, we waited outside for you to arrive."

"And by 'we,' you mean you and Vera?" Lieu asked.

"Yes, sir."

The lieutenant went to take a step into the house, but Barry threw up his hand and cleared his throat.

"Ahem. Cigarette out, please."

Lieu rolled his eyes and mumbled under his breath, "Oh, for fuck's sake." He took one last drag, then pulled it from his lips and flicked it onto the lawn near another officer. "Step on that, would you?" After blowing the smoke out of the side of his mouth, he entered the crime scene.

"Aren't you getting sick of this yet, Barry?" Lieutenant Garrett asked, pointing at the murder victim.

The body was lying on its side on a sheet of plastic in the center of the living room. Though the plastic had red smudge marks along much of its surface, there was no pooled blood. Like Judith Bentley before him, Stepan was not killed on the premises.

"I find the work intriguing," Barry answered, pulling a pen from his jacket pocket. "Case in point..," he brought the pen to the side of the dead man's head and used it to lift a clump of hair. "This gentleman is missing an ear."

"Christ!" Lieu blurted.

"It wasn't a clean cut," Barry added. "If you look here," he swirled the pen in a circular motion above the missing ear, "the edges of the skin are jagged and stretched."

"What does that mean?" I asked.

"It means it wasn't removed with a bladed weapon. See all the areas of removed skin from the victim?" Several patches of puzzle-piece-sized skin had been removed from Stepan's bare chest, arms, neck, and cheek. "From the look of it, I'd say our killer yanked the flesh off. Some muscle, too. There are some tight serration marks at many of the wounds, suggesting he used something like pliers or maybe channel locks."

"Fuck!" Lieu let out. "And this is what you call intriguing?"

"Well, there's more."

"Of course, there is," I jumped in.

Barry placed his gloved hand on the man's forehead and rotated it upward.

"He's also missing his eyelids," Barry pointed out. "They were most likely yanked off in the same fashion as his skin and ear. I'm sorry, correction. Ears. Plural. The other one is missing, too."

"Sick bastard, eh, Lieutenant?" Vera added, entering the scene.

He didn't say anything. He looked dumbfounded. I think he was shocked that Vera called him 'Lieutenant.'

"And, of course," Barry continued, "what victim would be complete without their very own number burned into their stomach? This one has the number 6."

Lieu turned to me. "What number was on the bakery chick?"

"Seven."

"Then it's true; the fucker is counting down."

Vera patted Lieutenant Garrett on the shoulder. "I bet that's gonna make Hayes smile, knowing she got something right for a change."

"Vera!"

"Sorry, Frank. Lieutenant."

"What about numbers, Barry?" I asked. "Did the killer leave any numbers for us?"

"He did. If you make your way over here," he waved us over to his side, where he was standing behind the body.

"Don't go messing up my crime scene," Vera yelled.

"We'll be careful," I said as Frank and I stepped closer to Barry.

"She's right," Barry stated. "Do *not* step on the plastic."

"Of course, I'm right, Gingersnap," she retorted.

We stood beside Barry and looked down at Stepan's back. It had been untouched except for a series of numbers written in marker.

"12369," Lieu verbalized. "What do you make of that?"

"I don't know," I replied. "Zip code?"

Barry jumped in on the guessing. "Locker number? Dollar amount?"

"Will you guys let the expert handle this?" Vera spoke up from across the room. "What are the numbers again?"

"12369," I repeated. "What are you thinking?"

"Give me a minute, Columbo." Vera stared at the ceiling, reciting the numbers. "12369. 12369. 12369." Then she stopped and looked at us. "Nope, I got nothin'."

Lieu tilted his head down and vigorously rubbed his forehead in frustration. "Vera, did I ever tell you, as a detective, you'd make a fine hairdresser?"

"Fuck, Lieu; I tried."

"Barry, what else can you tell us?" I asked, reeling things back in.

"The victim wasn't killed here," he answered, confirming my suspicion. "He was wrapped in the plastic and transported here after he'd been dead awhile."

"Any idea of timeframe?" I asked.

"Given the discoloration of the skin and darkened areas around the wounds and that the body is only in its second stage of rigor mortis, I'd say he's been dead approximately nine to ten hours. That's all I can tell you at this time. I've pronounced him dead. Vera and her crew can get started. I expect the body to be delivered to the morgue after she's done her part."

Lieu nodded. "Yeah."

"You heard the man, gents," Vera commented. "Time to clear out so I can get to work. I'll let you know when it's all set to come back in, Mick."

"Thanks, Vera."

We stepped outside, leaving the forensic team to their job. Lieutenant Garrett lit up another cigarette, unable to quell his nerves. I'd noticed he started up again after he and his wife almost divorced. I thought he would have quit after they reconciled, but I think the nicotine was the only thing that kept him calm enough for his wife to deal with. That woman must be a saint to have to put up with him.

"Dooley!" Lieu yelled, turning in my direction, not realizing I was beside him.

"Yeah, Lieu."

"You said the vic was a dealer at the casino?"

"Yeah."

"I want you to check with them and find out if they'll let you have a look at their camera footage from over the last twenty-four hours. Maybe Ben was there, scoping out his victim."

"People know his face, Lieu," I said. "I don't think Ben would..,"

"Goddamn it, Dooley!" he shouted. "He's picking his victims somehow. Do you have something better?"

He brought the cigarette to his lips to take a drag. I noticed his hand shaking uncontrollably.

"Are you all right, Lieu? You seem a little tense."

"Of course, I'm tense," he barked. "We've got a fucking lunatic out there playing a game with people's lives. Again!"

His hand continued shaking as he held the cigarette between his fingers by his side.

"Maybe you should take it easy, Lieu. Head back to the station. Better yet, back home. Let me, Vera, and the rest handle things here. We've got it covered."

"Ha!" he laughed sarcastically. "We've got shit." He turned to look at the open door to the house and dropped his barely-smoked cigarette to the ground. "Maybe you're right." He stepped on the still-smoldering cancer stick, pivoting his foot back and forth to ensure it was out. "This stuff is getting to me."

"I can tell," I said, patting him on the shoulder. "Go on," I encouraged. "I'll stay here a little bit to see if Vera comes up with anything useful. Then, I'll head back to the casino to see how cooperative they're willing to be."

"You do that," Lieu responded, pointing his finger at me. "As much as I don't like it, contact Agent Hayes to update her about this latest vic. Maybe she'll know something about those numbers."

"You got it, Lieu."

I watched him walk away, seeming a little ragged. I heard him yell to Barry as he got closer to his car. "I'm still waiting on your report from the last homicide. Now, you owe me two."

Barry put his hand up in a leisurely wave. He'd do everything he could to help us with the case, but he didn't take orders from the police. He'd take whatever time he needed to get everything right before submitting his report. Lieu knew that, but he always had to act the part of the hard-nosed cop – like Jimmy used to do. Like it was the only way he could feel good about doing the job. He'd better be careful. One of these days, the stress was going to get to him.

I shook my head and turned back to the house. "12369," I whispered to myself. What the fuck, Ben? Couldn't you make it a little easier for us dumb schmucks? For some reason, my thoughts went to Jimmy. Would he understand what his kid was telling us with these numbers? I had to get a message to him. That meant contacting Agent Hayes. Everything on my end had so far been a shit show. I wondered how things were working out on her end.

Chapter 12

Turmoil

The pacing was what disturbed me. It wasn't like Marion to dwell on things, yet she was creating a trough in the carpet with her back and forth. If it got any worse, the hotel was going to charge us.

"Will you stop for a minute and talk to me?" I requested, sitting at the foot of the bed. "This right here," I swung my arm from side to side to convey her linear travels, "is driving me crazy."

She stopped for a moment and gave me a harsh look.

"I'm sorry my thinking bothers you," she stated bluntly, the unrestrained sarcasm oozing from her lips. "At least I'm trying to figure things out."

"Hey, hey," I snapped back. "Is that *you* talking or your superiors?"

"What? What is that supposed to mean?"

"Come on, Marion. You've been acting funny ever since Vivian Yarrows showed up on the FBI's doorstep. Then, you lose your cool when questioning the poor woman. And now this non-stop back and forth. Are you going to deny it? Something is eating you."

"Nothing is eating me, and there's nothing for me to deny. I explained to you what that was about. We have a case. We have a suspect. And we have two victims with numbers burned into them. We both know there's more to come. Doesn't it bother you at all?"

"Of course, it bothers me," I replied. "Do you think I don't feel responsible for every death attributed to my son? My *son*, Marion. It goes through my mind every day - that he is the way he is because of how I raised him. Or how I *didn't* raise him. I wasn't there for him. I was selfish. I wanted the job more. Maybe if I cared more about being Ben's father when it mattered most, he wouldn't be like this. That's on me, Marion. It's something I'll never live down. But we're not talking about *me* right now. We're talking about you. You don't usually get bothered by stuff like this. But clearly, *something's* bothering you. What's got you rattled?"

She dropped her head and exhaled while she brought a palm up to rub her eye.

"Marion, it's me," I said in a gentler tone. "Talk to me. Tell me what's going on."

She dropped her hand and squeezed her eyes shut, struggling with something. I could see - whatever it was - it weighed on her.

"Jim, I..,"

Her phone rang, disrupting her thoughts.

"Hayes here," she quickly answered as if relieved about the sudden interruption. "What? Hold on; let me put you on speaker." She pulled the phone from her ear and clicked a button. "Okay, go ahead."

"*It looks like you were right about counting down,*" Mick said through the speaker. "*He's killed again.*"

"And you're sure it's him?" Marion asked.

"*There's a six burned into the man's stomach. If it's not him, then we've got one hell of a nasty trend on our hands.*"

I motioned to Marion, giving her a sign we'd practiced before.

"Mick, are you alone?" she asked.

"Yeah, I'm in my car."

Knowing it was safe, I threw my voice into the ring.

"You said the vic was a man?"

"*That's right. A Blackjack dealer from the casino.*"

"The numbers from the register," Marion expressed. "Twenty-one. Of course."

"So, he's not just targeting women," I said, more rhetorically, thinking out loud.

"*It appears not,*" Mick continued. "*And he's done his homework. The Blackjack dealer's address is also 21. Ben's game might be deeper than we thought.*"

I mumbled under my breath. "Why are you doing this, Ben?"

"What about numbers, Mick?" Marion asked. "Did he leave anything with the victim?"

"*He did. That's why I'm calling. We've gone over and over it and can't figure it out. I was hoping one of you two might understand. He wrote 12369 on the man's back. Does that mean anything to either of you? To you, Jim?*"

"Twelve thousand, three hundred sixty-nine?" I pulled out my phone and typed the numbers. I wanted to see them in case there was a pattern. I thought for a minute. "One plus two is three. Three plus six is nine."

"*Okay,*" Mick stated in a hopeful voice. "*What does that give us?*"

"Not a goddamn thing," I said, dashing his hopes.

"What if you keep the pattern going?" Marion interjected. "One plus two is three. Three plus six is nine. Six plus nine is fifteen. Does fifteen mean anything?"

I shook my head, unable to think of anything.

"*Nothing I can think of,*" Mick jumped in. "*We noticed all the numbers add up to twenty-one. Again. Could we be looking for another dealer?*"

"I don't think so," I replied. "I don't think Ben would make it that easy on us."

"What if it has nothing to do with the numbers we're seeing?" Marion chimed in.

"What are you talking about?" I questioned.

"*Yeah, I'm lost, too,*" Mick agreed.

"What if it's about the numbers we're *not* seeing? 4, 5, 7, and 8. Could that be something? 4578?"

"*I don't know,*" Mick answered. "*I wasn't good with numbers in school.*"

"We're not seeing things right," Marion said. "We need time to think about it. There's gotta be a clue in there somewhere."

"*That's just it,*" Mick responded. "*Do we even have that kind of time?*"

"Mick – when is the body going to the morgue?" I asked.

"*The body's being wheeled out now.*"

I looked at Marion and nodded. "Special Agent Hayes will meet you there in the morning. I'm going to think about those numbers for a bit. I hope to have some answers by then."

"Okay, guys. Thanks for the help."

"Mick," Marion grabbed his attention before he hung up. She took him off speaker and placed the phone to her ear. "You should know; It's no longer just me. The FBI is taking over the case. Chief Copelli has already been notified. I'm sorry, Mick; there's nothing I could do. It's out of my hands. I know. I wish it could be different, but you knew this was coming. I didn't want you blindsided. All right. I'll see you in the morning. Bye."

She ended the call and let out a heavy sigh.

"How did he take the news?" I asked.

"Surprisingly well," she replied.

"I understand that. I wouldn't want to be in Mick's shoes."

"You were.., you *are* in his shoes."

"That's different. I've got the stomach for this shit. Mick doesn't have the constitution. Plus, he barely had time to recover from The Letter Man spree before being thrust back into the muck."

"I think Mick is stronger than you give him credit for," she said in his defense.

"I hope you're right about that. I have a feeling this case is going to get a whole lot worse before it gets better."

"Which is why we need to find Ben. We need to put an end to this once and for all."

I felt a twinge in my heart. I knew what those words meant. Marion wouldn't say it to me outright. Ben had to be stopped - no matter the cost. I swallowed hard and gave her an understanding nod.

"Now, about what's been bothering you," I said, revisiting our earlier conversation.

"Jim, I can't do this right now," she replied. "There's too much going on. I'm sorry you can't accept that."

"Marion, I wasn't saying..,"

"Can we just get some sleep?" she cut me off and scurried into the bathroom to brush her teeth, putting an abrupt end to the conversation.

I shook my head, frustrated and defeated. I couldn't argue with the woman. She was too strong-willed to let me break through her defenses that easily. The conversation might have been over for tonight, but it wasn't over. Something had her shaken.

I crawled across the top of the bed and tucked myself under the blankets. I stared at the ceiling, my hands clasped behind my head on the pillow. Between the numbers rolling around my head and Marion's strange behavior, it was going to be a long, sleepless night. Lucky me.

Chapter 13

Those You Love

"Another rough day?" Gina asked as I walked into the living room. My face must have looked ragged and worn from the day I'd had. She was in her favorite chair, reading a book under the dim light of her reading lamp. She looked at peace. How much of that would change if I told her there was another murder? I couldn't keep it from her. It was better to find out from me than from tomorrow's newscast.

"It was a day, that's for sure. What ya reading?"

She flashed me the cover. "Emma," she said, by an author I'd never heard of. Then, she flipped the open book upside down and placed it over the armrest. "Dinner's on a plate in the oven. It should still be warm."

"I'm not really hungry. Thanks, though."

"Oh. I guess it *was* a rough day then."

She began to get up, no doubt to retrieve the food from the oven. She was obstinate about packing away food into the refrigerator as soon as we finished eating.

"Hon, it's okay," I stopped her. "I can take care of it."

"It's not a big deal, Mick," she argued, standing.

"No, really," I insisted, gently grabbing her hand. "I have something I want to tell you."

"It's bad, isn't it?" she questioned, sitting back down but on the edge of the seat. I continued to hold her hand as I sat on the corner of the coffee table, facing her.

"There's been another murder," I said softly, expecting Gina to freak out. Surprisingly, she didn't.

"Ben?" she asked.

I nodded. "We think so. It's the same signs. It matches the bakery owner."

Gina squeezed my hand. "I'm sorry, Mick. This whole mess must be eating you up inside."

"No, I'm okay," I replied. "I'm just worried about you and Stella Mae. I don't like that you're here alone while I'm at work. I can't think straight, constantly worrying about your safety."

"Babe, we're safe. You don't actually think Ben would do something to hurt us, do you?"

"I don't know. The kid is not well. The things he's done.., what he's doing. He's sick, Gina. I'm scared. I'm scared this isn't going to end well."

"What do you mean, baby? Not end well for who?"

"I don't know. For the police, for us, Ben, the city? He's jerking us around. He's planning something, and I don't have a good feeling. Jimmy said..,"

I froze, realizing what I just let out. My eyes widened in fear.

"Mick, what is it?" Gina asked, looking concerned. "Are you okay?"

Did she catch it? I had to assume she did. Maybe my nervous stare caught her off guard. I had no choice but to keep going, correcting my mistake.

"Jimmy used to say he'd get this feeling in his gut. It never let him down. Now *I've* got that same feeling, and it scares the hell out of me."

"But baby, we're okay. There's nothing to be afraid of."

I let go of her hand and rubbed the tension from my forehead. She hadn't yet heard what I was thinking. The hardest part was still to come. *Rip off the bandaid, Mick. It will be easier that way.*

"I think you should take Stella Mae and stay at your sister's house for a while."

"What?" Gina raised her voice.

"I want you and Stella Mae to stay with your sister. Not for a long time, just until we stop Ben. He doesn't know where Rosa lives. You'll be safer there."

"Mick, I'm not going to do that," she argued. "This is our home. I'm not going to run away every time someone in this city is broken or screwed up."

"Gina, listen." I had to find a way to convince her. I needed to keep her and Stella safely out of Ben's reach. "It's not just about that. Your sister lives alone, too. She doesn't know about any of this stuff going on. And she doesn't have a cop in the house to protect her. It's not just about protecting you and Stella Mae. It's about protecting all those you care about. I'll feel better knowing you two can watch out for each other."

"Mick.., I don't know."

"Please, Gina," I begged. "It's only for a few weeks. We'll have him in custody by then."

"How can you be so sure?"

"I wasn't until a few moments ago," I answered. "Remember that gut feeling I told you about?"

She nodded.

"Well, I've got a plan."

She exhaled heavily, giving me a look that said, *"You'd better."*

I leaned forward and kissed her on the forehead.

"It's going to be okay. I promise. Just do this for me."

"Okay, Mick," she agreed. "We'll go. But you'd better keep up your end of the deal."

I smiled and nodded.

"I'm going to bed," she said, clicking off her lamp. "Don't forget to put away the food in the oven."

"I won't"

"You said that before, and I found a plate of meatloaf in there two days later."

"I've got it," I said. "Go to bed." I didn't have the heart to tell her that, last time, I left the food on purpose. It was meatloaf, and her meatloaf tasted like wet cardboard. I had a bowl of cereal instead.

I watched her walk off toward the bedroom as I headed into the kitchen. I pulled the plate from the oven's bottom rack and threw it into the fridge unwrapped. It didn't matter that I wasn't hungry; I wasn't going to eat the chicken breast that tasted like a rubber tire or the burnt Brussels sprouts, anyway. If I didn't value my life, I'd sign her up for cooking classes.

I thought about the plan I'd told her I had. It was true; I did have one. And it was good, too. Sure to succeed. Unfortunately, there was more bad about it than good. I couldn't tell Gina that. I was glad she didn't ask. How do you tell someone that for your plan to work, five more people will first have to die?

Chapter 14

The Plan

By the time I arrived at the morgue, Barry was already deep into his explanation of Stepan's death. Special Agent Hayes stood across from him, hovering over the body on the cold stainless steel table. The medical examiner had already performed an autopsy, and the familiar Y-shaped incision in the corpse's chest and sternum had already been stitched back together. The body was a pasty white, having had all the blood drained from him. I'd now seen enough death that I didn't feel queasy as I approached the lifeless husk. That wasn't a good sign. Was I becoming lifeless, too?

"Ah, Detective Dooley," Barry announced, alerting Hayes of my presence. "I was just going over the details with Special Agent Hayes."

Hayes didn't budge from her position. Her eyes were locked onto the scarred number 6 on Stepan's abdomen.

"Hello, Special Agent Hayes," I greeted.

She offered no response or even a subtle movement to acknowledge me.

"Special Agent Hayes?" I repeated, lightly tapping her upper arm with two of my fingers.

She shook her head as if shaking away cobwebs, then turned to me, looking confused.

"Detective Dooley. Sorry. I was..,"

"Someplace else," I interjected. "I get it."

"Yes. Something like that."

"So," I turned my attention to Barry, "have you learned anything more about the victim - something that might lead us to Ben?"

"As a matter of fact," Barry began, "I was just telling Special Agent Hayes about the soot on Mr. Greguric."

"The soot?"

"Yes. I found traces of dry soot, oil-based, above and below the victim's eyes and mouth. He also had several cuts on the inside of his mouth along the cheeks."

"Ben cut the victim's mouth?" I questioned.

"No. Teeth marks," he continued. "Mr. Greguric cut the inside of his cheeks several times, trying to close his mouth. He had swollen tonsils as well. Stepan here was gagged. I believe he had a cloth around his mouth and another one around his eyes, which would explain the dried oil build-up in those areas. An oil-burning furnace will release trace amounts of soot into the air. In a humid environment, the moisture in the air will gather up the residue and collect on the skin. Higher levels of moisture would collect more oil. Because there were concentrated amounts of soot around the eyes and mouth, it stands to reason the man's sweat was absorbed into the fibers of the cloth, depositing the oily residue in those areas."

"The first victim told us she was blindfolded, as well," Hayes stated. "And she complained about the heat."

"So Ben is in a place where there's a furnace," I said. "Great! That doesn't exactly narrow things down."

"No," Hayes jumped in, "but it explains how he's burning his victims."

"Okay, but..," I paused, thinking about something. "Wait, he's branding his victims."

"Yes, we know that," Hayes commented.

"Where's he getting the branding irons? It's not like he's ordered them over the internet."

"There's a local machine shop that would do that kind of work," Barry said. "We've had them make the custom metal plaques you see over our freezers." He pointed to the freezer units along the side wall that store dead bodies. Above each one, cast iron numbers were attached to stainless steel plaques.

"Fancy," I said. "Can you give us the address of the machine shop?"

"Sure can," Barry replied. "I think I still have their business card. Give me one moment."

While Barry went off in search of that card, I thought it a convenient time to tell Agent Hayes of my less-than-brilliant idea.

"Special Agent Hayes," I said timidly. "I don't want to sound negative, but I think we need to discuss the possibility that we don't catch Ben before he finishes whatever twisted game he's playing."

"We'll catch him," she replied.

"But what if we don't?"

"We *will*," she reiterated louder.

I stared at her for a moment, showing concern on my face, hoping she'd understand the reality of the situation. We had no idea where Ben was or who his next victim would be, and he was stringing us along, making us play by his rules. It was time we switched the rules and made him play *our* game instead.

"And what if we don't?" I asked again, as serious as the circumstances that led us to this moment.

Hayes' eyes shifted downward. She faltered. For the first time, the woman who had been like a machine displayed a hint of doubt. Did I put that in her, or had it been there all along?

"And what do you propose, Detective Dooley?" she asked, looking back at me.

I noticed that, even though we were alone, she didn't call me Mick. She knew we weren't speaking as friends.

I drew in a nervous breath. "You said you believe Ben will try to go after Victim Ø. Vivian. I hope it doesn't come to that, but if he succeeds in this.., countdown of his, and we know she'll be his next victim, we should use that to our advantage."

"You want to use her as bait, don't you?" Hayes expressed angrily.

"If it gets that far..,"

"Absolutely not! That woman has already been through enough, and I swore I would protect her. I'm not going to give her up to that lunatic. Maybe you've given up already, but I'm not willing to let Ben win, and I'm sure as shit not going to let him get anywhere near Vivian."

"But Special Agent Hayes..,"

"I've heard enough," she yelled, cutting me off. "This isn't your case anymore. And though I appreciate your suggestion, the FBI will handle the decision-making from now on."

Hayes didn't let me reply; she stormed off to the stairwell leading to the exit. What was that about? I hadn't seen her like that before. She acted like I was willing to feed Vivian to the wolf. That wouldn't have happened. We'd be there to protect her. Why did I feel like I was suddenly the only one keeping my shit together while everyone else was falling apart?

"Here's the card, Detective," Barry stated, walking back into the room. "Um.., where did Agent Hayes run off to?"

I took the card from him and thought about the gentlest way to answer. "She got called back to the station."

"Ah, well, I had finished up here anyway."

"I should get going, too." I flashed the card in the air, "Thanks for this."

As I started walking away, Barry grabbed my attention. "Detective Dooley. If you're heading back to the station, I have the report Lieutenant Garrett's been hounding me about."

"I can take it," I responded.

"You don't mind?"

I waved my fingers toward me as if to say, *"Give it to me."*

Barry grabbed a folder from the far counter and handed it to me. "There's nothing spectacular in there."

I nodded. "I think we all expected as much. Thanks again."

I walked up the stairs with the folder and business card in hand, wondering if I should feed the information to the FBI first. I looked at the card and smiled. Heavy Metal Machine, with an image of a metallic guitar on its face. Nice. It was only three blocks away. I knew Hayes was trying to get her point across with this being the FBI's case but fuck 'em. I knew my job. And I was quickly learning my gut.

Chapter 15

Branding

I must have driven by the place a thousand times and never realized it was here. There wasn't much for signage on the small business except for some stenciling in the single window along the front and an unremarkable metal sign above the door that read, "custom machining." It was one of three businesses located in a shared, dilapidated building. The blink-and-you'll-miss-it machine shop was crammed into the smallest space, sandwiched between a hobby shop to its left and a tattoo parlor to its right. Upon pulling up to the sidewalk out front, the entire place looked closed, but then, what was I expecting in this neighborhood? Half the city's businesses were struggling to stay afloat, and that was in the "upscale" areas. Down here in "the slums," a business was lucky to remain open for longer than six months, and that was if they didn't get broken into every other week.

I checked the door, expecting it to be locked based on the appearance of the pulled shade and the absence of an "open" sign, but surprisingly, it opened when I turned the knob. I stepped into the dimly lit space and glanced around. Its size was quite deceiving. The shop was very narrow and jam-packed with large machinery, but it stretched a good deal toward the rear of the building. There was nobody present, but I could hear a low rumbling noise coming from the back beyond where I could see.

"Hello?" I called out.

I heard the steady rumbling slow and become quieter until it faded to silence. In the distance, a man appeared, weaving his way forward, maneuvering between machines on his way to greet me. He wore a black do-rag and brown smock over an olive-drab tank top, which displayed both tattoo sleeves down his arms. Small metal shavings covered the lower half of the smock and his boots, as did stains from machining residue. Streaks of black ran across his forehead and cheeks above and below a pair of safety glasses where he must have wiped away sweat with his blackened fingers.

"Can I help you?" he asked in a deep, rugged voice.

"Hi, are you the owner?"

"Owner, manager, and sole employee," he replied. "If you're looking for work, I can't help you."

I smiled, finding humor in his statement. Wearing khakis, a jacket, and a tie, did he really think I was machinist material?

"Thanks, but ah, I'm a detective with the Southbridge Police Department."

"Detective, huh? What kind? My cousin is a detective out in Jersey."

"I'm with homicide."

"Homicide? That's like murder and stuff, right? Hey, I may look like a tough guy, but I didn't kill nobody."

I put a hand up in front of my chest. "No worries," I said with a grin. "I'm not here to haul anyone in."

"In that case, what can I do you for?"

"I'd like to ask you a couple of questions."

"Sure. Go ahead. Shoot. Not literally, though. My ex-wife would kill me if the child support payments dried up. How else would she support her drug habit? The bitch."

"Probably a little more than I needed to know," I responded.

The man shrugged his shoulders.

I brushed aside his angry spousal comment and stuck to business. "Have you ever made custom branding irons?"

"What, you too?" he replied. "You're the second person in as many months who's asked about that."

"So you have made someone branding irons?"

"Yeah. Some douchebag punk came in here last month looking for a set. He was acting all squirrely, keeping his head down, hiding behind a baseball cap."

"Did you make them for him?" I asked.

"Yeah. Of course, I did. I got bills to pay, just like you."

"How many did you make?"

"I made eight. The guy told me he wanted numbers zero through seven."

That fit. Ben's already used three of them. He'll be looking to use the remaining five.

"Did you happen to ask him what he wanted them for?"

"What the fuck do I care if he's branding his dog or some shit?" he replied. "A paying customer is a paying customer."

I shook my head in frustration. "How did he pay? Card? Cash?"

"He paid cash. I told him he could pay when he came to pick them up. I told him two days. The dipshit left me hanging for almost a week, and when he did show up, he marched in here, handed me a wad of cash, grabbed the irons, and ran out. The son of a bitch shorted me a hundred bucks."

"Did he tell you anything about where he was or why he was late picking them up?"

"No; it's like I told you - he was in and out of here in a flash. The nervous piece of shit. Now listen; are you looking to get a set for yourself, or what?"

"What?" I questioned.

"If you're not here to order something, Detective, I've got to get back to work. We don't all make the salary of a homicide detective."

I smirked. "Right. I understand. But I'm actually gonna need you to come down to the station with me to give a written statement."

"Yeah, that's not happenin'," he replied.

"Excuse me?"

"I've got someone coming by in about an hour to pick up a hot order - which you're delaying me from finishing, by the way."

"I see. Can you swing by the station tomorrow morning," I asked.

"It's important, huh?"

"It is."

He rubbed his chin with his thumb and index finger as if pondering what to do. "I guess I can do that."

"Great! We'd appreciate it." I looked beyond him at the numerous machines and nodded. "I'll let you get back to it then. Thank you for your time."

I turned to exit. As I opened the door, the man called out.

"Detective. Whatever he did, if you catch him, I'd appreciate my hundred bucks before you send him off to the big house."

"Yeah," I nodded. "I'll see what I can do."

I walked out and closed the door behind me. I wanted to be upset at the guy but couldn't. He was only doing his job. How could he have known those branding irons would be used in the murder of innocent people?

Where the fuck did Ben get that sick idea from anyway? The kid had lost it. I saw that when I was visiting him in prison - the way he showed no remorse for his mother's death. If he felt nothing for *her*, why would I expect he'd feel anything for strangers, people he'd plucked on a whim? And for what? What was he hoping to accomplish? It couldn't only be to kill Vivian. He could have done that when he had her. Was he trying to prove his superiority over the police – to show how smart he was by eluding capture? Hadn't he already done that since he escaped prison six months earlier? *Why drag innocent people into your sick game, Ben?* Whatever his motivation, we needed to track him down and stop him. If that meant doing things a little off the cuff, then that's what I intended to do. After our last interaction, Hayes wouldn't agree with me. But then, she was getting a little too close to Victim Ø.., Vivian. She needed to stay focused and remain objective. I get that Hayes promised to keep the woman safe. We all would. It wasn't about that. It was about doing everything we could to stop a cold-blooded killer. Sometimes, that meant making hard decisions.

As I got in my car, my phone rang out.

"It's Mick," I answered.

The shouting began almost immediately. Lieutenant Garrett was in a mood. Couldn't that man ever speak in a calm voice?

"No problem, Lieu. I'm on my way in now. Yeah, Hayes warned me about that. I understand. I'll be there in a f..,"

He hung up before I could even finish. Well, today was looking promising. Dead bodies, uptight machinists, and now the FBI was taking control of the case. What next, a fourth victim?

Chapter 16

Burned

Staring at the glowing metal, I think back to the park. Early mornings bring early risers - young people trying to keep their youth and maintain their figure through the daily ritual of monotonous exercise. The joggers conceal their vanity under the guise of a healthy routine while wearing skintight athletic wear to attract the eyes of potential mates. They *want* to be watched. Some of us watch for different reasons.

Early mornings also mean less foot traffic. It's the perfect place for undesirables to go unnoticed. The homeless and downtrodden sleep away their miserable lives on bolted-down benches, drawing little attention from the eyes of uncaring passers-by. Like them, I received no recognition during my few weeks' stay among their kind. But *you*, my friend, were noticed by *me*.

Unlike the others at such an early hour, you had neither the interest nor the desire to run from the inevitable effects of age. You've welcomed it with open arms since the day she left you. You've prayed for the end, unable to take the necessary steps to join her. I can help you with that. It's what I do. I'm a messenger for death. And today, you will become a messenger for *me*.

"Benjamin," the man's weak voice let out. I didn't turn to face him, keeping my eyes on the reddening metal. "Why are you doing this?"

"You shouldn't concern yourself with my reasoning. Many would consider me irrational."

"This isn't who you are," he says, trying to reach me. Bad luck; I'm unreachable.

"You're wrong, Bernard," I respond. "This *is* who I am – who I've *always* been."

I let the iron continue to blaze in the open flame of the furnace as I turned to face the man who mistook me for a caring individual. We all make mistakes. His will cost him.

"Why?" the bound old man questions. "Why me?"

"I wish I could tell you it was to ease your pain," I reply. "I watched you for days, each morning visiting that same bench. You mumbled, speaking to the breeze. I was curious and had to learn. I sat beside you in a spot unknowingly reserved for someone else - someone no longer with us. The first time we spoke, you told me of your wife's passing – how she loved your walks together through the park. Even after the cancer took her, you continued to walk with her in spirit, hand in hand, while you waited for the day you could join her. I sat with you that morning and each morning after - neither of us alone. You didn't know who I was or what I had done. You didn't judge me as so many others had, an oversight for which I won't fault you.

"As a child, I learned to follow others' leads. I watched and listened, learning the delicate intricacies of emotional expression. I found ways to interact with those around me, showing them the subtle nuances in my face and demeanor to make them believe I cared about what they were saying. My conversations with you, Bernard, were no different. It's nothing personal."

The withering man is weak after what I had put him through. Bernard had been compliant through it all, remaining quiet as requested. He spoke softly, resolving each question I asked, only answering incorrectly twice. The first cost him a tooth, removed by my fist. The second cost him a finger – by my knife. It pained me to do it. Not because I felt sorry for him or languished with him in his pain. I felt nothing of that. It was because it was the finger that bound him and his wife together. The gold band would have earned decent cash from the pawnshop, like the previous one with which I used to buy my toys, but the ring slipped from his finger when I separated the digit from his hand. It hit the floor and rolled under the furnace. I was unable to retrieve it. Bernard's wife was no doubt somewhere smiling at my misfortune.

"I wonder if she was there?" I question, looking at the decrepit man.

"What?" Bernard speaks weakly.

"Your wife. I wonder if she was with us this morning when I took you? I wonder how she felt when I rendered you unconscious? Why didn't she save you, Bernard?"

A tear spills from his right eye, the first I'd seen. The pain doesn't hurt him as much as the loss.

"Have you finally accepted that she is not here with you?"

"She is," he whispers. "She's always with me."

I smile, letting him have his dream.

"I'm afraid I must cut our discussion short, Bernard. I'm on a schedule, and others are awaiting my wrath. As I mentioned earlier, I wish I could tell you I was doing this to ease your pain, but unfortunately, you were just another body for the taking, an easy target who stuck to the same dull routine. But there is some good news in all the bad. You will finally be joining your wife. So, if it makes you feel any better, you can think of this as a mercy kill."

"Don't do this, Benjamin," the weary man says, shaking his head. "You can still be forgiven."

"If only that were true, Bernard. Besides, I'm not seeking forgiveness. I'm sure even *you* won't forgive me after what I'm about to do."

I reach for the cloth around his neck.

"I do apologize, but the gag must go back on for this."

I pull it up onto his face and force it over his mouth. I give him a wink to comfort him before turning and grabbing the branding iron. I pull the metal from the flame, the branding end heated to a bright red. Like the others, this will be fun. I bring the burning number near my lips and blow, causing it to glow brighter. Bernard's eyes widen with fear.

"Try to hold still now," I say. "This is going to hurt. You've been a real trooper so far. Let's keep that streak going." A smile emerges on my face. Bernard is not comforted by it.

I turn the brand in his direction, watching his eyes follow it intently. He can feel the heat from a foot away. He begins to struggle harder than he'd done the entire time, mumbling incoherently into the cloth over his mouth. As I bring it closer to him, he turns away, giving me the perfect location. I press it against his cheek while the opportunity presents itself, his screams muffled behind thick fabric. The smoke from his scorching cheek fills the air above him with the stench of burning flesh. His skin melts under the intense heat of the metal. As I pull the iron away, some of his cheek around the burn sticks to the edge of the brand and tears free. The mark isn't as clean as I'd hoped. It's messy but still readable.

I drop the iron to the floor and reach for the knife on the table. Bernard has been a good sport, but I don't want him to pass out yet. He'd told me on more than one occasion that he wished to die so he and his dear, sweet Alice could be reunited. He had been nice to me. I want to grant him that wish. I lean in close, look into his tortured eyes, and plunge the knife into his gut just below his ribs. I watch his eyes flicker in shock as his body stiffens. He makes no noise; the pain from the blade isn't nearly as much as the burn.

"I'm glad you managed to stay with me, Bernard," I say, staring into his eyes from inches away. "Can you feel it? That's the life leaving your body." I tilt my head at a slight angle and smile. "Say hello to Alice for me." I give the knife a jerking twist, and it's over. All is quiet. Bernard has expired. There is something immensely satisfying in those few seconds before death. I exhale.

I pull the knife out, letting the blood drip from my hand as I place the blade back on the table. Lost ring aside, it has been a good day. We all have a part to play in this madness. Bernard played his magnificently, and he will further still. He will deliver a new message, and in doing so, he will grant my friends in law enforcement three days' reprieve. I hope they enjoy their vacation.

Chapter 17

...5

Before I made my way to the briefing room, I passed by Detective Stull on my way to my desk. He was one of the "lousy detectives" Lieutenant Garrett mentioned. He had his ear to the phone while taking notes. When he saw me, he pointed to the receiver and rolled his eyes. That was our universal sign that the caller was wasting our time.

"Yes, I understand, Mr. Baldino," Detective Stull stated in a frustrated tone, "but this is *homicide*. I'm very sorry you have a squatter in your building. Unfortunately, there's nothing I can do about it. I'm sure if you call the main number or stop by the station, one of our officers will be more than happy to assist you. Well, I appreciate that. Yes. But again, Mr. Baldino, this is *homicide*. Right. Okay. You take care now."

Detective Stull hung up the phone, barely containing his annoyed chuckling.

"Another live one, huh?" I said.

"Can you believe that guy?" Detective Stull replied. "He's called to complain three times this month. What doesn't he get about 'this is homicide'? How do these people even get my direct number? Christ. *I got squatters in my basement.*' Boo hoo. What the fuck do I care? Call a fucking exterminator."

"Why don't you tell me how you really feel?"

"Shit, that is how I feel, Mick. And then we got these bozos who come marching in here like they own the place." He pointed to the briefing room, where I could see two uptight-looking suits speaking with Chief Copelli, Lieutenant Garrett, and Special Agent Hayes.

"Get used to it," I said. "Until we have Ben Haddick in custody, they *do* own the place."

"Not for me, buddy. That's *your* case."

I shook my head and flashed a shit-eating grin. "Yeah, I know. You've got more important things to deal with. Like squatters." I grabbed a pad and pen from my desk and started toward the briefing room. Detective Stull commented back as if I was still interested.

"Squatters. Fuck. Unless one of them ends up dead, lose my number, you know what I'm saying?"

I didn't respond. My focus switched to the group awaiting me. I stepped into the room and closed the door behind me. The two unknown agents didn't see me enter as their backs were facing me, but Special Agent Hayes, who was standing next to Chief Copelli, alerted them to my presence when she waved me over.

"Detective Dooley," she began, as the two agents turned in my direction, "this is Agent Deitrich and Special Agent in Charge Samuels. They'll be heading up the investigation from this point forward." Then she introduced me. "This is Detective Dooley," she offered to the men. "He's been the lead on the case thus far and will fill you in on where we are with the case."

"Nice to meet you," I greeted, extending my hand. The larger of the two men, Special Agent in Charge Samuels, was a large black man who looked more like a linebacker than an FBI agent. He grabbed my hand firmly, applying pressure, asserting his haughty masculinity. When he released it, my fingers were a bit tingly. Nevertheless, I next offered it to the other agent, a timid-looking fellow who was smaller than Agent Hayes. He put up his palm to negate my effort and shook his head.

"Pass."

"You'll have to forgive Agent Deitich," SAC Samuels responded, defending the man, "he's a bit of a germaphobe."

"Ah, no problem," I replied, pulling my hand back and wiping my palm on my pants as if it were bacteria-ridden, though I have no idea why.

"Special Agent Hayes has told us you have some experience dealing with the alleged perp," Samuels continued.

"Not alleged," I answered. "It's Ben Haddick. We have fingerprints and DNA samples that confirm it. And yes, I have experience with the subject, as do all of us here, including Special Agent Hayes."

"I understand you *believe* it to be the Haddick boy," Samuels responded. "I appreciate that; I do. Hell, we have one of the killer's victims being held for observation right now who claims it's Ben Haddick, the infamous Alphabet Killer. The thing is.., the witness has endured a traumatic event and has been under a lot of stress; we can't rely on her word until she's been through a complete psychological evaluation. As for the evidence you spoke of, we have yet to see that for ourselves."

A bit agitated at his response, I raised my voice. "What, you think we're incapable of deciphering evidence and determining a suspect? Who the hell do you think you are?"

"Detective Dooley!" Lieutenant Garrett barked. "That's enough."

"But Lieu..,"

"I said, enough. It's out of our hands now. We've been instructed to hand over all the evidence on the case." The lieutenant grimaced a bit and grabbed his left shoulder. "They'll come to the same conclusion."

"If it's accurate," I heard Agent Deitrich say.

Disgusted, I shook my head. I wasn't going to win the battle. Not when my team wasn't in the fight with me.

"Well, speaking of evidence," I stated, "I have the report Barry promised you."

I slid the manila envelope from under my pad and tried handing it to the lieutenant, but our linebacker friend snatched it from my hand before Lieu could react.

"I'll take that," he said.

"Hey, do you mind, grabby?" I blurted, still upset about the situation.

"Detective Dooley," Agent Hayes stepped in, "a word please."

She walked past me, grabbing my arm on her way by, pulling me to the side. Once out of earshot, I let her have it.

"What the fuck, Hayes? Is this how it's going to be? *You* never acted like that asshole. And the other one.., Deitrich? A germaphobe? Are you fucking kidding me? How is he even an agent?"

"I understand you're upset, Mick."

"Oh, we're back to a first-name basis again?" I questioned snarkily.

"I was upset earlier; I admit it," she replied. "Now's not the time to revisit. I told you the FBI was taking over the case. It's bigger than I thought. The bureau's in a tizzy that they let their search for a wanted fugitive lapse over the past few months. They're worried that if this *is* Ben who's back to his old ways, they could be looking at some serious public backlash, including lawsuits. The higher-ups are nervous and taking this seriously. Samuels is not only in charge, he can have you suspended for obstructing justice or even arrested for hindering a federal investigation."

"So we're supposed to lie down and let them walk all over us?" I questioned.

"I'll have a conversation with Samuels," she replied. "I'll get him to be a little more subtle. In the meantime, do yourself a favor; keep the confrontational comments to yourself."

"Fine. But I don't have to like it. And what about the other one? What's his deal?"

"Deitrich isn't a field agent. He's what you might call an analyst. He's a numbers specialist. I fed him the numbers that Ben had left at the crime scenes. Without knowing anything else, he nailed it for both of the victims. The bakery and the casino."

"Well, fuck - where has he been all my life? What about the latest victim? Has he figured anything out with those numbers?"

"He's still working on it," Hayes replied.

Just then, Chief Copelli called out, "Special Agent Hayes, Detective Dooley - if you're finished with your discussion, Agent Deitrich has an interesting theory."

I let out a huff while Hayes nodded her head sideways for us to join the others.

"We're all ears," Hays said.

"Time," Deitrich stated without context as if we were supposed to know what he was talking about.

"Would you care to elaborate?" Hayes asked.

"12369 refers to time," he replied. "The quadrants of a clock. Twelve, three, six, and nine. Is there someplace in this city where that would make sense? A clock tower? A place that specializes in watches?"

Hayes turned to me for an answer. I looked at the lieutenant and the chief for the same. I shrugged my shoulders.

"That's just great, isn't it?" Lieu yelled, still rubbing his shoulder. "We have an answer but no place to go with it. Lots of places sell watches."

"Wait, wait," I said excitedly, raising my finger. "That place over on Shawmut Ave. The place with the clocks."

"That's right," Lieu jumped in. "That's all they sell: clocks, timepieces, watches." He pointed to his wrist. "My wife bought mine from there for our tenth anniversary. What the hell is the name of that place?"

"The Time Capsule," I answered.

"Right," Lieu acknowledged, snapping his fingers and pointing at me.

Special Agent in Charge Samuels spoke up. "Well then, I think we take a little trip to The Time Capsule, wouldn't you say? If Agent Deitrich is right, maybe we can get there before the killer strikes."

"Or maybe we catch him in the act," I added glumly.

"I know you're in charge, Special Agent Samuels," Chief Copelli noted, "but if you don't mind, I'd like my men to tag along." He pointed to me and Lieu. "They know the way, and an extra set of eyes couldn't hurt."

"Agreed," Samuels nodded. "Special Agent Hayes will ride with me. We'll follow you two. Agent Deitrich, you stay here and start looking through the evidence. See if anything stands out to you. Okay, we're on it, people. Let's catch us a killer."

And there it was. The man looked like a linebacker but sounded like a coach. I kept waiting for him to clap his hands and say, *"On three."* He could try, but I wasn't going to do it. I was barely a detective, never mind a football player. He could take his enthusiastic pep talk and shove it up his..,

"Let's go, Dooley," Lieu said in his usual gruff voice.

* * *

All appeared quiet on the western front as we pulled into the parking lot. I noticed the sign on the door almost immediately. The place was closed on Mondays.

Lieu purposely parked in a spot closest to the brick storefront, next to handicapped parking. He didn't want Agent Head-Up-His-Ass Samuels parking next to him. We both stepped out of the vehicle to meet with Hayes and Samuels to discuss our next step. The SAC didn't look too pleased. No amount of pep talk could help his cause if the small business refused to cooperate.

"So, where do we go from here?" Lieu jumped in, pointing at the sign as soon as the other two exited the large SUV.

"The plan remains the same," Samuels stated. "We assume Agent Deitrich is correct about the numbers. I want you to find out who owns the establishment. If the owner is the killer's next intended victim, the killer may know where they live. Lieutenant Garrett, I want a unit sent over to check on them and a uniformed officer stationed at their house throughout the night. Starting tomorrow, I want an undercover in this parking lot, keeping an eye on the place. Got it?"

"Yeah, I got it," Lieu replied. "Detective Dooley," he called out, not realizing I was standing right behind him.

"Right here, Lieutenant."

"Get on your phone," he ordered, rubbing the outside of his left shoulder and rolling it in a circular motion. "See what you can find out about this place. Who owns it? Where do they live?"

"You got it, Lieu," I replied. "You okay there?" I pointed to his shoulder.

"Yeah, damned pinched nerve or something."

"Okay." I walked away from the three of them and hopped on the internet. I hadn't ever been to this shop. It had a catchy name – The Time Capsule. While I looked up the website to see if the owner was listed, I wandered close to the entrance to take a peek inside. That was when I saw what I didn't want to see.

"Fuck! No!" I cried out, gaining the attention of the others. They ran over, already suspecting the horrible news.

"Get out of the way," SAC Samuels said, shoving me aside to glean the situation. He thought maybe there was a chance. I knew better.

Both Agent Hayes and Lieutenant Garrett were already on their phones. Hayes called for an ambulance, Lieu called for a backup unit. Agent Samuels reeled back, lifted his leg, and kicked the door open, busting the jamb. Splintered wood flew in all directions as he charged in, pulling his sidearm from its holster. I did the same, though I knew it was pointless. Ben wasn't here anymore – only the aftermath of another life he'd taken. Samuels swiftly ran into the back room of the small establishment and then a smaller bathroom near the rear while I checked on the body lying in the center of the floor.

"Clear!" the large agent's voice called out. "Shit!" he added, coming back to the storefront while holstering his weapon.

"He's dead," I said, removing my fingers from the side of the man's neck. "Son of a bitch!"

Hayes walked through the door. "Did we get here in time? An ambulance is on its way."

I shook my head.

Her shoulders dropped. "Don't touch anything else. I'll contact Mr. Hinkman." She looked at Agent Samuels to clarify, "The M.E." He nodded. "Lieutenant Garrett has a unit coming to cordon off the store, and he's on the phone with Vera now."

"Vera?" Samuels questioned.

"Vera Snell," she replied. "Chief Forensic Officer."

Agent Samuels looked down at the body and clenched his fists. "Goddammit!" He didn't question whether we believed this to be the work of the same killer. It was unmistakable. The lifeless man lay on his side, the number 5 prominently burned into his cheek.

Chapter 18

Heart of the Matter

When Barry asked us to clear out, SAC Samuels didn't budge. I don't think he trusted the state's medical examiner over bringing in one from the FBI, but there was no time for that. And, of course, once he stood firm, the rest of us stayed as well. Barry let out an aggravated sigh and bent down over the body.

"Our guy is leaving us with quite a collection," Barry stated, swiveling the deceased man's head upward to get a look at the rest of his face. "I'm sorry this happened to you, Bernard."

"Bernard?" Agent Samuels questioned. "Did you know this man?"

Barry took in a deep breath and let it out. "Unfortunately, I did. His wife, Alice, was a friend of my mother's."

"Was?" I asked.

"Yes," he replied. "Alice passed away two years ago. They used to stop by and visit with my mom every so often. After Alice died, Bernard never stopped over again."

"Okay, so what can you tell us?" Agent Samuels inquired.

"Give me a moment, please." Barry stared silently at the old man for about thirty seconds, paying his respects, and then began. "His name is Bernard Tussle. He owns the.., *owned* this store. He's right around my mother's age. I believe he's either seventy-five or seventy-six years old." Barry rubbed his gloved hand across Bernard's opposite cheek. "Agitated skin. He was gagged like the others. There's no redness around the sides of his eyes or ears. He wasn't blindfolded."

"What does that mean?" I asked. "The others were. Why not him?"

"The killer didn't care that the man saw him." Agent Samuels answered.

"Or he didn't bother to hide his identity because he wanted to put fear into the man," Agent Hayes added.

Barry continued his assessment. "There's some swelling and dried blood on Bernard's lips." He used his thumbs to separate the victim's lips. "Yup. He's missing his front tooth. It broke off at the gum line. If I had to guess, I'd say our killer struck him – probably with his fist. And probably several times."

"Christ," Lieu's voice echoed out from behind us. "Ben would hit an old man like that?"

"Thank you for that, Lieutenant," Agent Samuels said, "but again, we haven't determined who the perp is yet."

"Bullshit!" Lieu raged. "We know who the son of a bitch who did this is." He winced and grabbed his left upper arm.

"Please calm down, Lieutenant Garrett," Agent Hayes stated.

"The hell I will," he responded angrily. "We know how to do our fucking jobs, and we know Ben is doing this."

"I appreciate that you feel..,"

"I don't need your goddamn appreciation," Lieu barked, interrupting the SAC. "I need you to start listening to what..," He paused for a second, making a funny face. "To what..,"

I saw his hand clench his arm tighter before his eyes rolled back.

"Lieu?" I called out, reaching for him, but it was too late. He dropped to one knee and then collapsed to the floor. "Lieu!" I yelled. "Oh my God; get the paramedics in here."

Hayes ran out the door, calling for the ambulance crew. They had stayed, waiting for the coroner's vehicle to arrive in case they were needed to help move the body when Barry was through. I put my ear to Lieu's mouth.

"He's barely breathing. Come on, Lieu, hang in there."

Barry stood while Samuels stepped over the lieutenant's legs to race to the door.

"Let's go, let's go," he yelled. "Get those men in here."

A couple of uniformed officers ran to the doorway to check what the commotion was about. Expressions of dread draped across their faces when they saw Lieutenant Garrett sprawled on the floor, looking white as a sheet. A second later, they were shoved out of the way by Hayes.

"Out of the way, officers," she screeched. "Let us through."

The paramedics rushed in, large medical bags slung over their shoulders. They scrambled to Lieu's side.

"Out of the way, sir," one said to me. He placed his hand on my shoulder and gave me a slight nudge. I fell back onto my butt and slid backward, staying on the floor, watching the two men work while my heart raced. I could feel Barry standing behind me. He was staring down at Lieu's motionless body. I brought my fist to my mouth and felt my hand shaking. I couldn't control it. My thoughts were all over the place as I caught only pieces of what the paramedics were saying.

"... myocardial infarction ... oxygen ... he's slipping ... come on, come on ... stay with me ... we're losing him ..."

Then, everything came blaring at me at once with five words.

"He's gone into cardiac arrest."

I began to mumble under my breath, "No, no, no, no, no. Don't do this, Lieu. Don't do this. Breath, damn it!"

"Starting chest compressions," one of the paramedics announced. "Get the defib ready." The other unpacked a defibrillator from his bag and began charging it.

I looked up in time to see Hayes cover her eyes and turn to step out of the door. She squeezed by the officers who were still standing in shock.

I looked back and watched the second paramedic tear into Lieu's shirt while the first pumped oxygen into his lungs with a little hand pump over his mouth and nose. The second paramedic placed the defibrillator pads on Lieu's chest and yelled, "Clear!" I watched Lieu's chest heave upward, then flop back to the ground. "Still not breathing."

"Fuck, fuck," I whispered. "Don't you die on me, Frank." It occurred to me that was the first time I addressed him by his first name. It felt strangely weird but comfortable.

The defibrillator recharged. "Clear!" A second jolt passed through Lieu's body. Again, the rise and fall of a dying man. But then, a glimmer of hope. "I've got a pulse!"

My head slumped to my chest, a sliver of relief felt by all in the room. I couldn't help myself; I had to know.

"Is he going to make it?"

"We have to get him to the hospital." The paramedic nodded to his partner, who immediately darted out the door. "Your friend has had a heart attack. We'll do everything we can to try to keep him stable." He continued pumping oxygen into Lieu's lungs. "He's not out of the woods yet. He may have a partial arterial blockage, restricting blood flow to his heart. We'll inform the hospital to have a surgeon waiting for us, along with the ER staff."

The other paramedic reappeared in the doorway, carrying a canvas blanket with looped straps at each end. He laid it down beside Lieu. They gently rolled him onto his side and slid the blanket under him. After they squared him onto the canvas, they lifted him up while one of them yelled, "Clear the way, please." Everyone jumped out of the way as fast as they could to give the paramedics room as they shuffled out the door to a waiting gurney. With the aid of Barry, I managed to get to my feet and walk to the door to see them wheeling Lieu to the ambulance. Hayes had her head down, still covering her eyes. The officers were on their phones, no doubt calling their friends at the station.

"Get him there," I yelled to the paramedics, who paid me no heed. They knew their job; they knew what they had to do. I turned to SAC Samuels to tell him I had to go, but he already knew before I could get the words out.

"Go, Detective," he said, shooting his thumb toward the vehicles. "Special Agent Hayes and I will take care of things here."

Hayes heard her name and looked up from her sullen state. She saw my worried face and nodded. She had gotten close to Frank over the past couple of years, working with the Southbridge P.D. on these seemingly neverending, goddamn cases, but she wasn't one of us.

"Thank you, Agent Samuels," I said. I grabbed one of the officers and directed him to his squad car. When almost there, Hayes cried out, "Mick..?"

I looked at her, and even from a distance, I could see how bloodshot her eyes were. She didn't have to say anything more. I nodded and yelled back, "I will."

She wanted reassurance Frank was going to make it. I wanted to give her that. He *was* going to make it. He had to. Ben caused this. He's taken too many lives already. He wasn't going to take Frank, too. I've seen enough. I didn't care what Hayes thought; if there was a chance to catch Ben using Victim Ø, I had to convince her. Ben was a rabid dog who needed to be put down. I knew that now. There was a time when I thought maybe he could be saved, but that time had passed. There was no saving the monster he'd become. If I had an opportunity to take him down for good, there's nothing anybody could do to stop me. It was his life or the lives of innocent people. There was nothing to think about. As far as I was concerned, Ben was a dead man walking.

Chapter 19

The Waiting Game

I felt helpless as I watched them wheel Frank through the sliding glass doors of Cooley General. A couple of off-duty officers were already there, having been notified by their coworkers. I had called Gina along the way; she told me she'd meet me here. I told her not to worry about it, but she insisted. She and Frank always got along well. I was thankful she listened to me about staying with her sister, Rosa. It put my mind at ease, knowing she wasn't alone at the house. Rosa was gracious enough to babysit Stella Mae. She and I didn't always see eye to eye, but she loved that little girl. Family is family. And right now, in mine and Gina's eyes, one of our family was in the OR, fighting for his life.

"Baby, I got here as fast as I could," Gina expressed, stepping into the waiting room. She ran up to me and gave me a sympathetic hug. I needed it, but I think it was more for herself. "Have you heard anything yet?"

"No," I answered. "They took Lieu into the OR right from the ambulance, and we haven't heard anything since. He's been in there an hour already."

"What happened?" she asked.

I wanted so badly to keep the news of another victim from her, but I made a promise. She was a cop's wife and had to deal with the bad as much as the good (but was there *ever* any good?).

"We were at a crime scene.., another of Ben's."

"He killed again?"

"Yeah. And Lieu got a little riled, raising his voice at the new FBI agent in charge of the case. The next thing I know, he collapsed. The paramedics said he had a heart attack. His heart stopped for a minute, but they managed to get it going again."

My thoughts jumped to Jimmy and what he'd been through. He and Hayes told me he'd died on the way to the hospital after he got shot. The paramedics managed to bring *him* back, too. Then his heart stopped again while in surgery. The lucky bastard was revived again, though none of us knew it. Hayes managed to cover that up with Karen's help. I still can't believe all of that happened. And Karen knew. And now, *I* knew, and it killed me that I couldn't say anything.

"I should have seen it coming, Gina."

"Mick, why are you doing this to yourself? How could you have known?"

"He kept grabbing his left arm and shoulder. He said it was a pinched nerve, but I should have known better. He doesn't take care of himself; he's dealing with so much stress. He's been a walking heart attack waiting to happen for years."

"Hey, hey," Gina said, grabbing my chin and forcing me to look at her. "You have a lot of stress, too. You're not Frank's babysitter. He's a grown-ass man. You can't keep watch over him, and you certainly can't blame yourself for not knowing it was coming. You said it yourself - even Frank thought it was just a pinched nerve."

"But, Gina..,"

"I don't want to hear another word about it, Mick. You aren't a doctor. It's not your job to know anything more than what Frank said it was. But he's with the doctors now, and he's going to make it through this."

Bless this woman I married. She was the level-headed one. She kept me together whenever I felt I was going to fall apart. I'll never understand what she saw in me back in high school.

"Where's Madeline?" Gina asked about Frank's wife, looking around the room.

"She's on her way. She was at the outlets."

"That poor woman must be a wreck."

"Well, we're about to find out," I responded. "Madeline's here now." I gestured out into the hallway, where a nervous-looking Madeline Garrett was gazing from side to side, confused about where to go.

"I'll get her," Gina said.

She walked to the doorway and called out, "Maddie." Frank's wife turned to acknowledge her name, and immediately upon seeing Gina, a half-ton of weight fell from the woman's shoulders. She dashed to Gina and embraced her, tears forming in her eyes. She looked over Gina's shoulder and saw me. I nodded and gave as optimistic a smile as I could, knowing her husband's heart had already given out once before. She released Gina with one hand and extended it toward me, urging me over. I felt compelled to join them if only to offer Madeline comfort.

"Oh, Mick," she said with teary eyes, grabbing my hand and squeezing it. "Tell me he's going to be all right."

"He *is*, Maddie," I replied. "You know better than to think otherwise. Your husband is a tough SOB. He wouldn't let something like this keep him down."

I hated being positive simply for the sake of comforting another, knowing damn well it was all a lie. Frank could be dead right now for all I knew, and I was giving this woman false hope, only to have the truth come crashing down upon her. I couldn't stay around this.

"I'm sorry, but I have to make a call. You'll stay with Madeline, won't you, Gina?"

Gina separated from Madeline's grasp. "Of course. Come on, Maddie; let me buy you a coffee."

They walked off down the hallway toward the right; I went to the left. When I got to a quiet area, I pulled out my phone and dialed a number previously given to me, whom I had listed as J. Ghostman in my contacts.

"Hey, it's me," I began. "I know I wasn't supposed to call unless it was an emergency, but we need to talk."

I hated myself for this, but things were getting out of hand. Too many innocent lives had already been lost, and we still had no clue where to find Ben or how to catch him. And now *this*. We had one solid chance, and Hayes was being uncooperative. I hoped this little stunt would change that without costing me too much.

"He's killed again. You knew this would happen. It's not going to end until *we* end it. That means he has to be stopped by any means necessary. And now the whole mess with Frank. What? You mean Hayes hasn't told you? Frank's in the hospital; he had a heart attack at

Ben's latest crime scene. A bunch of us are at Cooley General now. We're still waiting to hear from the doctor. Listen, I know you don't want to hear it, Jimmy, but this is all on Ben's shoulders. I know he's your kid, but he's gotta be taken down. I understand that. We're all doing what we can, but you've seen firsthand what he's capable of. Hell, if it wasn't for him trying to make you out to be this city's savior, we might never have caught him the first time he was doing this shit. Yeah. Well, as a matter of fact, I do have an idea. That's why I'm calling you."

He wasn't going to like what I had to say, but he was going to listen, damn it. If he was still the same Jimmy I once knew, he'd realize it was the right thing to do.

"I know how we can catch him," I continued. "But I'm going to need your help. It's going to get personal, Jimmy. I hope I can count on you."

Of course, he was agreeable; he had no idea what I was about to ask. Things would probably get ugly from here. I took a deep breath and thought, *here we go.*

"This is my idea."

Chapter 20

The Past Never Dies

The idea was circling in my brain. Mick had a valid point. Even with the FBI stepping up their game, there was no guarantee they'd catch Ben before he completed whatever the fuck crusade he was on.

Marion told me about the new SAC from Washington. He sounded like a no-nonsense kind of guy, but he had no idea the kind of nasty shit Ben was capable of. Until he lived it like we all had, in his mind, the killer was just another scumbag ready for him to take down. But Ben was different. He was smart. Calculating. He knew how to stay hidden and when to strike. He had a plan mapped out – something the authorities did not. We've all just begun playing his game, but he's been playing it for months. He's up to something big; He's telling us as much. It's bigger than just killing innocents, and until we figure it out, we'll always be chasing his smoke. That's why Mick's plan is solid. Marion won't think so, but that's why he's enlisted my help. Sure, let me do the dirty work - as if that woman ever listened to anything I had to say.

I stood at the hotel window, peering out at the traffic lights speeding by, contemplating how to communicate my thoughts to Marion in a way she wouldn't find counter-productive to her own. She was strong-willed and didn't often let anyone lead her in a particular direction. Once she had her mind made up, it was difficult to change. I had to try.

I heard the door-lock buzz from the key card. Marion had arrived. When she entered, she was on her cell phone. I greeted her with a smile; she reciprocated with a sour look and a subtle shake of her head, indicating it was not a good day.

"Yeah, I'm sorry I didn't make it," she spoke into the phone. "It's been one hell of a day."

That wasn't a good sign. If it's already been one hell of a day for her, then my discussion with her would send her over the edge.

"Yes, I plan to stop in tomorrow," she continued. "You'll be fully briefed on Mr. Hinkman's findings. There's no need to worry about that; SAC Samuels is now on board with our suspicions that the killer is Ben. Yeah. He changed his mind after Agent Deitrich filled him in on all the evidence thus far collected. Yes, of course. Thanks again, Mick. I appreciate the update. I'll see you tomorrow."

She hung up and tossed the phone onto the bed while kicking off her shoes. She was looking a little ragged. Her hair had come slightly undone from her usual tightly-formed bun. She pressed her fingers to her temples and let out a relieved breath.

"It looks like you had a tough day," I opened with to gauge her temperament.

"There was another murder and..," She hesitated, looking for the words. "Frank Garrett's in the hospital. He had a heart attack."

"I heard," I responded.

"How did you..?"

"Mick called me. It sounded like you received an update on his condition."

"He was in surgery most of the day. He had a lot of scarring on his heart. It turns out he had multiple minor attacks leading up to the big one that almost killed him. He had a blocked artery. They put a stent in. Because of the damage to his heart, they want to keep him in the ICU for a day while they monitor his condition before transferring him to a regular room. If all goes well, he'll be home on Wednesday."

"That's good to hear," I expressed.

"Yeah. I'm sorry I didn't tell you about Frank sooner. There'd been a lot to take in today. I need to take a shower."

"Before you do that," I said, reaching for her hands. "We need to talk about something else."

"Something else?" she questioned.

"When he was on the phone with me earlier, Mick told me about his idea to use Vivian to catch Ben."

"Oh, he did, did he? Did he also tell you that idea was off the table?"

"He told me you were against it, yes."

"Damn right, I'm against it."

"The thing is, Marion.., it's the best shot you've got to catch him."

"No, we know his plan. He's counting down. He plans to kill four more people before coming after her again. We'll stop him before it gets that far. We're learning more every day. We'll catch him."

"Will you?" I said frustratingly. "Do you even have any idea of a pattern he might be following? Two women of different ages and backgrounds, a young man barely in this country legally, and an elderly man who sells clocks. Ben's not working a pattern at all. He's taking whoever's convenient. You have no idea where he is or why he's playing this game of his. He's been ahead of the police the entire time. The only thing we know for sure, and that's if we're interpreting his threat correctly, is that he'll be coming back to finish what he started. Victim Ø is his end game. He doesn't know we know that. But if you hold onto her, he'll catch on real quick. If that happens, he may decide to start his little game all over again. The FBI has got to let her go. *You* have to let her go."

"Jim, I can't do that," Marion retorted, shaking free from my hands.

"Why not?"

"I don't use victims as bait. I promised I'd protect her."

"That's bullshit! You protect people every day. You've never been like this with anyone else. You've been acting funny ever since that woman came knocking on the FBI's door. What makes this one so special?"

Marion began to rub her forehead as she paced to the window, taking her turn to oversee the traffic. She looked at me through the reflection.

"I just need to keep her safe, okay? You wouldn't understand, Jim."

"Help me to understand, Marion. What's going on here? Why is this Vivian woman so important to you?"

She put her hands on her hips and dropped her chin to her chest. She knew I wouldn't give up until she opened up to me. I told her a couple of years ago that we were a team. I'd have her back when she needed it. But if she refused to let me in, to give me a reason why, that showed a lack of trust on her part. And if she couldn't trust me, maybe we weren't the team I thought we were.

"Marion..?"

"Jim, I.., I never told you why I decided to join the FBI."

"No," I replied. "Does it matter?"

"It does now - with this case."

"What do you mean?"

She turned and walked to the edge of the bed, keeping her head down as if she were ashamed to look at me.

"When I was sixteen years old," she began, sitting down and fiddling her thumbs, "my younger sister was abducted on her way to school one morning."

"Marion, I..,"

"No, let me finish. Brittany was such a sweet girl. She was so caring and giving. She had a smile that would light up the room and make people forget about their troubles. She was smart and witty. She had so much personality, you know? People fell in love with her, and she was a friend to everyone who met her. But she was too trusting. She wanted to believe everyone had a good heart."

Marion's eyes welled up as she choked back tears.

"Roy David Willmecki," she continued. "That was the son of a bitch who took her, though nobody knew who it was for weeks. He had tricked her into helping him retrieve his cat that had just run under a bush on the side of his house. Like a good little helper, Brittany marched right up the lawn. There was no cat. It wasn't even his house. The couple that lived there were away on vacation. When she bent over to look under the bush, he snatched her. He covered her mouth to keep her from screaming while he carried her to his truck. I always prayed she got some good kicks in."

"My God, Marion. I didn't know."

"How would you? I don't go around advertising it."

"Still," I responded, somewhat confused, "what does any of that have to do with Vivian?"

"The local authorities were of no use, making excuses every chance they could to retain a little bit of positivity in the public's eye. It was only after the FBI got involved a couple of weeks later that things started to change. They turned up the heat and started putting pressure on everyone they believed fit the profile of the kidnapper. A week later, Roy David Willmecki turned himself in. He claimed the entire kidnapping wasn't as exciting as he thought it would be. But, it didn't stop him from..,"

Tears trickled down Marion's cheek. I hadn't seen her this vulnerable before. I sat beside her and grabbed her hand.

"Hey, hey," I tried to console her. "It's all right."

"No, it's not," she said, using her free hand to wipe her tears away. "There's more. When they recovered Brittany's body from that scumbag's basement, she had been beaten and raped several times."

She pounded her fist on the mattress beside her.

"Ten years old! The sweetest girl you could ever know, and that animal beat her and raped her, and when he was through having his fun, he killed her. And do you want to know why I have to protect Vivian? Why she's different? Because Roy David Willmecki took a branding iron and burned a zero into my little sister's back. *'So she'd always be mine,'* he confessed. So you see – Ben's clearly done his homework. He's dug into my past. He's taunting me. He's trying to get into my head. He sent Vivian right to my doorstep to rattle me. He tried to handicap us before we'd even begun looking. Well, I refuse to let him win. My sister was the first Victim Ø; I won't let Roy kill another."

Clearly, Marion was more distraught than she believed.

"You mean, Ben," I corrected her.

"What?"

"You said you weren't going to let *Roy* kill another. We're not dealing with Roy. We're dealing with Ben."

"Right. That's what I meant."

"Uh-huh."

"It's because of what happened to Brittany that I'd decided I wanted to join the FBI. I've dedicated my life to taking down the criminals who think they can get away with anything they do. This case is no exception. But I'll be damned if I do it by placing Vivian in harm's way. Setting her up as bait is not something I'm comfortable with."

I wrapped my arm around her and squeezed her into me. The anger she felt had dried up the tears.

"Marion, I'm so sorry that happened to you and your family. It shouldn't happen to anybody, but it does. It's a shitty world we live in. But if there's a chance Vivian can..,"

She brushed my arm from around her and stood.

"I told you, it's not going to happen," she stated adamantly. "This is the FBI's case, Jim, not yours. Not Mick's. That means I call the shots. Vivian stays in protective custody at our field office."

"Marion..,"

"I'm taking that shower now."

She walked away and closed the bathroom door with a little more force than expected. Had it been her place instead of this hotel, she would have slammed it harder, making sure to get her point across. Believe me, her point was across. Sending Vivian out there was a no-go. Marion was strong-willed. Once she made her mind up, it would take an act of God to change it. She was committed to seeing justice done. That's one of the reasons I fell in love with her. The thing was, I truly felt she was wrong. But that didn't matter. Whether I agreed with her decision or not, she was in charge. It was going to play out her way. I only hoped she could live with the repercussions of that decision.

Chapter 21

Money Talks

The coffee wasn't going down as smooth as I'd hoped. It had been too rough a night. Between staying at the hospital way too late, consoling Frank's wife, and having to eventually part ways with Gina as she returned to her sister's house, it wasn't the best sleep. I was hoping the office could provide a bit more comfort.

I walked to my desk, needing distractions. I peered over at Frank's darkened office, the sound of silence strangely piercing into me. In my head, I heard him shout out a thunderous order, "Get in here and shut the door, goddammit," and I felt a comforting grin take shape.

"What's that weird-ass expression for?" Detective Stull asked, directing a pencil at himself and air-drawing an awkward smile to imitate mine.

"Nothin'. I was thinking about Frank and hoping for a quick return."

"Oh, it's 'Frank' now, is it? You're on a first-name basis with our fearless leader?"

137

"No, I'm not," I answered, feeling embarrassed. "I guess I just..,"

"Relax, Dooley," he cut in. "I'm just ragging ya. Yeah, we're all feeling that way about Lieu. I don't think a guy has ever been so hated yet so loved as much as that cantankerous son of a bitch. I hope he gets back in here soon. Meanwhile," he pointed the pencil he'd been holding toward the briefing room, "we've got our new bosses over there, stroking the egos of Captain Redfern and Chief Copelli, making them believe they know what they're doing."

"They're not our new bosses," I retorted, referring to the FBI. "They're only here to help with the case."

"Well, whatever they are, that agent woman Hayes didn't seem very pleased when she got here at 5:00 this morning."

"5:00?" I questioned. "Jesus, Stull, what are you doing here that early in the morning?"

"I've got three daughters," He replied. "When you live with four women as I do, you try to get up as early as possible and leave the house before they all wake up and start yapping about who's taking too long in the bathroom and who's been wearing whose clothes? Christ, it's like I'm living in *their* house instead of them living in mine. No, thank you. I'd rather be here. At least here, I have peace and quiet when I'm on the shitter. Anyway, I think you're supposed to be in there."

"I'm trying to avoid that if I can help it."

"I'm afraid you're not going to have much choice. Captain Redfern has already stepped out twice looking for you."

"Dooley!" a voice yelled from behind me, startling me.

"Speak of the devil," Detective Stull jibed.

I turned, forcing a smile. "Yes, Captain?"

"Gather up your paperwork on the case and meet us in here. We've got things to discuss."

"Right away, Captain," I replied, regretting leaving my empty house. I didn't have much paperwork. I hadn't started my official report yet, just notes and scribbles I'd kept along the way. With everything that'd gone on, I'd fallen behind. I was hoping to get a jump on that today.

I gathered my notepad and pen, scooped up my tumbler of semi-burnt coffee, and proceeded to the briefing room. I heard Detective Stull's phone ring.

"Detective Stull," he answered. "How many times do I have to tell you, Mr. Baldino - this is Homicide? Hom-i-cide."

I couldn't help but shake my head and smile. Detective Stull thought he had it rough dealing with cranky landlords. At least he wasn't going into the lion's den smelling like steak. And seeing Hayes' dour expression as I opened the door told me she'd already had that talk with Jimmy. I could tell I wasn't exactly on her favorite person's list.

"Detective Dooley," Chief Copelli greeted. "Good to see you, son. I know you and some of the other boys were at the hospital quite late. I appreciate that; I know Lieutenant Garrett would, too."

"Thank you, sir," I responded, trying not to drop anything as I shook his outstretched hand. "Is there something going on with the case I should know about?"

"What's going on," Special Agent Hayes stated pointedly, stepping forward, "is that we all need to get on the same page as the killer. We have four victims, three of whom are dead. We have reason to believe the killer will be going after at least four more before he's finished. There doesn't seem to be any connection between the victims. The only pattern we can tell the perp is following is that he's leaving us clues at the scene, directing us to his next victim. So far, we've surmised each of them, only we've always been too late."

"Hold on," I jumped in. "Let's be clear. Ben isn't leaving us clues to his next victim. He's leaving us clues as to where his next victim's body will be."

"Right," Hayes agreed. "Which means we need to figure out his clues faster and work our way backward to the intended victim before Ben strikes."

"Was there any clue left behind with the latest victim?" I questioned.

Agent Deitrich, who'd been standing at the periphery of the room, away from the rest of us germ-infested folk, took that as his cue.

"Bernard Tussle, branded #5 in the killer's countdown, had these three Monopoly bills in his pocket."

He held up a plastic ziplocked bag with colorful play money inside. There was a ten-dollar bill, a five-dollar bill, and a one-dollar bill."

"That's it?" I questioned.

"No," SAC Samuels spoke up, perhaps feeling left out. "He also left a game piece and one of those little green, plastic houses, which Ms. Snell is currently working on in her lab. Oh, and a quarter, though that could have been the victim's own."

"What are you expecting Vera to find?" I asked.

"At this point, anything," Samuels replied. "We need to figure out what the clues left with Mr. Tussle mean.

The quicker, the better. Does anybody have an idea? Everything is on the table."

"What was the game piece that was left?" I questioned.

"The automobile," Agent Hayes answered. "Are you thinking something?"

"I'm thinking more about the little green plastic house," I replied. I turned to Captain Redfern and Chief Copelli. "Don't we have some greenhouses in Southbridge? I mean, the flower growing kind, not the color."

"You don't think it could be that simple, do you?" SAC Samuels blurted.

I shrugged my shoulders, "You said everything's on the table. It's worth a shot."

"There's that nursery down off of Peacock Road," Captain Redfern answered. "They've got a few greenhouses on their property."

"Send a unit to check things out," SAC Samuels ordered. "Find the owner; tell them not to go out anywhere alone."

Captain Redfern nodded agreeably and stepped off to the side to radio dispatch.

"What else do we have, people?"

"Maybe we should check out green-colored houses, too," Hayes added.

"We can get a few patrols going," Chief Copelli responded, "but we don't have the manpower to check the entire city promptly."

"Understood," SAC Samuels came back. "Start what you can. We need to be proactive. Have your men calmly remind residents they should remain observant of their surroundings. If at all possible, when leaving their home, they shouldn't go out by themselves."

"That's a tall task," I stated.

"We have to do our due diligence, Detective."

"What about the car and the money?" Hayes asked.

Samuels glanced over at Agent Deitrich, "Any thoughts, Agent?"

"The car could signify that the next location is not nearby. Like, one would need to drive to get there."

"That's not very helpful," I retorted. "And the money?"

"Well, it's not much to go on," Agent Deitrich began. "We could be looking at a bank or financial institution. Or, the bills might represent simple numbers: 1, 5, and 10. When added together, it's 16. When subtracted, it's 4. When multiplied, we get 50. When divided, only 2. Again, not much to go on."

"You mentioned a bank," I lit up. "We have a TD Bank on Oliver Street. Their color is green. And they're quite a distance from The Time Capsule. That hits all three of the clues."

"Good. Get over there," SAC Samuels demanded of me. "Meanwhile, Agent Deitrich, I want you to continue working out numbers. I want to look at all the options. Also, we need a Monopoli board. Maybe there's something on it that correlates with someplace in this city."

"I can pick one up on my way back from the bank," I volunteered.

"All right, you *do* that. Special Agent Hayes and I will work with Agent Deitrich and Officer Snell. Let's do this. We're going to get that son of a bitch."

And like that, I was off. We had officers on the street, checking out several locations. None of us knew what we were looking for or what we'd find, but it felt good to do something instead of sitting around, *wondering* what to do. It would also keep my mind preoccupied, so I wasn't dwelling on Lieutenant Garrett.

I didn't get a chance to speak with Hayes. That might have been a blessing. She didn't look like she was in the mood to discuss things. Hopefully, one of us would get lucky, and this would all end before we needed Vivian's assistance. If not, then we'll be seeing a lot more death come our way. I didn't want to think about that right now. One task at a time. Get to the bank, talk safety with the employees, then pick up a gameboard. It should be pretty straightforward.

Chapter 22

Somedays

I stepped into the lobby of the small TD Bank branch, a heavy smell of perfume permeating the air. I'd made it a habit to check my surroundings to gather what information I could. Jimmy taught me that when I was a rook. There was a small line in front of me, and I could tell the overbearing fragrance was coming from the woman at the rear of the line who kept rubbing her fingers through her recently styled salt-and-pepper hair. Her nails were polished with a glossy turquoise color with wavy patterns of sparkly silver glitter. She looked like she'd just come from the salon.

There was an older gentleman in front of the woman. The personal check he held shook wildly in his trembling right hand. He wore a thin, unzipped navy jacket and a baggy pair of tan khakis, which were incredibly wrinkled along the back of his legs. I don't think he was as concerned about his appearance as the woman behind him was of hers. The "Vietnam Veteran" cap atop his head was skewed slightly to one side as if he were trying to fit in with the younger generation who wore their hats like that on purpose.

One customer stood at a prep counter to my left, pulling out a withdrawal slip from an acrylic holder. His nails had black gook along each of his cuticles and weren't nearly as flashy as the glammed-up ones the woman was flaunting. He wore ripped jeans that had brown stains smudged across his upper thighs, where it looked like he might have wiped his dirty hands. He had on a crew-neck sweatshirt that rode up a little in the back, exposing a flannel shirt underneath.

The young man kept glancing up to look at the three tellers behind the counter before going back to staring at the paper in front of him. I noticed for the few minutes I'd been in line that, though he'd been holding a pen the entire time, he hadn't actually written anything. He glanced up again, nervously biting his lower lip as he scoped out the tellers. He turned his gaze to the three of us in line, which was when I noticed a bead of sweat trickle down the side of his nose. His eyes then shifted back to the tellers and to the cameras mounted at the ceiling line behind them. I knew what was going on here. The man was interested in a different kind of withdrawal.

I stepped from the line and nonchalantly strolled to the customer prep counter, pulling a deposit slip from the holder and positioning myself between the young man and his view of the tellers. He swiveled his head to the side to try and glance around me.

"How's it going?" I said, flashing a slight smile to not alert him of anything suspicious. He narrowed his eyes, giving me an annoyed glare. I shook the pen I held and dropped it onto the counter. "Figures," I groaned. "Would you mind if I borrowed yours?"

"What?" the man said, looking confused. He probably wondered why I was disturbing him from his determined task.

"Your pen," I replied. "Are you still using it? Mine's dead."

"Oh. No, you can use it." He handed me his pen, keeping watch on the line just as a customer finished up with their banking and walked by. As the elderly veteran at the front of the line took his place at the now-available teller window, the skittish young man beside me swallowed hard and stepped from the counter, squeezing the withdrawal slip tightly in his grip.

"Don't you want to fill that out first?" I questioned, gaining his attention again.

"What?" he asked.

"I noticed you hadn't filled out your slip there." I pointed to the paper in his hand.

"Man, why are you talking to me?" he questioned, his annoyance raised.

Calmly, I continued. "I just think you should fill out the slip before you get up there. It makes things go more smoothly that way."

"I don't need you telling me what to do, man."

I put my hands up defensively. "Pardon me. I was only trying to help."

"Well, shut up," he responded. "I don't need your help." He took another step to get in line before I disrupted his plans further.

"Oh, one more thing," I said, putting my index finger up. "I'd think long and hard about what could happen."

"What are you talking about?" he questioned, agitated.

"You know, if you decide to go through with it."

"You don't know what you're talking about, man. You should get outta here."

"Okay," I said. "Maybe I don't know what I'm talking about. Maybe you're a smarter guy than I give you credit for. I mean, I don't see any cops around, do you? Although.., I guess that doesn't mean there isn't one."

"What?" he questioned surprisedly. "A cop?"

"Yeah, you know, an undercover cop. Or one who's off-duty. You never can tell. That'd be a shame. All the planning that went into this, only to have such bad luck as to choose the one bank where a cop was doing his banking. Although, it would be funny, don't you think?"

"Shut up, man. You don't know nothin'."

"You could be right, but as I said, you should think long and hard about what could happen."

The nervous young man looked forward as the line shifted again. He looked back at me and saw how dead serious my eyes were. I think he understood as his stern look suddenly softened. He looked down at the crinkled paper in his hand and licked his lips.

"I didn't want to bank here anyway," he stated, trying to save face. "The customers here are whack." He strutted to the exit, dropping the withdrawal slip to the floor.

"You want your pen back?" I questioned, smirking.

Two middle fingers were his response as he walked out, hopefully deterred enough from a later attempt. I suppose I could have done a little more - expressed I was a police officer and asked for identification. He wouldn't have had to give it to me, and I certainly wasn't going to haul him in on suspicion of wanting to rob a bank. I'm sure he wasn't the first person to think about that. People were having hard times. Unless he brandished a weapon or carried through with the deed, there was nothing I could legally do. Besides, I had more important things to worry about. Stopping and catching Ben was first and foremost on my mind.

I resumed my spot in line, now next to be waited on. I looked at the three tellers, all in their late teens or early twenties, and wondered if Ben would really go through with harming an innocent kid. I quickly shrugged that off. I had no idea what Ben was capable of anymore. He beat and killed an elderly man. He was twisted and deranged. He was unpredictable. People – maybe even young people – were nothing to him. That made him even more dangerous. That made me more angry but also more fearful.

"Can I help you, sir," the young woman called out from behind her station. I stepped up to greet her.

"Hi, can I speak with your manager, please?"

"Oh, I *am* the manager," she replied. "Is there something I can help you with?"

"You? You're the manager?" I'm sure that came out wrong. I didn't mean to be offensive to the young woman; I wasn't expecting someone so young to be managing a bank.

"Uh-huh," she nodded, seemingly unfazed by my comment.

"Um, I..," I stumbled. I wasn't sure how to approach the subject with someone only a few years out of high school. My thoughts jumped to Stella Mae. Would I want my daughter to discuss this subject with an officer if she was this girl's age? Probably not. But here's the thing.., I'm a homicide detective who had a job to do. Doing the right thing sometimes meant doing the hard thing. If it meant saving lives, there wasn't a choice at all.

"My name is Mick Dooley. I'm a homicide detective with the Southbridge Police Department. I don't want to cause alarm, but we're searching for a dangerous individual who is targeting people who are alone or possibly find themselves in secluded areas away from others. We're warning the public to try to stay in groups of two or more."

"Homicide?" she questioned.

"That's right," I answered. "But believe me when I tell you there is nothing to worry about as long as you stay close to others. Can you do that? Can you let your employees know?"

She looked at me with wide eyes and an even wider mouth as she nodded her response. "Uh-huh." I think I just scared the young lady half to death. But maybe that will keep her from being *all the way* dead.

"Good. Now listen to me. Have you had any employees not show up for work recently? Maybe within the past couple of days?"

"No. Everybody has reported to work as usual."

"That's good...," I glanced at the young woman's name tag, "Shelly. That's *very* good. I'm going to give you my card." I reached into my pocket and handed her the last card I had on me. "Now that's my direct line." I pointed to the card. "If any of your employees miss work unexpectedly, I want you to call that number. If I don't answer, I want you to call the second number on that card. That's to the police station. Do you understand me?"

"Uh-huh," she nodded rapidly. "I mean, yes."

"Good. If you call, I want you to tell them that Detective Dooley stopped in and spoke with you and that I asked you to call. And then give them the name and address of the employee who didn't show up. Do you have all that?"

"Yeah, I think so," she answered timidly.

"Okay, great. And please tell your employees not to go out alone. *All* the employees. Not just these two."

"I will," the manager answered.

I looked at the other two tellers whose stares told me they heard some of my conversation with their boss. I'd leave it at that. If being scared meant they would be more cautious, then I did what I could do.

I walked out feeling good about myself. Maybe I was wrong about the bank, or maybe Ben hadn't yet struck, and I just made it harder for him. Either way, I felt I saved those young people in there. If not from a sadistic killer, at least from a potential bank robbery. Somedays, being a cop was better than others. Chalk this up to one of the good days. It may not have gotten us closer to catching Ben, but I'd take what successes I could. Now, it was off to pick up that monopoly board. Maybe that would help steer us in the right direction.

Chapter 23
Cover

Why did I put myself in this situation? It was too risky. Did I think an overcoat and baseball cap would keep those who knew me from recognizing me? Fat chance. So, I stayed clear of people, keeping my head down. I was just an anonymous visitor, wandering through the corridors like everyone else. Except this visitor was supposed to be dead, and nobody was the wiser.

Marion would throw a fit if she knew I came here. She'd worked so hard, risked everything - her career, her reputation, to ensure my "death" went off without a hitch. Her bosses weren't pleased, but they came around. They'd since taken advantage of the debt I owed. For the past three years, I'd been behind the scenes as a sort of liaison, occasionally helping them with cases. I'd kept a close eye on the FBI's progress after Ben escaped prison, but I wasn't getting involved. A part of me was happy he'd gotten out. I'd hoped he'd run off someplace and start a new life for himself, leaving all the darkness behind. I thought Ben could learn to be good again. I was wrong.

It's bad enough I had to convince Marion's superiors to let me in on this case. Then I talked Marion into letting me tell Mick I was alive. He was the only detective I could trust and the only one who knew Ben like I knew Ben. Maybe even better since he'd visited Ben all those times in prison. But now, how would the FBI feel, how would Marion feel, if they knew I was risking it all to check on a friend? *Was he a friend? Or just a respected colleague?*

Frank and I had had our share of bad blood over the years, especially after he'd had an affair with my wife, but he was always a straight-shooter. He expected only the best from his officers. It was that obstinance that made us.., that made *me* a better detective. He didn't have manners, he didn't have class, but he always had my back. He was passionate about cleaning the streets of Southbridge, and he demanded the same passion from his subordinates. No matter what my personal feelings were about him and my late wife's infidelity, I respected him professionally. I hoped he'd recover from the heart attack, but I had to come and see him in case.., well, this could be the last opportunity I get to pay my respects. To hell with the FBI. They couldn't keep me away.

The young woman at the reception desk told me Frank was on the second floor, Room 217. I had to be careful; it was still visiting hours. I took a chance that all available officers were out searching for Ben's whereabouts. There could be some stragglers, but I remained cautious, keeping my head to the floor, only glancing up to look at room numbers. After Room 215, the hallway opened up to a large vestibule. A circular nurse's station was in the center of the floor, where two nurses sat at monitors. The setup allowed me to walk to the far side of the station and peer into Frank's room from a distance, where I could keep safe from familiar eyes.

Frank's wife, Madeline, was by his side, holding his hand. Frank appeared to be sleeping, unaware anyone was there at all. I stood motionless, stiff, watching for a minute before one of the nurses took notice.

"May I help you, sir?" she greeted me with a smile.

Admittedly, it caught me off-guard, and my mind shifted to defensive mode as I brought my hand up to rub my forehead to disguise my face.

"I was looking for Room 217 to visit a friend," I replied, "but I see his wife is currently with him."

"Ah, yes. Mr. Garrett. He's recovering nicely and should be going home tomorrow morning. You're welcome to go in. He can have up to three visitors."

"Thank you, but I'd rather stay out here if it's all right with you. Mr. Garrett's wife never cared much for me. I'd hate to start any drama."

She looked at me as if she'd heard more than she wanted and relaxed her smile.

"I understand, sir, but I can't have you standing in the hallway like this. Would you care to have a seat in the waiting room?"

Still keeping most of my face covered and feeling like a suspect in a crime, I shook my head. "No, thank you. If you could allow me one more minute, I promise I'll get out of your way and leave."

The nurse dropped her shoulders and huffed. "I'll give you two minutes. Then I'm going to have to ask you to either visit with your friend or go somewhere else – perhaps the cafeteria? But you can't stand here."

"I get it," I responded. "Thank you."

As luck would have it, I only needed *one* minute. Madeline got up from Frank's side and walked out of the room. It wasn't to use the restroom, as there was one in Frank's room. I was hoping she was leaving, but it was more than likely she was going outside to get some air or to the cafeteria to get some food. Either way, it was my chance, and I didn't need much time.

I walked over to Room 217 and leaned in the doorway, staring at what looked like a frail man. I'd never seen Frank like that before. He was always larger than life, puffing out his chest like he owned the room. Now he was pale, his cheeks were sunken in, and he looked like a shell of the man he used to be. How could people have not seen this coming? *Take it easy, Jim.* Easy to say from someone who hasn't seen the man in three years.

"Jimmy? Is that you?" I heard to my left.

Shit! I let myself get too distracted. That's it; it's all over. My secret is out. I quickly turned away from the sound of the voice, hoping they'd think they were mistaken. I took a step, but the voice called out again, this time in a hushed tone.

"What the hell are you doing here?"

That was when I realized it was Mick. Relief washed over me as my shoulders dropped. I felt my eyes roll as I turned to face him.

"Keep it down, would ya?" I said as I glanced down at a Monopoly board game Mick was carrying under his left arm.

"Keep it down?" he questioned. "You're walking around where everybody can see you. Someone could recognize you."

"I'm being careful."

"Right, because I didn't just notice you," he said, not disguising his sarcasm. "So what are you doing here?"

"I had to come. I wanted to make sure Frank was all right. If something happened, and I didn't get a chance to see him..,"

"I get it, but still. I can't believe Hayes agreed to this."

I diverted my eyes, checking in on Frank again, a clear sign of guilt.

"She.., doesn't know you're here, does she?"

I shook my head.

"Jesus Christ, Jimmy. Are you *trying* to get caught? Hayes will have your ass if she finds out."

"Then, I guess it's a good thing she's not going to find out," I stated, glaring at Mick to get my point across. "What's with the board game?"

Mick looked down at the game he was carrying and then back to me. "We're looking into something from Ben's last clues. I bought two. I dropped one off at the station for Agent Deitrich to study, and I was bringing the other home with me. I didn't even realize I carried it in until I got on the elevator."

"What were the clues?" I asked.

"I thought you'd know by now. Don't you and Hayes communicate? Wait, of course not. You're at the hospital without her knowing about it."

"Let's just say Marion and I have had our disagreements about the direction of this case."

"No kidding; I could tell she was in a mood when..,"

"Haddick?" a weakened voice called out.

I immediately saw Frank out of the corner of my eye, struggling to sit up. I ducked my head out of view under the rim of my hat and scrambled past Mick, tapping him on his upper arm as I walked by. I didn't go far, standing just out of sight as Mick entered Frank's room. I listened while Frank suggested he must be losing his mind since he thought he saw a dead man. Mick covered for me, telling Frank I was someone looking for directions to the elevators. *Thanks, Mick; I owe you one.*

As much as it could have been a bad situation, I was relieved to hear Frank's voice and to see him sitting up. The old jalopy still had some gas left in his tank. That was a weight off. I felt a smile invade my face, and I made my way to the elevators. If I knew Frank, he'd want to dive right back into the case as soon as he was discharged. Thankfully, Chief Copelli had his head on straight. He wouldn't let that happen.

I pressed the down button for the elevator and looked back down the hall toward Frank's room. He'd be home tomorrow, where he could take it easy for a while. He'd be gone from this life one day, like all of us would be, but I was glad it wasn't this case that took him down. That would be too much, even for me.

Rest up, old friend. You've had our backs for so long; it's time we had yours. Sit this one out. Mick and I will end this. I'll make sure of that.

Chapter 24

The Road to Nowhere

There had to be something. What were we missing? I'd studied this Monopoly board for two days straight, and I didn't see a connection with anything in Southbridge. Even Agent Deitrich had exhausted his efforts to determine what everything meant. Was Ben feeding us more of his mind game bullshit to keep us chasing our tails? Was he manipulating us, leading us astray so we didn't get close to him?

Nothing seemed to make sense. Maybe that was the point. Why would Ben want us to figure things out before he could kill again? We had three different denominations of fake money, a little plastic house, a pewter car, and a coin. I pulled out my phone and swiped to the pictures I'd taken of the items. Vera wasn't happy I'd disturbed her while I snapped away, but I obviously needed something to stare at for hours and hours with no clue as to what I was looking at. And for what? Nothing seemed special about them. Everything looked the same as what I pulled from the game I purchased. And the coin? From what I could tell, it was an ordinary quarter with George Washington on the front and an eagle on the back. It was dated 1998. Did the year mean something? I'd already looked up information about the quarter and found that 1998 was the last year it was in production before switching to the new quarters. What did that tell me? Oh, I know – diddly-squat.

The clues Ben left were too much for me. Figuring out the numbers 3, 1, and 4 represented PI was one thing; deciphering this random shit was something else entirely. If Agent Deitrich couldn't piece things together, did I think I had a chance?

I stared at the board, the silver automobile game piece positioned on the "GO" square, all revved up with nowhere to drive. The three bills were in front of me, laid out in the center of the board. The plastic house was off to the side. Ben left $16 as part of his messed-up clue, but nothing in the game was that cheap. What was he trying to tell us? Was I supposed to play the game? I shook my head in frustration; this was ridiculous. I looked at the dice and rolled my eyes. Was I really going to do this? Would it kill me to try? With determination, I swiped the dice from the table.

I hadn't played the game in years, but what I remembered most was how long it could last. I wasn't sure how it would work with only one player, but I had no intention of playing longer than one trip around the board. I shook the dice in my hand and rolled them onto the table. If it were an actual game, it wasn't a good start. I rolled a six. I slid the car forward six squares, landing on Oriental Avenue. It cost $100 to buy. I glanced at my paltry amount, a $10, $5, and a $1 bill, and thought, *not today*. That was fine. I had no intention of buying properties anyway. I reached for the dice for a second roll but stopped before picking them up. My hand hovered over the dice as I stared at the numbers. I didn't know why, but something at that moment struck me. I had rolled a 1 and 5 to make six. I looked at the play cash, of which I also had a $1 and a $5, and then back to the dice and thought, *maybe..?*

I pulled the car back to the start, looked at the three bills one more time, and then counted out 16 spaces. I had to grin at the result. The car sat on St. James Place. Was it a coincidence, or did I just hit upon something? In Ben's letter to Hayes, he hinted at his reasoning for playing this game. He was enacting some warped sense of retribution for what happened to his father. St. James' place? Shit. Could Ben be going after whoever bought Jimmy's house? I had to get over there.

I grabbed my jacket and ran out the door, dialing Agent Hayes to let her know what I'd come up with. By the time she answered, my stereo's Bluetooth had picked up.

"This is Hayes."

"Special Agent Hayes, this is Mick. I might have something from the clues Ben left."

"Are you alone?"

"Yeah."

"Hold on, Mick. Let me put you on speaker."

I heard a quiet click, and then Jimmy's voice rang out.

"Whatta you got, Mick?"

"Honestly, I'm not really sure. I'm on my way to your old house now."

"My old house? Why?"

"I've been going out of my mind studying the game," I answered. "Ben left us $16, and, for whatever reason, I counted out 16 spaces on the Monopoly board. Jimmy, it was St. James Place. I don't know if that means anything, but I didn't want to take the chance."

"Good call, Mick," Agent Hayes' voice rang out. "I'll call and brief Samuels and have him send a unit. Don't do anything until backup arrives."

"I can't do that, Agent Hayes. If there's a chance to bring in Ben and stop this madness, I'm taking it."

"Don't be foolish, Mick," she responded.

"Marion's right," Jim agreed. "Ben is dangerous; he's out of control. There's no telling what he might do. Even to you, Mick."

I kept hearing Lieutenant Garrett's voice in my head. *You can't just pick and choose what you want to do. You signed up for this. We've all got a job to do, and that's to protect the citizens of this city. And need I remind you, that includes your wife and kid.*

That's all I wanted – to protect Gina and Stella. They were my motivation. Then, Gina's words from the day before she left clamored in my head. *We'll go. But you'd better keep up your end of the deal.* That's what I intended to do. I wouldn't let my girls down.

"I've gotta try," I replied, ignoring their advice. "I'll keep you posted."

As I reached for the "end call" button on my dash, I heard Agent Hayes squeak out a final "Be careful, Mick." I appreciated the sentiment, but nothing was going to happen to me. I had too much to live for. Ben, on the other hand, needed to watch his back.

I hadn't been over that way in months. After Jimmy was gone and Ben sentenced to prison, the house fell into foreclosure. Karen was a little upset about that at first. In those early months after Ben's arrest, she thought it was all a big mistake, and that her son would be released and could then move into his father's house. But it wasn't a mistake. Ben had killed nine people and would never be a free man again. Well, he wasn't supposed to be. Who could have imagined he'd escape?

Anyway, a new owner swept in and began updating Jimmy's house at a fever pitch like he was going to flip it for a profit. Surprisingly, he didn't. At least, not yet. When I first pulled up, the house looked very different from what I'd remembered. It was a different color because of the new siding, and the owner had since added a front porch. It looked good and made me instantly think about what I could do to spruce up my house, but then I remembered what my salary was and quickly dismissed the crazy idea.

Everything seemed quiet as I stepped from my car. There was a dark blue Chevy Silverado in the driveway. That was a good sign. I stepped up onto the recently constructed porch and rang the doorbell. The curtains on the windows were drawn, preventing me from seeing inside, which made me a bit nervous for no apparent reason. I heard footsteps approaching and instinctively placed my hand on my sidearm. Was it Hayes' *"Be careful"* that had me rattled or the idea that I could be right and this could be Ben coming to the door? My nerves heightened with the sound of each step.

The door opened a few inches, and a man's head peered sideways from around the backside.

"Who are you?" he said loud and curt.

"Sir, I'm..,"

"I don't want any. Go away!"

He shut the door before I could explain myself. He seemed very nervous. Was that his nature, or was he hiding something? Or someone? I quickly knocked and announced myself, hoping for a better response.

"This is the police; please open the door."

Right after I said it, a cruiser pulled up behind my vehicle. If nothing else, the backup helped to verify my statement. I saw the man peek his head out from behind the curtain, peering curiously at the officer walking up his lawn. It was the rookie, Riley. I caught myself rolling my eyes. The department *must* be short on officers if the chief was willing to send the rookie out here alone. It might be wrong of me, but I couldn't help but think, if this *did* turn into a nasty situation, did I really want the rookie backing me up? The front door flew open, surprising me and causing Riley to draw his weapon.

"What's going on here?" the man asked sharply.

I patted my hand in the air, signaling Riley to holster his gun.

"Sir, we don't mean to alarm you," I began. "Is there someone else in the house with you?"

"What? No, there's nobody else here. What's this about?"

"We're sorry to bother you, but we received information that someone might be in trouble at this residence."

The man quickly stepped onto his porch and walked by me, looking toward his neighbors' houses on either side of his own. With his door left open, I leaned forward and glanced around inside, looking for any sign of suspicious activity. All seemed normal and calm.

"It was that rat, Harlowe, wasn't it?" the man said, pointing to the neighbor on his right. "He's never liked me from the day I moved in."

"I can't say where the information came from," I replied, "but I assure you, it wasn't any of your neighbors."

The man swung around, his face displaying agitation.

"What? Just great! Now, who's after me?" His eyes squinted, and he waved his index finger back and forth, pointing at me and Riley. "It's you, isn't it? You're one of *them*."

Taken aback, I looked at the rookie and then back to the man. "I'm sorry?" I questioned, confused. "One of who?"

"Don't come near me," the man yelled, diving between us back to the safety of his open door. "You're not going to probe me!"

I shook my head, utterly perplexed. "Sir, we're not..,"

"Get back to your ship, heathens. Go back to wherever you came from."

He slammed the door shut; I heard the deadbolt click. A second later, he popped his head between the opening in the curtains, flashed us a nasty grimace, and then yanked them closed.

I threw my hands out questioningly toward Officer Riley. "What the actual fuck was that?"

It wasn't meant to be funny. Regardless, the rookie almost burst out laughing. I came here thinking someone might need help, but the kind of help that gentleman needed was above my pay grade. From my brief glimpse inside, the house looked clean. There was no indication of anything out of the ordinary, no signs of a struggle. Maybe I was wrong about St. James Place. Or maybe I'd arrived before Ben took a victim. I didn't get the chance to warn the man. I doubted he'd open the door again. It was *his* problem now. With the rookie being here, it was clear we didn't have enough resources on the force to have a unit parked out front. As much as I'd earlier hoped I was right about Ben's game, I now hoped I was wrong. The paranoid conspiracy theorist inside had better pray that I was.

I looked at the rook and nodded my head toward the vehicles.

"Let's get outta here."

He silently concurred and strolled back to the cruiser. Before getting in my car, I peered back at the house – *Jimmy's* old house – "James' Place," and shook my head. I'd have to report back that this was a bust. Maybe we'd find out in a day or two that I was right all along when somebody stumbled upon the man's dead body. I hoped it wouldn't come to that. Until then, it was back to the drawing board. Or Monopoly board.

I hopped into the car and let out an exhausted breath. As Riley pulled around me, waving as he drove off, a thought sprang into my head. It sure would have been nice for something to go right for a change.

Chapter 25

So Right, So Wrong

I thought it would be a good idea to visit Vera in her lab for no other reason than to get my head straight. She had a way of keeping things in the moment. Unfortunately, it wasn't helping. Whatever she was talking about, I missed the majority of it. My thoughts were scattered. The case, Jimmy being alive, Lieutenant Garrett's health, Ben's motives.., and my family. I missed my family. I wanted them back, but I knew they were safest with Rosa. I video-chatted with Gina every night, and she would let me see Stella's incredible smile, but I missed holding them. I missed their smell. I wanted this to be over so we could be a family again. I wanted..,

"My *ass*," Vera's voice clamored, snapping me back to the conversation I'd been absent from.

"What was that, Vera?" I asked, noticing Danny out of the corner of my eye, shaking his head as if asking Vera to repeat herself was a mistake.

"I said, then he grabbed my ass. Can you believe that? I had a mind to pick him up and carry him off like he was my bitch if I wasn't having such a good time enjoying the strippers."

"Wait, did I miss something?" I questioned. "Strippers? I thought we were talking about the case - how it's been almost a week since the well has run dry."

"What the frick, Mick? That was like ten minutes ago. Where have you been that whole time?"

"First of all.., did you say 'frick'?"

"Don't get me started," Vera replied. "Danny's been telling me how I cuss too much."

I glanced in Danny's direction. He nodded, his eyes wide as if to say "*way too much.*"

"But you just got through saying how you wanted to make someone your bitch," I reminded her.

Vera shrugged her shoulders. "My Mother Teresa membership card expired last week. Bite me."

I didn't know what to do with that, so I continued my thoughts.

"Anyway, I'm sorry, Vera. I've been a little distracted lately. We've come up empty at every turn. There was nothing with the greenhouses – or green houses. My bright idea about Jimmy's old place turned out to be a dud. Agent Deitrich is trying his best to come up with something from the nonsense clues Ben left. And for all we know, we're being led in the wrong direction."

"You're taking this way too hard, Mick." She turned and looked at her lab tech. "There's a joke in there, but *someone* won't let me say it."

Danny looked up from the eyedropper he'd been using and grinned victoriously. If I didn't know any better, I'd think there was a devious little shit hiding away in that odd young man.

"You have to ask yourself," she continued, "what would Jim do?"

My heart quickened, and my eyes grew. Why would Vera say that? Did she suspect?

"Jim?" I questioned. "Um.., why?"

"He wouldn't worry about that shi.., um.., poop. He'd get out there, stick his nose to the pavement, and let his instincts take over. That's what made him such a good detective. You can too, you know. Follow your instincts, I mean. I have faith in you."

"You mean the instincts that led me to that dead end at Jimmy's old house?" I questioned sullenly.

"Hey, you figured out the casino before anyone else did."

"And where did that get us? Just another dead body."

"My point is, you got us there. You can do it again."

"Thanks, Vera. I appreciate..," my voice trailed off as my phone rang. I pulled it from my pocket and looked at the screen. I then looked at Vera with what must have been a nervous gaze. "I.., I've gotta take this."

"Don't let me stop you." She brushed her hand forward to shoo me out. "Get the fudge out."

I gave her an awkward look. She winked.

Stepping out of the lab and onto the staircase leading up to the Detective Bureau, I answered the call coming in from J. Ghostman.

"Hey, what's going on?" I inquired. "Do you think it's a good idea, calling like this? Okay, it's your fault if your cover gets blown. Hayes? I imagine she's upstairs. I'm heading there now. She's not answering your calls, huh? Did you two have another spat?" I froze halfway up the staircase after Jimmy raised his voice. "Okay, okay. What is it? What? You're shitting me? Holy shit! No, no, I got it. I'll let them know. We'll get there."

I hung up the phone and sprinted the rest of the way up. Turning the corner, I saw Chief Copelli in a meeting with Agents Hayes and Samuels. They weren't going to like it, but I needed to interrupt. I didn't bother to knock on the briefing room door. Instead, I swung it open like I owned the place. And at that moment, with the announcement I had, I did.

"The post office," I blurted. "That's where Ben is leading us."

"What are you talking about?" SAC Samuels said in his condescending way. "How do you know that?"

"I was right about the $16 representing spaces on the Monopoly board. St. James Place. I was wrong about it being Detective Haddick's house. It's 'Jimmy's Crib.' That was a local band from years ago. They used to plaster their signs up on the bulletin board at the post office."

"I remember them," Chief Copelli spoke. "It seems odd that Ben would know of them. He would have only been seven or eight years old when they were together."

"I'm telling you, Chief, I have a feeling about this."

Agent Hayes' eyes narrowed. "You know what, I do too. I think it's worth checking out."

SAC Samuels huffed. "All right. You and Detective Dooley get down to the post office. Find out if there have been any mail carriers or other personnel missing from work. Report back with what you find."

Hayes nodded. "Got it." She walked by me, grabbing my sleeve and pulling me along. She kept a good pace on her way out. I had a hard time keeping up with her.

"Mine," she shouted as we exited the police station. I followed her to the waiting SUV. I don't think I had my second leg in the door before Hayes gunned it out of the parking lot.

"That came from Jim, didn't it?" she questioned. "He mentioned something about recalling the name James' Place or Jim's Place, but he couldn't quite remember what it was."

"Yeah," I replied. "He called me. He said he tried calling *you*, but you weren't answering."

"I couldn't exactly answer in that meeting, could I?"

"I suppose not. Jimmy made it sound like you two had been arguing."

I watched as Hayes pursed her lips. Her eyes faltered, too, lowering to the steering wheel before looking back out the windshield.

"He's still trying to convince me to involve Vivian," she said, maintaining her forward stare.

"If all goes well at the post office," I responded, "and we catch Ben before anyone else gets hurt, you'll no longer have to worry about that."

I didn't know what else to say. I was the one who planted that bug in Jimmy's ear. Was I trying to convince myself that Vivian's involvement wouldn't be needed? I still believed it was the right call. Hayes and I didn't speak anything more about it. In fact, we didn't speak at all for the rest of the trip.

The SUV came to a screeching halt in the parking lot. We both threw our doors open, rushing to be the first to make it inside. Or maybe we were both rushing to get away from the uncomfortable silence.

When we stepped into the lobby, I took a sweeping glance around for my own reassurance. To our right, a woman and her child were pulling mail from a PO Box. There was another woman in front of us at the counter being helped by a postal worker. Hayes and I patiently stood in wait for our turn. I watched the woman with the child as they wandered in our direction toward the exit. The boy was so excited to have helped his mother, and I wondered if Stella would be as excited about such trivial things when she got older. The mother glanced in my direction, and I flashed her a warm smile.

I turned back to face front, realizing Agent Hayes and I still hadn't spoken a word since the early moments of our trip here. I didn't want this to remain an uncomfortable situation. I tapped her upper arm to gain her attention. When she looked at me, I pointed to the wall on our left, where a bulletin board was hung, displaying a disorganized smattering of flyers and business cards.

"That's the board Jimmy was talking about," I said. "He told me Ben used to get so excited to see the Jimmy's Crib flyers because he thought it was cool his father's name was up there where everyone could see it."

"I could see where a young boy would be impressed by something like that," Hayes responded coldly.

Thankfully, the woman in front of us finished up, and we could go back to official business, where we didn't have to pretend we were enjoying each other's company.

"What can I do for you today?" the man behind the counter asked.

Hayes took the lead. "We're here on official FBI business." She flashed her badge. "We're wondering if there have been any employees who haven't reported to work recently? Maybe unexpectedly? Maybe without officially calling out?"

"No," the man said, shrugging and rolling his lower lip. "Not that I'm aware, anyway. We've been on a good attendance streak lately."

"What about any chatter from other employees?" Hayes inquired. "Has anyone complained about a customer acting peculiar? Maybe making them feel uncomfortable?"

I watched the worker's face scrunch in curiosity. "I can't say that I've heard anything. What's this about, anyway? It sounds serious."

"We're not at liberty to say," Hayes replied. "I would ask, however, that you or one of your coworkers contact me directly if an employee neglects to show up for their scheduled shift."

She pulled out a card and handed it to the inquisitive postal employee. He held it in front of his chest while he inspected it. My eyes drifted slightly from the card to the embroidered emblem above his shirt pocket, a blue and white eagle.

Hayes continued, "Thank you for your time. I appreciate.., *we* appreciate your cooperation."

Oh, *now* she recognized me. As she turned to leave, I grabbed her sleeve, stopping her.

"Hold on a sec." I pulled out my phone and navigated to my photos. Pulling up the picture of the quarter with an eagle on one side, I stared at the date for a moment before turning my attention back to the employee. "Can you tell us who PO Box 1998 belongs to?"

The man softly chuckled. "I'm afraid I can't. We only have 850 boxes."

I felt my shoulders drop in disappointment. I really thought..,

"You ready to go?" Hayes urged.

"Yeah," I replied, still staring at the numbers. The numbers. "Wait!" I quickly did the math in my head. The numbers in the date added up to, "27," I announced. "Can you tell us who PO Box 27 belongs to?"

"I'm afraid I can't without proper documentation," he answered.

I looked at Hayes; she saw how serious I had become. She immediately stepped away, jumping on her phone.

Fifteen minutes later, Hayes stepped back up to the counter and flashed her phone, displaying a signed court order by the district judge. "Will this do?" she questioned.

The employee courteously smiled and began typing away at his computer. "Let's see. Box 27 belongs to Chester and Rudy Greene."

I looked at Hayes in shock. "Greene. Fuck!" I watched as her jaw tightened and her nostrils flared.

"We're going to need an address," she said through clenched teeth.

Chapter 26

I Am Vengeance

"You shouldn't waste your tears. It's unbecoming. After all, I let you live longer, didn't I?"

I turn my back on the man to retrieve the instrument that will deliver my gift to him - a permanent scar marked upon his flesh. The flame from the furnace has once again done its job to perfection. The metal's orange glow, as I pull it from the open panel, radiates with vile intention. The foul stench of burning flesh in the air will only thicken with what I am about to do. The art I create brings me joy. It is a necessary evil.

I feel no malice toward this man, nor did I toward his brother. They will serve as merely messengers. Though their deaths offer me pleasure and comfort, I will not rest until the raging turmoil within me has quelled. Victim Ø will pay the ultimate price for my boundless fury, but her unwitting sacrifice will save countless others from my wrath. I may have been wicked and revolting to those whose lives I have taken, but I have always had reasons for my.., unpleasant behavior. *She* will learn true wickedness.

I hear the faint mumbles behind me, a desperate attempt by a desperate man to prevent the inevitable. His senses have awoken. He has felt my pent-up anger in every blow I have unleashed. He has breathed in the smell of what my unrelenting temper is capable of. He has tasted the salt of every tear and the metallic tang of every drop of blood that has met his tongue. He has heard the cries and pleas of a loved one softly diminish into silence. And, finally, he has borne witness to what the end looks like through the inescapable expiration of his dearly departed, pitiful brother.

I slowly turn to address the frightened man's concerns. My hand shakes not with anticipation of what is to come but from the nagging ache I feel from the weight of the branding iron. I use my other hand to steady my grip while his eyes target the heated number 3 that will soon become his legacy. His face displays scars matched only by the torn skin on my knuckles, the reason for the constant stinging. I feel what each victim feels. I endure the pain so they understand how dire their situation is. But still, they fail to recognize how lucky they are. The hurt they feel, the pain I deliver upon them, always comes to a merciful end. But my agony, my torture, continues even after their deaths. They find peace, whereas I find only hatred in its purest form.

"I wish I felt sorry for these things I do," I tell the man as my eyes drift to his deceased brother's forearm, where the number 4 had moments before been tattooed into his flesh by searing heat. "I don't. Feelings have never been a part of me, only faked emotions I learned to mimic and hoped they could one day be real. Or, perhaps,

I felt something real at one time. If I had, those emotions faded years ago. The only times I feel anything are when others feel pain and anguish. Their terror soothes my ache."

I set the heated metal on the table beside the bloody knife. The man squirms violently in his chair as if he had hope of freeing himself. It never ceases to amaze me why people constantly give up on things in life, only to struggle so vigorously when life is about to be stripped from them. I smile playfully, hoping to ease his worry. A second later, he feels the bitter sting of my good hand as I slap him across the face to make him realize his worry is warranted.

"Don't!" I state, waving my finger in front of his face. "You brought this on yourself. Your brother did so well, answering seven questions correctly, prolonging your life." I point to the body slouched in the chair behind me. "He died with dignity, knowing he spared his brother from so much pain. You, however, answered only two questions correctly, to your brother's misfortune. Pathetic. I understand how watching your brother suffer with each incorrect answer you uttered might have somehow affected your ability to think clearly. I was lenient when you couldn't tell me how many stars made up Orion's belt, which awarded Rudy that slice across his chest. Not everyone takes the time to admire the skies. The answer was 3." I point to the branding iron sharing the same number. "But, come on, who doesn't know there are seven continents on the planet? I can only give you so many strikes. After your brother's performance, I expected better of you. I'm quite sure Rudy wished you'd done better."

I step behind Chester's dead brother's chair, keeping an intent watch on the living brother's reaction. I grab a clump of the deceased's hair and yank his drooped head up so his brother can see his bloody face. I lean forward with my lips beside the dead man's ear and speak.

"Hey, Rudy. Did your brother fail you this badly while you were alive?"

I reach around and snag the ends of his lips, making them open and close at my will.

"Yes, he did," I say in a higher-pitched voice, impersonating Rudy and teasing the living sibling with my uncaring actions.

"How could you stand being his brother when he doesn't have a brain in that head of his?" I ask.

"I felt sorry for him," I answer in the same high voice while playfully manipulating his lips. "I couldn't leave him on his own."

The living brother, Chester, jerks his body ferociously, his bindings keeping him tethered to the chair, my comments getting a rise out of him.

"I understand that," I continue. "If not for you, the cold hands of Death would have come for your brother years ago. But today, Death has returned to claim her prize." I throw Rudy's head forward as it slinks heavily to his chest.

Chester's protests become louder, cloaked behind the gag. He shakes his head from side to side, his eyes watering through the anger, confusion, and fear.

"What's the matter; you didn't like my little puppet show? In my defense, I've never had any formal training as a ventriloquist. That was my first time handling a dummy. Oh, wait. It turns out *you* were the dummy all along. Oops."

He shouts something unintelligible through the cloth. I think I'll humor him.

"What was that, now?" I pull the cloth down onto his chin and reach into his open mouth, pulling free the wadded-up fabric within.

"I'm going to kill you, you goddamn freak!"

I jam the ball of cloth back into his mouth, all the while smiling. "Is that what you think?" I say, sliding the second cloth back over his mouth. "I'm afraid not, Chester. You see, *I'm* going to kill *you*. But don't worry; I'm not Death. She would take you quickly. I'm vengeance. I'm going to take my time."

I reach for the handle of the branding iron. I feel waves of heat still radiating off the far end of the steel. That's good. My new plaything is ready.

With my other hand, I grab the knife and stab it vertically into the tabletop. Chester's eyes explode with fear. I tilt my head like a curious puppy, wondering what could be going through his head at this exact moment. It doesn't matter. Something else will be going through his head soon enough. I give Chester a devilish smirk.

"Shall we begin?" I ask rhetorically. "Your brother earned a less painful death than what I have in store for you. He didn't have to endure the searing pain of his flesh burning - to bear the smell of his skin melting away. You won't be so lucky." I imagine Chester's fear-stricken expression was because of the gleam I have in my eyes as I thrust the burning number 3 against his chest.

Chapter 27

Dead Ahead

Special Agent Hayes and I stepped into the Forrest Hill Apartment building, and I couldn't help but wonder how it got its name. There wasn't a forest nearby, and the landscape couldn't be flatter. It must have been a name meant to attract potential renters, making the place sound better than it was, like how Greenland was named, to trick people into moving there.

The interior lobby floor was carpeted with what used to be a beige or light-colored tan, as seen along the fringes, but had since turned a darker brown from dirty shoes and the lack of regular cleanings. Dark brown paneling covered the walls, maintaining a gloomy feel even with the overhead lights working at full capacity. There was a stale thickness in the air that you could taste when you opened your mouth, which was a good enough reason to keep my mouth shut.

There were two apartments on the first floor along the wall to our right and a staircase along the left wall, leading to other apartments. There was no elevator in sight. I felt sorry for the folks who had to lug their groceries to the upper floors. Thankfully, Chester and Rudy Greene lived in apartment 2 on the ground floor, so we didn't have to walk far.

Hayes took the lead. We approached the door cautiously but with a sense of urgency. My heart was pounding through my chest, and I wondered if Hayes could hear it. Was she feeling the same, or had her FBI training prepared her to remain calmer in these situations? I didn't know why I was so nervous. We didn't know anything yet. We couldn't even be sure I'd made the right call. Everything seemed to fit with the clues Ben had left us, but if he was smart enough to elude capture for as long as he had, he was smart enough to lead us on a wild goose chase.

"You ready?" Hayes asked quietly, standing by the door.

The look in her eyes told me she meant "*be ready for anything*," and I instinctively placed my hand on my sidearm. I nodded.

Hayes knocked on the door and then gave me a side-eyed glance. She was nervous, too, which made me feel better about myself but also uneasy. After a minute with no response, she knocked again, more forcefully.

"Chester or Rudy Greene," she announced. "Please open the door."

I put my head down, listening for any sound beyond the door. There was nothing. I looked at Hayes and shook my head.

"Maybe they're not home?" I questioned. If I couldn't convince myself of that, how was I expecting to convince Hayes?

"Or maybe we're too late," she replied, giving me a solemn glare. "We'll know more when the landlord arrives."

Hayes had contacted the landlord on the way over and.., *encouraged* him to meet us at the building. If nothing came of it, we could at least ask that he take any resident complaints regarding strange people or activities going on at the property seriously.

"What time did he say he'd be here?" I asked.

She looked over my shoulder toward the front door and nodded, "I think that's him now."

I turned to see a rather rotund man approaching the exterior glass doors. He had a strip of hair combed over his scalp from his right ear to his left, trying to mask his balding head. A lit cigarette was dangling from his lips behind a five o'clock shadow that looked more like a ten p.m. shadow. He wore an undersized, coffee-stained tee shirt that revealed more of his stomach hanging over the waist of his pants than I'd cared to see. I now knew why the place was unappealing. If the landlord couldn't present *himself* decently.., what chance did the building have?

The man walked in, retaining the cigarette clenched in his lips. Hayes stepped by me to greet him.

"Mr. Candalario?" she asked.

"It's Candalari," he replied. "No O at the end."

"Sorry. I'm Special Agent Hayes with the FBI. We spoke on the phone a little bit ago. I appreciate you for taking the time. This is Detective Dooley from the Southbridge Detective Bureau."

I reluctantly held out my hand. "Nice to meet you."

Mr. Candalari's eyes looked down at it and then back at my face. "Are you the one who sent my cousin up the river?"

"Oh, ah, no," I answered uncomfortably, pulling my hand back and wiping my palm on my pants as if he'd accepted my greeting, and I needed to rid myself of whatever he'd inadvertently passed to me. "At least, I don't think so."

"Nah, you're taller than the other guy," he acquiesced. He took a drag from his cigarette and blew it in our direction. Clearly, he didn't hold authority in high regard.

"Must you?" Hayes asked. She waved her hand in front of her face to clear the smoke.

"Oh, I'm sorry," he replied, pulling the cigarette from his lips and wagging it back and forth in front of her. "Is this bothering you?"

Hayes didn't bat an eye, staring the man down like she was ready to go a few rounds with him. I think he got the hint because, a second later, he tamped the cigarette out against the wall paneling. He carefully placed the remainder of the cancer stick into his front pocket.

"So, what's this about, anyway?" he questioned.

"Mr. Candalari," Hayes began, "we have reason to believe the tenants in apartment 2 might be in danger."

"Ha!" he bellowed. "In danger of getting evicted if they don't pay the rent they owe. I told them – the first of the month."

I shot Hayes a concerned look. Not because Mr. Candalari was an uptight jackass but because today was the fifth of the month.

"Would you be able to open the door for us, Mr. Candalari?" Hayes asked. "We don't have a warrant, but we fear something may have happened to the brothers, and it would be in your best interest to let us take a quick look."

"I know how this works," he said. He put his nose in the air and began sniffing. "Is that smoke I smell?" he questioned facetiously, winking at Hayes. "Oh no; I'd better open the door in case of a fire," he continued nonchalantly.

I guess he did know how it worked. The man squeezed between us, lumbering toward apartment 2. "Something better *not* have happened to them until I get my rent," he barked. "What are you two investigating that's so dangerous anyway?" he asked, fumbling for the right key on an over-crowded keychain. "Is there something I should know about these guys? If they're dealing drugs or involved in human trafficking, I swear to God, they're going to be out on their ears. I don't need none of that shit in my fine establishment."

He inserted the key (finally) into the doorknob and gave it a turn. My thoughts fell back to his words. Was he being sarcastic, or did he really think this was a fine establishment? He opened the door, and my thoughts snapped back.

"Would you look at this mess," he stated, pointing down at a pile of papers and a slew of unopened mail scattered just inside the doorway. "I have half a mind to tell them to find another place to stay."

The landlord bent down to pick up the papers, and when he did, his pants rode halfway down his ass cheeks. It was bad enough seeing his hairy lower back peak out at us from under his shirt; it was another thing altogether being blinded by the full moon of the man's hairy ass crack opening wide for all to see. Hayes threw her head upward in disgust while I turned away to keep from dry-heaving. Not that it mattered. It was too late. We'd already seen the nasty sight that would give us both nightmares for weeks to come.

"Oh, shit!" Mr. Candalari exclaimed, standing back up. That brought our attention back to the apartment. "Oh, fuck! Oh, shit!" he continued, dropping the papers he'd just picked up and pointing to his left as he stumbled backward out of the doorway.

I quickly pulled my gun and stepped into the apartment, aiming it where Mr. Ass Crack had pointed. In less than a second, I felt my chest tighten, and I struggled to gather air into my lungs. It suddenly felt like I was holding a cinder block as the weight of my weapon caused my outstretched arm to fall to my side. My legs crumpled slightly under my weight, and I staggered backward against the wall to prevent myself from falling. Hayes' eyes shot open, reacting to my loss of balance and general appearance of dread. Even as the landlord continued his horrified mumbling while backing away toward the front entrance, Hayes peeked her head around the doorframe to gather a look. Mr. Candalari's large, hairy ass was no longer our biggest concern.

"Oh. My. God!" Hayes expressed, covering her mouth.

We now had a new image to haunt our nightmares.

Hayes quickly stormed in with her gun drawn, weaving in and out of each room, clearing them of any immediate threat. When she was through, she grabbed my arm and pulled me back into the hallway, closing the door behind her.

"Looks like we'll need that warrant, after all."

Chapter 28

...4...3

This was one of those times I wished I'd been wrong. Why does this keep happening? Why can't we figure Ben out sooner instead of walking into.., *this?*

"Move out of the way, please," SAC Samuels grunted to the inquisitive tenants who'd gathered in the open lobby of the apartment building, their nosiness sparked by the flashing lights of three cruisers parked out front. "Officer Riley, get these people out of here," he barked to the rookie.

Officer Riley had been standing in the lobby as well, off to the side of the small crowd, unsure of how to handle the onlookers. Another officer had kept them at bay for the most part, not allowing them to step any further than the staircase banister.

"Yes, sir," Riley answered, jumping into action at the Agent's command. "Let's go, folks, back to your apartments. Give us some room to do our jobs, would you? C'mon, now." He gave a friendly nudge to a few of the bystanders, directing them back up the stairs. They expressed their dissatisfaction through the various groans and grumblings they let fly on their way back to their units. They didn't realize it, but they were better off. Nobody should have to bear witness to the gruesome scene left for us inside apartment 2.

With SAC Samuels' arrival, I pushed myself from the doorframe where I'd been uncomfortably leaning to block the curious tenants' view of the crime scene. I stepped out into the hallway and brushed by him.

"I've gotta call my wife."

"What the hell, Dooley," he snapped. "We're in the middle of a homicide investigation."

I turned to him, my face feeling flush. "I just need a minute. I need to hear Gina's voice. Nothing we can do until Barry gets here."

I heard him mumble something under his breath, much like I imagined Lieutenant Garrett would have done if he were here. I didn't care. He made it clear that this was the FBI's investigation. Last I checked, my identification read "Detective," not "Agent." They wanted it; they could have it. This case was *their* nightmare sideshow. I was just the unlucky bastard along for the ride.

I stepped through the front glass doors into the parking lot. A couple of officers were standing off to the side, comparing notes about what they'd seen as if they were sharing recipes. Mr. Candalari, the landlord, had his back pressed against the passenger door of his car, puffing away on a cigarette, his fourth, judging by the spent butts at his feet. He glanced over at me and shook his head in disbelief, his hand shaking as he removed the cigarette from his mouth. I gave him an understanding nod. I'd been there. It wouldn't help.

I pulled my phone from my pocket and dialed Gina. Listening to the rings, I stared back through the apartment building doors at the scene unfolding within. The uniformed officers scrambled to maintain order while Special Agents Hayes and Samuels conversed in the open doorway where a horrific murder had taken place like it was no big deal. I couldn't do that. I couldn't pretend it was just another day at the office. The world could be a dark place. But rather than accept that and live in the muck, I needed a reminder that there was still good in this life, something and someone worth crawling out of the darkness for.

"Hey, it's me. No, nothing's wrong; I just wanted to hear your voice. Do I? I hadn't noticed. Maybe I'm coming down with something. How are things at your sister's house? I know, baby. It won't be much longer; we're getting closer to catching him. How's Stella? I miss you guys so much. Can you put the phone near her? I want to hear my baby girl."

I could hear only some muted breathing and Gina telling Stella to *"Say hi to Daddy,"* but it was enough. My little girl was there, and I knew she was smiling. She and Gina were the beacons of hope that kept me clawing for the surface when dirt kept piling up on top of me. They kept me going.

Gina retook the phone. "Hi. Yeah, I'm feeling better already. Thanks. I should probably get back to work. Yeah, you too. I love you. Tell the munchkin I love her too. Okay. Talk to you later. Bye."

I hung up the phone and stared at the screen for a few seconds, letting out a breath. I felt the tiniest twinge of a smile come upon me. The agents could live in their world all they wanted. My world was better.

Barry pulled up along the front walkway beside me in his large white medical examiner's van, drawing my thoughts back to reality. He stepped from the vehicle with his medical bag in one hand while his other struggled to find the opening to the sleeve of his half-dangling navy blue ME jacket. I opened my mouth to say something, but Barry stopped me before any words exited.

"Don't, Detective. It's already been a rough morning."

"Well, get ready," I replied. "It's about to get rougher."

I opened the door for him just as he managed to finagle his jacket over his shoulder. Both agents glanced over at the sound of air rushing into the building. The other two officers paid no heed as they continued to herd stubborn tenants back up the staircase.

"It looks like I'm late to the party," Barry joked.

"Yeah, well, this is one party you'll wish you hadn't been invited to."

"To be clear, Detective.., I never *want* to be invited. I'm beginning to think you guys only need me for my brains and good looks."

"It's a curse, isn't it?"

"Yeah, except I don't have good looks, so where does that leave me?"

"Mr. Hinkman," Special Agent Hayes greeted with a nod. "We're glad you could make it on such short notice."

"Such is the life," he responded. "Now, let's see what all the fuss is about," he continued, squeezing between the two agents into the open doorway before stopping only a foot in. "Ah, I see now."

SAC Samuels looked at me funny. "You all set, Detective, now that you've had your little 'minute'?"

"Are you married, Special Agent Samuels?" I asked, my eyebrows furled.

"Divorced," he replied.

"I wonder why?" My response said it all. Samuels' lips snapped shut as he diverted his eyes from me and into the apartment. I probably would have felt bad if he wasn't such a dick.

"What do you make of this shit, Mr. Hinkman?" he asked, quickly bringing the subject back to the crime scene. "Brothers Chester and Rudy Greene. The landlord confirmed until we have positive identification."

"Well, not exactly the paint color I would have chosen," Barry answered, glancing at the wall to his left. "I'd say Ben's making a statement."

"That he's a sad, delusional fuck!" Agent Hayes blurted.

I whipped my head in her direction, shocked at her response. That wasn't like her. She usually remained cool.

"That could be part of it," Barry acknowledged. "I think he's also telling us he's stepping up his game." He took another few steps into the room and faced the front wall. "I especially like how he's decorated *this* wall," he said, waving his hands in front of him. "Writing messages in blood is always an attention-getter. '*I'm getting closer to Ø every day*,'" he read aloud. "Catchy. And, of course, the numbers *9, 7, 2, 4*. Any idea about those?"

"We sent a picture of it to Agent Deitrich," SAC Samuels answered. "We haven't heard back yet."

"And we won't," Agent Hayes said, sounding frustrated. "At least not before Ben kills again."

"You don't know that," SAC Samuels responded.

"Look at this, Special Agent Samuels," she said heatedly, pointing into the apartment. "This is what we're up against. We've figured out every one of his little numbers games, and we're still miles behind him. He's killed five people since his prison break. He killed eight before that to land him in prison in the first place."

"I thought he killed nine," Barry interrupted, no doubt counting Jimmy among Ben's victims.

"Whatever," Hayes said in an annoyed tone, realizing she slipped up. "My point is, the bodies keep piling up, and we have nothing to show for it. Ben is going to keep killing and killing until we do something about it. I can't let that happen."

Hayes stormed past me toward the exit.

"Where do you think you're going, Special Agent Hayes?" Samuels cried out.

"To do something about it."

"If you walk out that door..," his words trailed off as the door closed behind his partner.

"Damn it!" he grunted, slamming his fist against the door frame. "What is that woman up to?"

"I can tell you what *I'm* up to," Barry said, unfazed by the loud, uncomfortable exchange. "Like the others, neither of these men was killed in this apartment."

Against my better judgment, I stepped into the doorway. With Hayes gone, I felt I needed to do my part.

"What do you mean, neither was killed here?"

"As I stated, Detective. Both men were killed elsewhere and then dropped here for us to find."

"But the blood..,"

"Isn't theirs," he cut me off. "At least, not all of it. There's an empty five-gallon bucket stashed under the table over here with residual blood in it. That's what he used on the walls."

"Shit!" SAC Samuels said. "Do you think he's been collecting blood from all his victims?"

"It's hard to say without analysis. There could be some of the victims' blood in that mess. But unless Ben has killed another ten people that we don't know about, it's unlikely the blood is theirs at all. Two walls covered in the stuff. None of the victims, including these two, bled enough for the amount we're seeing."

"Or is it even blood at all?" I questioned.

"Oh, it's blood," Barry answered confidently. "The smell is very distinct."

"Great! Another mystery," I said. "You might as well take us through the rest of this, Barry."

I looked at the two deceased men while holding back the bile that had built up in my stomach. One of the brothers was lying on his back on the couch. His arms were resting by his side, the number 4 displayed in burnt flesh on his left forearm. The man's head and eyes were facing up toward the ceiling. Had that been the only thing facing up, it would have been one of the milder scenes we've encountered. But then, that wouldn't have been like Ben. Like straight out of a horror movie, the victim's feet and lower legs were pointing skyward, having been broken at the knees and forced to bend in the opposite direction from normal. And worse, as gruesome as that looked, it was nothing compared to his brother.

The other Greene sat upright in a leather chair, his feet upon the ground and his arms positioned naturally on the chair's armrests. Clumps of hair had been removed from his head, as had some of the skin from his scalp. His nose, lips, and ears were all cut from his face, and his eyes removed from their sockets. The large handle of a knife, most likely the weapon used to create such uncaring devastation upon the victim, stuck out from the man's temple, the blade buried deep in his skull. His collared shirt was unbuttoned, exposing the prominent number 3 burned into his chest.

"Well," Barry began, standing beside the couch, "based on the discoloration of the skin and the advanced stage of rigor, this man.., shall we call him Victim 4," he questioned, pointing to the burn in the arm, "was killed several hours before our friend over there in the chair."

"Several hours?" SAC Samuels questioned.

"That's right. The question is, *how* did this one die? Like the other victims, these men were both bound by their wrists and ankles, at the mercy of their killer. At first glance, we can assume the victim in the chair died from the knife being plunged into his head, though I imagine it took more than one attempt; the skull is pretty hard. But this one..,"

Barry began inspecting around the head, looking for a similar knife wound, sliding his fingers under the lying man's head to feel for any openings.

"No visible gashes on his front. Nothing on his head."

Barry leaned in closer to the body, his face inches from the victim's, and pulled the man's eyelids down.

"Uh-huh. That's what I'm looking for," Barry continued, still inspecting the man's face. "It appears he died of asphyxiation."

"You can tell that?" I asked, amazed at what someone in Barry's profession could see where others wouldn't even know what to look for.

"Petechiae," he said confidently. Like we were supposed to know what that meant. "There's some tiny areas of hemorrhaging along the eyelids."

"Strangled?" I asked.

"No. There are no noticeable marks around the neck or throat. There's no abnormal swelling of the tongue. He wasn't gagged or smothered. If I had to guess, I'd speculate he had a plastic bag placed over his head. He would have expired in four or five minutes, suffering the entire time."

"All while his brother watched, I bet," I said, pointing to the other dead body.

"Ah, yes," Barry responded, stepping toward the chair. "Victim 3 here is quite a mess. The streaks of blood down his face at his dismembered features indicate he was most likely alive during the malicious act."

"Fuck!" SAC Samuels let out with a gasp.

"I agree," Barry continued. "That's not a very nice thing to do. The eyes, especially. There are no cut marks around the sockets. It wasn't a knife that did that. I'm thinking.., maybe a spoon?"

"Ugh! That's disgusting," I said. "I think I'm going to be sick."

"Hold off on that, Detective," Barry urged. "At least until I'm done, anyway. Judging by the wound around the blade on the side of the head, it looks like I was right about multiple attempts. At least twice, anyway. The poor bastard."

"I can't deal with this anymore," I expressed. "I need some air – preferably some that doesn't smell like death."

"Well, you're in luck, Detective; that's all the information I've got right now until I can perform an autopsy."

"Thank God," I stated, feeling my stomach gurgle in disapproval. "I'll be right back."

I backed out of the apartment and hastily walked toward the exit. As I got to the door, Vera and Danny were entering with their kits in hand.

"You don't look so hot, Mick," Vera said as I dashed past her.

I didn't listen for anything more, instead concentrating on not decorating the walkway with the morning's breakfast. Breathing slowly, I was able to keep things down. I glanced over at Mr. Candalari, who, based on the pile accumulating at his feet, was inhaling cigarettes at an astonishing pace. My eyes scanned the parking lot. Special Agent Hayes' SUV was gone. She left me here to find a ride back to the station. Thanks, Hayes.

Her words came back to me. *"To do something about it."* What was she up to? Did I even want to know? Would she do something to put herself in danger? That would be just like her, wouldn't it? What was I worried about? She could handle herself; she knew what she was doing. I, on the other hand, felt like this case was bigger than me. But Lieutenant Garrett had enough faith in me, even if I didn't have faith in myself. And Jimmy risked his new identity, or whatever the hell that whole thing is, to drag me into this mess. Gina, too, believed in me. Was I the only person who doubted my ability? I needed to shake that. They all believed in me for a reason. I wasn't going to let them down. For them, I'd suck it up and get back to doing my job. I had a case to solve.

I took a deep breath, opened the front door, and headed back inside. I'm sure Vera stored up enough inappropriate remarks by now to hurl in my direction. That should be enough to keep my mind distracted from the horrific scene. Then, Hayes' words popped into my head again. *"To do something about it."*

I wondered what she meant by that. What was she doing?

Chapter 29

The Right Thing

"**A**re you sure you want to do this?" I asked.

"Weren't you the one who tried to convince me it was the smart thing to do, Jim?" Marion replied.

"I did. But of the two of us, who's the smart one here?"

Standing beside Marion, Agent Dipshit chuckled at the comment. I gave him a nasty look. He immediately fell silent.

"Still," I continued, turning my view toward the two-way mirror where, behind it, Vivian was waiting quietly in the next room. "Will that be enough to convince *her*?"

"There's only one way to find out."

Marion placed her forearm on the other agent's chest and brushed him back a step to clear him from her path. She had her mind set, and you didn't want to be in her way. She exited the observation room, hellbent on getting Vivian to cooperate with us.

194

Marion had informed me that Ben had struck again - brothers, both dead. She didn't elaborate on what she encountered earlier in the day, but whatever it was had her in a mood. She'd been against using Victim Ø to draw Ben out since the first mention of it. Suddenly, it'd become her top priority. I can only imagine the scene that could have provoked such a change of heart, and I'm sure my imagination was downplaying it.

She stepped into the room where Vivian had been waiting patiently. The woman remained silent, stiff, brooding. Only her eyes shifted to greet her visitor. Marion pulled out the chair across from her and eased into the seat.

"Hello, Viv. I have something I'd like to..,"

"Have you talked to my little brother and sister?" Vivian asked, cutting off Marion. "Are they safe?"

"They're with your aunt, just as you asked. They're safe. You know you don't have to stay here, right? Our doctors have cleared you. You're free to go home anytime you'd like."

"I can see my brother and sister again?"

"Of course."

"But what about.., *him*? The Alphabet Killer? I know he's still out there."

I watched Marion's shoulders slump even as her expression remained unchanged. She gave a subtle nod.

"Ben Haddick is still out there, yes," she answered.

"He said the countdown would end at zero." Vivian looked down at her arm and rubbed her fingers over the scarred Ø in her flesh.

Marion's stern look cracked and gave way to a look of sympathy instead.

"Viv, I..," her words silenced, and she shifted her glance toward the mirror on the wall. It was like she was looking at us right through it. Her eyes glossed over. I could tell her thoughts were on her sister. All of the fear came back to her in an instant.

I nodded as if she could see me. "Come on, Marion," I mumbled. "You can do this."

Marion turned back to Vivian. "I won't let that happen. You're safe here. You can stay in the hospital until we catch him."

I dropped my head in disappointment. Marion caved. I couldn't be upset with her; her traumatic past had a deeper hold on her than even she would care to admit. The sick fuckers of the world take innocent lives without realizing how much damage they do to the ones that remain. The living carry the invisible scars of their deceased loved ones for the rest of their lives. Sometimes, we learn to suppress the pain. Sometimes, the damage is irreversible.

"You know he won't stop," Vivian said, her voice quivering. "He's going to keep killing until he gets me."

"We'll stop him, Viv."

The room went silent. I looked down at the floor, shaking my head in frustration, knowing Vivian was right.

"Let me help you," the scared woman spoke.

I looked up, shocked, wondering if I'd just heard what I thought I heard.

"He wants me," she continued. "Let him come after me."

"Viv, you don't have to do that," Marion said, trying to sway her. "You don't understand what Ben is capable of."

"Don't I? He held me captive, Special Agent Hayes. He beat me, tortured me. He marked me with a goddamn branding iron. I know better than anyone what he's capable of doing. But I can't sit here, pretending everything will go away. If he can't get to me, he'll kill someone else. And then someone else after that. And it will keep happening. And I wouldn't be able to live with myself knowing that I could have done something to stop it. I can't keep being scared. I want to see my brother and sister. I want to go on with my life."

"Viv, you need to understand what you're asking. It will be dangerous. You'd be putting yourself in harm's way."

"You'll keep me safe," she replied. "I trust you, Agent Hayes."

Marion bit her bottom lip, contemplating her next course of action. She knew Vivian was right. Hell, she'd initially gone in there to convince Vivian of that. Instead, Vivian convinced Marion it was the right thing to do.

"We'll have to get the press involved," Marion responded. "Ben needs to see that you're no longer afraid - that you're going home."

"I understand," Vivian nodded.

"We'll get you set up back into your apartment. We'll have an officer stationed outside, keeping an eye out. I'll be checking in on you regularly. Unfortunately, your brother and sister will need to remain with your aunt for the time being until Ben is in custody. We can't risk putting them in danger."

"I know," Vivian agreed. "But I can speak with them. I'll let them know that we'll be back together soon."

"Viv.., are you sure you want to do this?"

I could tell from Marion's demeanor that the question was less for Vivian to answer than it was for her to overcome the question she was asking herself. *Are you sure you want to let Vivian do this?*

The woman dubbed Victim Ø bravely responded, "Yes, I'm sure. I have to do this."

Marion reached across the table and gently squeezed Vivian's hand. She put on a confident face and flashed the woman a fake smile. "Okay. Give us a few days. We'll set up a press conference. We want to make this highly visible. We want everyone talking about the woman who survived an encounter with The Alphabet Killer."

I watched Vivian's hand tighten around Marion's in reciprocation. She pursed her lips together and nodded. Marion released her grip and stood, continuing to stare at the woman. Then she turned her head toward the mirror with a solemn, almost fearful look and nodded. She stepped toward the door and opened it, looking back at Vivian one last time.

"You're a very brave young woman, Brittany." Then she stepped out of the room.

I wonder if she realized she accidentally called Vivian by her sister's name. Maybe it wasn't an accident. Maybe Marion felt this was her chance to make things right with her sister – to avenge her sister's death. She could take down Ben before another Victim Ø would ever have to endure what her sister endured. To her, Vivian was Brittany all over again. Only, this time, she could do something about it. This time, she could change the outcome. This time, things could end differently.

Chapter 30

Out Here in the Field

After catching a ride back to the station with Officer Riley, I hoped the rest of my day would be uneventful. I'd seen enough death and misery in the last couple of weeks to last a lifetime. A few hours spent sitting quietly at my desk wasn't too much to ask. If anything, it would be a much-needed reprieve. But, as we stepped through the front door, that thought was quickly stripped from me.

"Why don't you just do your damn job?" a man's voice echoed loudly against the tile walls. I knew who it was immediately. Like James Earl Jones or Morgan Freeman, his voice was unmistakable. Officers had surrounded the agitated man to keep the situation from getting out of control.

"I assure you, Mr. Woodruff, we will look into the matter as soon as we have an officer to spare." Sergeant Hannidy was trying to keep the peace, but Bowden Woodruff was an ornery man on the best of days.

"A spare officer?" Bowden retorted. "What are all these men then, Boy Scouts?" he waved his arms in a circle, pointing out the officers around him. "Is it because I'm a black man I can't get justice?"

And there it was. As it often happened, Bowden Woodruff blew things out of proportion whenever he didn't get his way. It didn't matter that three of the six officers near him were African-American. In his mind, the police wouldn't help him because of the color of his skin. That couldn't be further from the truth. The police didn't like dealing with him because he was an irritable blowhard who constantly called the station, complaining about everything and everyone. He was like the boy who cried wolf – only on steroids. Everyone was out to get him. He made sure we knew about it, too. Every. Single. Time.

"Mr. Woodruff," Sergeant Hannidy announced, "that's enough. You know as well as I do there's a killer out there. My officers are doing everything they can to keep people safe. They can't be running off, half-cocked on some fool's errand."

"But what about my cow?" Bowden yelled. "Tess was a good milking cow. That's taking right from my pocket. I may not be a cop in a fancy uniform like you, Sergeant, but I still got bills to pay, just like you. Somebody has got to pay for what they did to her."

I thought it prudent to step in.

"Mr. Woodruff.., you know me." Officers parted to give the man a clear view of who was speaking. "You've known my family for years. My brother and I used to visit your farm when we were kids. My dad would help you unload bales of hay in exchange for two gallons of milk. You let me name one of your calves. Do you remember?"

"I remember," he replied. "You named him Robert."

I smiled. "That's right. Good memory."

"It was a stupid name," Bowden responded. "I renamed him Digger after you and your folks left."

I grinned, letting out a slight chuckle. "Yeah, I guess it was a stupid name. But, listen, why don't you come upstairs and tell me what the problem is? These officers work hard, and they've got a lot going on. I happen to have some free time. What do you say?"

"Are you going to listen to what I have to say?"

"I'm listening now," I replied, waving him toward the staircase. "Let's hear what the problem is."

I didn't want to hear it. I shouldn't have gotten involved. I was a homicide detective in the middle of a high-profile murder investigation. But I wore the uniform for years. I knew what those other officers went through day in and day out. If I could de-escalate the situation before Bowden found himself in cuffs, spending an all-inclusive, one-night stay in our glamorous accommodations, it would be a win for all of us.

I gave a quick wave to Sergeant Hannidy. He shrugged his shoulders and flashed a rueful smirk. I made my way up the stairs to the Detective Bureau. Bowden Woodruff was in a huff, hot on my heels. I figured I could take a few notes and pass them along to Sergeant Hannidy to dole out to one of his officers when they had the time to check it out.

I strode to my desk and pointed to a "guest chair" along the side of it. Mr. Woodruff swiveled his head in both directions, looking around the room before taking a seat as if he were suspicious of others sneaking up behind him. I pulled out a pen and tapped it a few times on a pad in the center of my desk.

"Mr. Woodruff," I began, "what can I help you with?"

"First, I wanna say your daddy was a good man," he said. "And I was sorry to hear about your brother."

I felt my heart skip a beat and a tingling sensation down my spine.

"Thank you, Mr. Woodruff. I appreciate that. Now, tell me what's going on. You mentioned a cow?"

"That's right. Tess. I found her in the field this morning. Somebody done killed her."

"Was she shot? You have a lot of woods behind your pasture. Hunters sometimes carelessly get a little too close to people's property. Could it have been a stray bullet?"

"Detective, do I look like a damn fool to you?" he questioned, his voice raised. "My Tess wasn't shot by no stray bullet. Somebody sliced her neck open."

I drew back, shocked at the statement.

"Oh. Yeah, that's ah..," I lost my words for a minute. "That's not a hunting accident."

"No, it's not," he responded, slapping his palm on my desk. "Now, I want to know what you plan to do about it."

"Well, Mr. Woodruff, this is a highly unusual situation. I don't usually handle cases like this."

"You're a homicide detective, ain't you?"

"Yes, but we investigate *people's* deaths. This is more a state police matter. I can write up a report and get it over to them. I can also refer you to the MSPCA. They have a law enforcement division that looks into things like this. I assure you, they will do a full investigation. But honestly, Mr. Woodruff, I'm not sure how much help they could offer in finding the responsible party. It could have been some kids on a dare, thinking it would have been a 'fun thing to do.'" I motioned my fingers in air quotes.

Bowden Woodruff stood angrily. "So that's it then? My Tess won't get justice?"

"I didn't say that. We take crimes against animals very seriously. Once I get the report over to the state police, they will open a full investigation. But I don't want to give you false hope, Mr. Woodruff. In a situation like this, a random cow killing, it might be difficult to catch the person or people who did that. I'm very sorry. As I said, I can give you the number to the MSPCA. They can also aid in the removal and disposal of the cow."

He flopped his hand over in disgust. "You keep it." He stomped his way back to the staircase before stopping and turning. "You know what I don't understand," he said. "What were those kids thinking they were going to do with her blood anyway?" He turned back to descend the stairs.

"Wait!" I cried out, stopping the older man in his tracks. "What did you mean by that?"

"I mean, I don't know why they was trying to collect her blood."

"Why would you think that?" I asked, getting up from my desk and walking toward the man.

"I found a bucket out in the field that had some blood in it. There was blood all around it on the ground, too. It looked like the handle gave way."

"A bucket?" My thoughts jumped back to the apartment, where the walls had been bathed in blood.

"Mr. Woodruff, I've changed my mind; I'd like to check that out."

* * *

I bent down over the dead animal, careful not to get my shoes stained with blood. I used the eraser side of a pencil to lift a flap of the animal's cut neck. I wasn't an expert like Barry, but it looked like a clean slice- a machete or something similar. It was a deep cut, slicing through major arteries and the animal's windpipe. The cow's tongue sticking out from the side of its mouth was a sickening sight. I imagined its struggle to breathe, gasping for air while it bled out. I shook my head and sighed. I turned and looked at Mr. Woodruff standing over me.

"Can you show me the bucket?"

He frowned and nodded, pointing his finger toward the far side of his field. I stood and backed away from the cow, looking down at my shoes. They had a little mud on them but were still clean of blood.

I followed Bowden deeper into the pasture until we came upon the mess. A yellow bucket, like the one in the Greenes' apartment, lay on its side in the mud, the majority of its contents spilled all around. The bucket's wire handle was twisted out of shape, by the look of it, broken out of its housing from the sheer weight of the liquid.

"Do you know when this happened?" I asked.

"I found her this morning," Bowden answered. "But I was out of town the last two days. That's why she was out here. All of my cows were. I don't like keeping them cooped up in the barn when I'm away."

"I understand. Well, sir, I think I've seen enough. I'm going to call this in. Please don't touch anything until I get a forensic team here. They'll need to clear the area. I'll ask some questions and see if anybody has ideas about who could have done this." I knew who did this, but I couldn't provide that information. "If I find out anything, I'll let you know."

Mr. Woodruff pressed his lips together and raised his chin. He stuck out his right hand in appreciation. I returned the gesture.

"Thank you, Detective," he said. "I appreciate you coming out here, even if it was only to indulge a grumpy old man."

I smiled. "Not at all, Mr. Woodruff. You were always nice to me and my family. It's the least I can do. And I do plan on getting to the bottom of this."

"Whoever did this, he better hope I don't catch him before you do."

I nodded and followed Bowden Woodruff to the gate. He wasn't going to catch who did this. We'd already been after Ben for over two weeks without so much as a clue where he might be. It's horrible enough he's killed innocent people to satisfy his morbid, psychotic urges, but now he's killed a cow, too. A cow? For what? To show us he's capable of anything, no doubt. I couldn't believe the sick piece of shit he'd become.

I stepped to my car door and looked over my roof at the dead cow lying in the field. I let out a heavy breath. Then I took a final look at my shoes and shook my head. I had blood-saturated mud soaked into the sides and tops of them. Dammit! Those were my favorite shoes. I suppose it could have been worse, it could have been..,

And then the smell hit me.

Shit!

Chapter 31

The Smell That Surrounds You

Getting dressed in the morning didn't feel the same without slipping into my usual work shoes. I had left them with Vera to analyze the blood. She wasn't too happy about the smell. I wasn't pleased about it, either. They'd already stunk up my car on the way back to the station. And the drive home.., I couldn't tell you the last time I'd driven a car wearing only socks. It wasn't horrible; it just felt funny on the toes.

Before heading out the door, I dialed Gina as I did every morning. She started and ended each of my days.

"Hey, babe. Good morning. I slept okay. You? Oh no; did she keep Rosa up, too? That's good, at least. Is she feeling better? Hey, hold on. I'm making a coffee. I'm gonna put you on speaker."

"*...and she's got another tooth coming in,*" she continued without missing a beat. "*I'll try to send you a picture of it. She misses you. We both do.*"

"I miss *you* both."

"I think she's been trying to speak. I mean, I know she's still too young, but I swear it sounds like she says 'Mama.'"

"I bet you're feeding her that word so she'll say it before she says 'Dada.'"

"I promise; I'm not, Mick. But Rosa has been spouting her name all day, every day, so don't be shocked if Stella calls out my sister's name before either of ours."

"She will," I heard Rosa's voice in the background.

"When you get back here, we'll make sure to erase Rosa's name from the little peanut's vocabulary. But listen, I gotta go." I picked up the phone from the counter and clicked off the speaker. "I love you, too. Give my other favorite girl some kisses for me. Okay. I'll talk to you tonight. Bye."

I always felt better after our morning call. Unfortunately, things always went downhill from there. I locked the house and opened the door to my car. The foul stench of cow manure was still present, making me regret not keeping the windows cracked to air it out. I could only hope the smell wouldn't stick to me; I'd never hear the end of it from others at the station.

On the ride in, my mind splintered in all directions. I thought of Lieutenant Garrett and wondered how he was feeling. I should have probably stopped by and checked in on him or at least called and updated him on the case. Wait! Not that. That would only increase his blood pressure. Then again, seeing or hearing me might do that anyway.

I also thought about Ben and the horrible killings. How could he.., how could anyone do that to other people? It's disgusting. And not only kill them but torture them and transport them and do things that convince me there is nothing left of the Ben I once knew. And why kill a cow? Pointless.

Then there's Agent Hayes. She stormed off to who knows where. Not that she reported to me, but I thought I would have heard something by now. If not from her, then from Jimmy. I could have reached out myself, but I was afraid I'd learn something I didn't want to hear about.

I arrived at the station in what felt like record time. It wasn't, but that's how far my thoughts were adrift. I walked into the station, already feeling uncomfortable from the spare shoes I wore, but made more so when they began squeaking with every step. I went directly to Vera's lab, hoping to wear the soles out enough to minimize the sound before heading upstairs. Vera saw me traipsing down the stairs and met me at the locked glass door.

"Hurry, get in," she said. "I don't want that crotch rot Samuels coming down and seeing me. He's already been down here once this morning and.., ah, what the shit, Mick?"

"What?" I questioned.

"I just told you.., SHIT! You smell like you just came from the city sewers. Didn't I get enough of that shit last night? I literally keep saying the word because you put it back in my brain again. Dipshit! Holy shit, there it is again."

I heard Danny snicker over by a large stainless steel sink.

"You too, Danny?" I said, raising my arms in a questioning manner. His eyes shot open nervously, and he ducked his head back into the large metal basin.

"So, Mick, you coming down here.., what's this shit about?"

"Can we stop with the shit jokes?" I asked nicely but probably showing irritation on my face. "The smell's from my car."

"All right, all right," she said, flopping both hands forward at me. "You want to know about the blood, don't you?"

"If you've got the results."

She picked up a sealed plastic bag containing my shoes and plopped it on her desk.

"The sample from your shoes matches the blood we scraped from the apartment wall. It's the cow's blood. Ben's become a real sick fuck."

"He has been all along," I responded. "I know that now. You got anything else for me?"

"Yeah. Danny pulled some trace amounts of oil residue from one of the vic's shirts."

"Like you might find coming from a furnace?" I asked.

"Yeah. Dried sooty residue."

"Just like Stepan Greguric had on his skin," I said. "There's a connection there. Ben's holding his victims and maybe killing them in a basement somewhere. Someplace with an open boiler. That's how he's burning them, too."

"Good luck figuring out where," Vera added. "The old bones of this city.., there must be a hundred buildings with those old boilers in the basement."

"Tell me about it." I let out a frustrated sigh. "Thanks for the information, Vera. When can I get these back?" I pointed to the wrapped shoes.

"You're going to want them back?" she questioned. "You're better off buying a new pair."

I gave her a sullen look. "That's a shitty thing to say." Then I smiled. "See what I did there?"

"Get out of here, Mick," she said, pointing to the door. "Give me a few days to finish typing up my report. Then they're all yours. Good luck getting that smell out, though."

"I'll figure it out, Vera. Thanks."

I exited the lab and squeaked my way up the stairs. Damn shoes! When I rounded the corner into the Detective Bureau, SAC Samuels was standing by the copier, scanning some files. He was chatting with Agent Deitrich. I glanced around the room. Detective Stull was at his desk on the phone, scratching his head with the backside of a pen. Chief Copelli was walking down the far hallway toward his office. Still no Special Agent Hayes. It was quiet. I never thought I'd miss the loud, raucous, on-the-verge-of-workplace-harassment screaming coming from Lieu's office. Yet here I was, wishing he'd bark an order to me.

I strolled to the copier, treading lightly to keep my shoes from making obnoxious noises. I heard the tail end of a sentence from Agent Deitrich, "*...nothing on the numbers yet.*" I announced my arrival by clearing my throat, though I was sure they heard my shoes way before.

"Excuse me, Special Agent Samuels. Has there been any word on Special Agent Hayes?" I hoped I didn't sound like I was worried. I guess I was a little. I didn't need him to know that. Hayes had originally thought Ben was out to seek revenge on her. It was all just part of his twisted game to get her involved in the case. But then she goes off on her own like she's Rambo. Doesn't she realize he's still dangerous?

"Special Agent Hayes is setting up a press conference about Vivian Yarrows," SAC Samuels replied.

"Victim Ø?" I questioned. "What about?"

"She's going back home. We're letting the public - and that son of a bitch Haddick - know all about it. If he's going to try to get to her, we're going to be all over it."

"Does she know she's being used as a guinea pig to draw Ben out?"

Samuels grinned. "She volunteered."

"Really?"

"She trusts Special Agent Hayes. Plus, there will be an undercover officer stationed outside her apartment. She'll be safe."

"I hope we catch Ben before it comes to that. I don't need two more deaths on my conscience."

"Yeah, well, you should prepare for the worst. That lunatic could be anywhere, and Agent Deitrich has hit a wall with the numbers Haddick left us."

"And I just learned he killed a cow," I added. "That's what the blood in the apartment was from."

"A cow?" Samuels questioned. "Is that why I'm smelling manure?"

I shook my head in embarrassment. "My car didn't air out. The smell clung to my clothes."

"You'd better get that..," his words ended, interrupted by his phone ringing. He no longer acknowledged me. He turned his back and answered his cell as if he wasn't interested in what I had to say. Maybe he never was.

I shrugged my shoulders like it wasn't a big deal, then turned to make my way to my desk. Along the way, I heard Detective Stull raise his voice.

"I'm not saying that, Mrs. Bonderman. I'm just saying that this is the police. There's nothing for me to do. I understand that. Yes, I know you've complained about it before. Have you tried contacting a plumber or an HVAC company? Well, there you go. That's who you should be contacting. I'm sure they'll be more than happy to check things out for you. Okay, Mrs. Bonderman. No, not a problem at all. That's right. Have a good day. Bye now."

He hung the phone up and glared at me. "Jesus Christ, is there a full moon out tonight or something?"

"It sounds like you're getting all the live ones," I said, smiling.

"I'm telling you.., these people. That woman's called twice now, complaining about the smell coming from her heating vents. She called last week, too."

"Her heating vents, huh?"

"She says it kinda smells like burnt skin every time the heat kicks on."

"Burnt skin?" I questioned.

"Yeah. And I already had the apartment building owner, Mr. Baldino, call me again earlier today. He was complaining about squatters in the basement again."

"Wait. Both calls were about the same apartment building?"

"Yeah."

"What's the address?" I asked, standing from my desk.

"It's the Springdale Apartments over on Chelsea. Why? You thinking about arresting some squatters?"

"Nah. I'm sure it's nothing. I'm just gonna go check it out. Besides, we could use some good public relations about now. I'll let you know if Mrs. Bonderman gives me any trouble." I gave him a smirk before turning away.

It could be nothing, but I figured, what could it hurt? Best case: Detective Stull is right about tonight being a full moon. Or maybe I'll bust a squatter or two. Worst case: well, I didn't want to think about that.

Chapter 32

Setting the Trap

My heart pounded as I watched the monitors from inside the FBI's mobile command center. A camera panned over the gathering crowd of media correspondents and newspaper journalists, the views displayed on the monitor to my right. Social media bloggers and YouTubers were also among the press, looking to dazzle their few thousand followers. Beyond them, a mob of curious spectators congregated to see what the commotion was about. On my left, a monitor displayed a close-up of a solitary podium set atop the concrete steps in front of Pierre's FBI field office. I would have preferred if the press conference took place indoors in a more controlled setting, but it wasn't my call. Marion wanted it out in the open, in the light of day, and in the public spotlight to accentuate Vivian's regained confidence and positive outlook. She wanted it on everyone's lips. The more the word spread, the better chance of success that it would reach Ben. If he wanted to go after her, he'd be paying attention.

The FBI had already enlightened the voracious media hounds about the reason for the conference. They came in full force to report on the one victim who had been held captive by The Alphabet Killer and lived to tell about it. They didn't need to know the reason why - that Ben promised to hunt her down and kill her as part of some sick countdown.

The buzz of the horde was palpable as reporters and their camera crews squeezed ever tighter on the crowded steps, anxiously awaiting the arrival of Vivian Yarrows. How ironic that she had survived her encounter with a deranged killer only to find herself about to become the victim of the unruly mongers of the press.

As two agents and I watched from inside the sardine can on wheels, a hush fell over those in attendance as the large doors of the Bureau opened. Ushered by several agents, with Marion in the lead, Vivian stepped into the sunlight for the first time since her decision to aid in Ben Haddick's capture.

Led by Marion, the dark-suited agents escorted the nervous-looking woman to the podium, her eyes scanning the onlookers as if worried her tormentor was among them. Marion took to the microphone first.

"Ladies and gentlemen of the press, thank you for coming. My name is Special Agent Marion Hayes of the Federal Bureau of Investigation. As many of you know, the city of Southbridge has had a killer walking the streets over the past few weeks, stalking innocent individuals in some heinous and twisted pursuit. It isn't the first time our neighbors to the west of us have had to endure such unthinkable circumstances, and the FBI and local law enforcement have been doing everything they can to ensure the safety of the citizens of that fine community.

Today, because of a brave individual who has come forward after having escaped from her captor, we now know the identity of the killer.

"Make no mistake," Marion looked square into the closest camera, "and I'm talking to you, Ben Haddick." A loud gasp fell over the crowd. "Your days are numbered."

Much like a feeding frenzy after chum had been thrown into shark-infested waters, the media ate it up and came back with a flurry of questions.

"Agent Hayes, are you saying Ben Haddick is responsible for the recent murders that have plagued Southbridge? Is The Alphabet Killer back? Do you know his whereabouts? When do you expect to have the killer in custody?"

I watched Marion's expression on the monitor become firm and determined.

"The FBI has recovered evidence linking Ben Haddick to the crimes," Marion answered. "And with the help of Ms. Yarrows," she motioned toward the woman, "we now have positive confirmation that the killer is, in fact, the same man who once called himself The Alphabet Killer.

"After having been through a harrowing ordeal and having to recover from the wounds inflicted upon her by that brutal maniac, I am pleased to report that Ms. Vivian Yarrows survived her attacker and is heading back home, ready to resume her life. We hope that her strength and courage will give hope to the enduring people of Southbridge during this dark time.

"With that, I would like to turn things over to the incredibly brave Ms. Vivian Yarrows."

Marion stepped away from the podium, gesturing for the anxious woman to step forward. Vivian lifted her head from her chest, looking over the sea of people, her face showing more worry than Marion let on to the public. Vivian had already been coached on what to say but in the heat of the moment, with cameras shoved in her face, things could go off script fast. She needed to show confidence, that she wasn't afraid anymore. She needed to be believable that she wasn't worried about leaving the FBI's close watch.

She stepped forward, bowing her head again to gather her thoughts. I saw her chest heave as she took in a deep breath. Then, she raised her chin, a deliberate smile on her face to convey her delight.

"Thank you, Special Agent Hayes, members of the press, and all those in attendance. A little over three weeks ago, I was kidnapped, held against my will, beaten, and tortured. The man who did these things to me didn't try to disguise his face. He wasn't hiding in the shadows, letting the darkness conceal his identity. He wanted me to know who he was. He wanted me to be afraid, to give up. He wanted me to know he was in control. That man.., was Ben Haddick.

"He tried to break me - to break my will. He thought of me as only a victim. Well, I stand before you today, not as a victim, but as a survivor. My name is Vivian Yarrows, and I am not a broken woman. I am alive, I am free, and I am going back home."

And then the questions came.

"Ms. Yarrows, how long were you held against your will?"

"I don't know," she replied. "I was unconscious for a time. There were no clocks. It was hours, maybe a day."

"Did Ben Haddick tell you why he was doing these things?"

"No, but I believe he is a sad little man who needs others to feel weak so he can feel strong."

Vivian was doing just as she rehearsed with Marion. Demean Ben; make him angry. The goal was to make it so that he had little choice but to carry out his promise. She was to make herself a target. If he went after her, The FBI would be there to apprehend him.

"What will you do now that you have your life back?"

"Honestly, I haven't thought of changing anything. I'm just glad to be going back home."

"Ms. Yarrows, how does it feel, knowing you're the only person to have lived through an encounter with the infamous Alphabet Killer?"

"I feel fortunate to be alive," she answered. "But I also feel great sadness for the families of those who weren't as lucky."

"You mention luck," one of the reporters shouted. "You standing here is a testament to how lucky you were. Can you take us through the events leading up to your escape?"

I saw the sudden nervousness in Vivian's eyes. The question rattled her. She'd forgotten her response. Or perhaps she couldn't run from the truth. It wasn't luck that she survived. Ben released her so she could warn the FBI he was back. He wanted a challenge. He set her free so he could take her life at a later date. As Vivian said, Ben wanted to be in control. He would finish his game on his terms. And it would be right out from under the FBI's nose. Or so he thought.

"I...I..," Vivian stumbled.

Marion jumped in and spoke into the microphone. "I'm sure you all still have questions, but as you can imagine, this has been a very trying time for Ms. Yarrows.

She has been through a great ordeal and is very excited to be going back home to Southbridge. Her family is also anxiously awaiting her return. We want to get her back there so she can put all of this behind her. Thank you all for coming."

Marion turned and slung her arm around Vivian's lower back to steer her toward the Bureau's entrance. From there, she would guide Vivian to the lower garage, where Marion's black Escalade awaited. They would drive back to Southbridge to deliver Vivian back to her apartment. She would stay there until further instructions. She wasn't to leave the apartment.

The U.S. government had graciously paid for enough groceries and other supplies to last a few weeks. Hopefully, it would all be over by then, and Ben would be back in custody.

I kept telling myself this was going to work out. It was the plan we laid out. The trap was set. Vivian was safe. Marion was committed to ensuring that. The rest was up to Ben. If they couldn't stop him from killing two more people, he'd be coming for her – Victim Ø.

Marion was counting on it.

Chapter 33

Last Thoughts

I'd been to the Springdale Apartments before. Not since I made detective, but several times when I was your run-of-the-mill uniformed officer. I couldn't tell you how many times I'd hauled an abusive spouse out of there. I wouldn't be surprised if some of the carpeting in those units still had blood from a few of those beatings. I wouldn't say I missed those days, but dealing with the shit I'm neck-deep in right now, maybe I did. In those cases, at least you knew what you were dealing with when you arrived. Rarely in a spousal abuse situation did the abuser run. They wanted to control the situation and often the narrative of how things went down. Sometimes, they became violent. Sometimes, a weapon was involved. Those were all things an officer prepared for when responding to such a call. But the stuff I'd witnessed during my time as a homicide detective.., those were things for which you could never prepare. I hoped my hunch about this latest visit was wrong.

219

I pulled into the half-empty parking lot at the rear of the four-story building, its appearance unexceptional. Nothing about the outside of the building seemed unusual. I stepped from my vehicle and scanned the brick face of the tenement, then proceeded to walk the exterior perimeter. Everything was quiet.

I stepped through the front door into a tiny vestibule where, along the left wall, a built-in panel with little white buttons was present for guests to buzz tenants, allowing them access through a second locked door. I skimmed down the labels of handwritten names until I came to the one I recognized from Detective Stull's conversation: Bonderman. Henrietta Bonderman.

I pressed the little button for apartment 7, hoping the woman was home. A crackling noise similar to a cheap walkie-talkie sounded from the speaker. And then a woman's voice.

"Hello?"

"Hello," I replied. "Is this Mrs. Bonderman?"

"It is. Who is this?"

"Mrs. Bonderman, I'm Detective Dooley from the Southbridge Police Department. You called the station earlier regarding a smell."

"I did. But you're not the officer I spoke with."

"No, Ma'am. Detective Stull was pulled away on another assignment and asked if I could check in on you."

"He sounded like it was a bother."

"Not at all; we try to do what we can. But, um.., would you mind buzzing me in so I can check out that smell?"

A few seconds of silence passed before a weak-sounding hum came from the door, followed by a clicking sound. I tugged on the handle, and the door swung open with a nerve-tingling squeaking sound. My mind went to how easy it would be for a stranger to gain entrance. Press all the buttons; someone was sure to buzz you in.

Apartments 1 through 4 were down the hall to my left. I navigated the right hallway where apartments 5 through 8 resided. I stopped at door 7 and quietly knocked three times. The same voice I'd heard over the speaker rang out.

"Who's there?" As if she hadn't just let me in.

I cleared my throat. "It's Detective Dooley, Mrs. Bonderman."

"Show me your badge through the peephole," she insisted.

I unclipped my badge from my belt and flashed it to the door's small glass lens. A second later, the sound of a chain lock slid across its housing. Then, a deadbolt unlatched. The door creaked open a few inches, and a pair of eyes, surrounded by wrinkled skin, peered out.

"Mrs. Bonderman?" I questioned with a smile.

The woman opened the door the rest of the way to allow me entrance.

"Can never be too careful," she said, backing away.

"That's true," I nodded, yet I got in with little resistance.

"Well, come on," she instructed, waving her hand onward as she turned her back to me, her slippers scraping across the floor due to her legs barely lifting. "There's a little here, but the smell is heaviest in the other room."

I followed her a short distance, where she turned left into the next room. The smell hit me like a brick wall as soon as I reached the doorway into the room. It wasn't overpowering, but it was that unmistakable stink you'd smell after burning your hand on a stove. The odor had a hint of what smelled like burnt hair, as well.

"You smell it, don't you?" she asked, but as less of a question and more of a, *there must be something wrong with you if you don't,* kind of statement.

I scrunched my face and nodded to let her know the scent was prevalent. "And you say the smell is coming from your vents?"

"That's right, though I've blocked off most of them. It seems to come and go every few days. I told the landlord about it, too."

"Mr. Baldino?" I questioned.

"That no good piece of..," She hesitated. "Well, I don't cuss, mind you. But you can fill in the blank."

"Mr. Baldino called us as well," I informed her. "He thought there might be squatters trespassing in the basement. I should take a look while I'm here. Make sure someone isn't starting fires down there. Could you point me in the right direction, Mrs. Bonderman?"

"It won't do you no good. The door's always padlocked. And good luck getting ahold of that good-for-nothing rat to unlock it for you."

I grinned. "Well, I still think I'd like to check it out just the same. As you said, you can't be too careful."

"Suit yourself," she said, leading me back to her door. "Go back the way you came. At the end of the far hall, take a right. The basement door will be on your left."

"Thank you, Mrs. Bonderman." I opened the door and stepped out into the hallway. "I'll let you know if I discover the source of that smell."

"Eh," she responded, then shut the door.

Okay then, I thought. *Maybe I won't let you know.* I followed Mrs Bonderman's instructions, passing by all the units on the first floor to the end of the hall. She wasn't wrong; as soon as I turned the corner, the door to the basement was right in front of me on my left. And as she said, there was a padlock in place. But as I stepped up to the door, I noticed the arm of the lock wasn't closed, only made to look like it was. From a distance, one wouldn't realize it was unlatched.

I lifted the padlock from the metal loop and swung the hasp open. The door creaked open slightly. I hung the padlock back on its loop and opened the door wider. The smell immediately punched me in the face. It was the same smell as in Mrs. Bonderman's apartment, only enhanced tenfold. I covered my nose and mouth with my left hand and placed my right hand on my weapon. I didn't spot a light switch, but there appeared to be a dim glow coming from beyond my sight. Was there a light on, or was it coming from the furnace? Maybe there were squatters down there, after all. I announced myself and listened for any stirring.

"This is the police. Is there anyone down there?"

Nothing.

"I'm coming down," I spoke loudly. I pulled my sidearm from its holster. "No sudden movements."

I shuffled down the concrete steps, keeping my eyes focused and my senses on alert. The heat radiating from below, mixed with the lingering odor, was almost unbearable. As I neared the bottom, the room opened up into view, and my heart slammed against my ribcage. My breath became shallow, and a sudden chill shot through me as I discovered the origin of the horrible smell.

I raised my gun, waving it aimlessly in the dim light, my heart pounding heavily in my chest while sweat streamed down my cheeks. In front of me, facing away, a man was sitting in a chair, his arms and legs bound. The chair was in front of a large wooden table, and to his right was an old boiler furnace with an access panel open to an intense flame. With adrenaline flowing through me, I rushed forward to check on the man, my gun still poised firm in my grip, pointing into the darkness beyond the furnace.

"I'm here!" I yelled instinctively, hoping to reassure the man that help had arrived. I hadn't known it was a wasted breath until I got to him and saw he was already dead, his throat cut. The man wore a red-stained white buttoned shirt that had been torn open, and upon his exposed hairy chest, the number 2 was still oozing. Blood trickled down from his neck, flowing over the burnt number and mixing with the puss. That was when it hit me that the wound was still fresh and must have just happened within the last few minutes. That meant that Ben might still be..,

The sound of a footstep behind me caused me to swing my body around, my arms extended, ready to fire. I never got the chance as a metal rod slammed against my wrists, causing me to drop my weapon. I heard the bones in my left wrist shatter. My right wrist was intact but had gone numb from the strike. I stumbled back, crashing into the deceased man and knocking his chair over. I lost my balance as well and tumbled to the floor, landing on my right hand, which collapsed under my weight. I turned my head and looked up at my assailant, a branding iron raised over his shoulder. As he swung it downward, I managed to twist just enough that it missed my head but smashed against my shoulder. I cried out in pain and rolled onto my side, trying to get to my knees. The shoulder was burning, sending flairs of jolting pain down my arm. I couldn't let that stop me. I secured one knee under me and pivoted my weight around to get my other underneath me. That was as far as I got before I felt my own gun pressed against my forehead.

Ben Haddick stood before me, clasping my gun in one hand while the other held the still-heated branding iron. His face was pale and thin but masked behind an ungroomed dark mustache and beard. He had dark blotches on his forehead where he had wiped his oil-residue-stained fingers across. And at that moment, he had a look of pure hatred in his eyes.

"I didn't want it to be like this, Mick," he said. "You weren't supposed to be here. You've ruined everything."

"Ben, calm down," I said with a lump in my throat. My left hand had been shaking from the break, but just then, my right hand began quivering to match. "You don't want to do this."

"Oh, I do, Mick. There is still so much I intend to do."

"Let's just talk about this," I said, trying to remain as calm as a man with a gun to his head could be. "You've killed a lot of people, Ben. You don't need to kill anymore."

"You mean, like you?"

He pressed the barrel harder into my forehead.

"Please, Ben. Don't do this." I felt my wife's hand brush tenderly against my cheek. I heard her whisper in my ear *Promise you'll never leave us*. I saw my little girl's smile and the sparkle in her eyes. "Ben, please. Gina and my little girl..,"

"What?" he interrupted. "They wouldn't be able to live without you? I've heard it before, Mick. They all beg for their lives. I expected better of you. You're right about one thing, though. Gina and your little daughter, they won't be able to live without you. Because after I'm through with you, I'll be paying a visit to them."

"Don't you dare!" I yelled

"I dare whatever the hell I want!" he seethed, spit flying from his lips. He let out an irritated breath. Then, in a calm voice said, "Goodbye, Mick."

I watched as his index finger twitched by the trigger. I closed my eyes tightly, the images of Gina and Stella Mae burning into my skull. Their faces will be the last thing I see before I die, and I am at peace with that. I hear Ben inhale deeply and in the next second..,

"Bang!"

My head jolted back, and my eyes opened to the sound of Ben laughing. It took me a moment to realize I wasn't dead - that the loud bang wasn't my gun going off, but Ben yelling the word instead.

"Oh, man," Ben said in between his laughter. "You should see your face. I can't kill you, Mick. You're like family. And you didn't really think I would do anything to Gina and your little girl, did you?"

Just as quick as Ben's laughter began, it ended, and he shot me a serious look, his eyes burning into my soul.

"Don't get me wrong, Mick; I'm a monster. But I'm not that kind of monster. You've ruined what I had going here, but the plan remains. You won't stop me. I *will* finish what I started. I'm letting you live this time, but don't go thinking you're safe from all of this. Get in my way again, and I won't hesitate to kill you."

I think I was in shock that I was still alive. Otherwise, I might have been able to react faster to prevent what happened next. I watched Ben's hand with the branding iron rise, seemingly in slow motion, yet still too fast to do anything about it. As it swung down upon me, I heard an awful cracking sound before everything went black.

Chapter 34

...2

Echoes. The sound reverberated in my ears, waking me. Was I underwater? No, I could feel myself breathing. My eyes slowly, painfully crept open to a blur. Gray was the first color I saw, followed by a black shoe. The world appeared sideways. Wait; *I* was sideways.

My head rested on the hard concrete, my right shoulder numb, buried beneath my weight. Where was I? The answer quickly came to me from the stinging sensation felt on the left side of my head. The blur in my eyes faded, and I shoved myself upward onto my butt.

"Whoa! Take it easy," the woman's voice said.

She was pressing a damp cloth against the gash in my forehead, the reason for the sudden shock to my system.

"You're pretty banged up," she added.

My eyes focused first on the woman's uniform, a paramedic, the name J. Clarke embroidered above her right breast pocket, then, they shifted to my surroundings.

"Where is he?" I yelled.

"Oh, good, you're awake," a voice came from over the paramedic's shoulder. "What the hell happened here?"

It was Special Agent Samuels. I was sure he intended to be sensitive because of my current condition, but it came out like an interrogation.

"It was Ben," I stated, lifting my left arm to swipe away the paramedic's hand from my head. A sharp pain shot through my forearm before I managed the feat, causing me to wince and squeeze my arm to my side.

"Your wrist is broken, sir," the young brunette tending to my injuries informed me. "Try not to move it. We'll get that bandaged up in a moment, but you'll need to go to the hospital for a cast."

"Later," I said, rubbing my left shoulder where Ben had hit me with the branding iron.

"We know it was Ben," SAC Samuels responded, sounding annoyed. "Not only because he left us a goddamn corpse with the number 2 stamped into his chest, but because he left you a love letter." He swung his torso around to point at the table while keeping his eyes locked on me. "What I want to know is, what the hell were you doing here without backup?"

"I was here checking on a..,"

I froze mid-sentence. What was I supposed to say - I was investigating a heating problem? A strange smell?

"Well?" he requested. "You were checking on a what?"

"A hunch," I answered.

"A hunch? You were checking on a hunch? Let me remind you..,"

"Excuse me!" I raised my voice while getting a foot underneath me. "And you, miss," I said unintentionally gruff to the young paramedic. "Will you stop fussing over me? I'll be fine."

I pushed myself to my feet as the paramedic backed away.

"As I was saying," I continued, "I had a gut feeling. Detective Stull received some phone calls from tenants complaining about a smell. A burnt fleshy smell. Something in my gut told me I should check it out."

"Something in your gut?"

"That's right. A damn fine detective once told me you could rely on your gut as much as any evidence. And he was right. Here we are."

"Yes, here we are," he repeated, only in a sterner tone. "You almost got yourself killed, our suspect escaped, and all we have to show for it is another dead victim to add to the list. If you trusted that gut of yours so much, why didn't you request another officer go with you? We could have had our man in custody by now."

He wasn't wrong. It was a solid argument. I could have grabbed Riley or another officer to accompany me. I was careless, and it almost cost me my life. It was dumb of me.

"Excuse me, gentlemen," the familiar voice of the medical examiner rang out. "If you two are through bickering, I'd like to concentrate here."

I leaned my head to the side to peer around SAC Samuels. Barry was kneeling by the fallen chair, inspecting the victim's face by manipulating the man's head from side to side. A forensic photographer was snapping pictures. Two uniformed officers were standing watch – one covering his mouth with his palm, the other staring down at the blood-stained floor with his forehead cupped between his thumb and index finger.

"Where's the rest of the gang?" I questioned.

Samuels looked at me stone-faced. "Ms. Snell and her assistant are on their way. We've got an officer posted at the door upstairs and three others going door to door, looking for the Haddick boy."

"And Special Agent Hayes?" I asked.

"She was getting Vivian settled into her apartment. I left messages with her, but she hasn't returned my calls."

"How did you know I was here?"

"Detective Stull mentioned you went out on some fool's errand. I tried to reach you several times, but as a recurring theme around here, nobody picks up their phones. I sent a unit to retrieve you. But then.., this."

I pulled my phone from my pocket and saw I had several missed calls. I also noticed the time and realized I'd been unconscious for almost an hour. I slid my phone back into my pocket and glanced down at my swollen left wrist, which I'd clamped tightly to my side to minimize its movement, and then to the paramedic who was pulling her hair back into a ponytail.

"You got anything for the pain?"

"You really should let us bandage that up and take you to the hospital," she replied.

"I'll get there," I answered. "I just need something for right now."

She reached into her bag, "I'll give you a couple of Ibuprofen; it should help take the edge off."

"I'll take three."

She handed me two sealed packets, each containing two pills, along with a small 8 oz bottle of water. My shoulder, my head, my wrist.., fuck it, I took all four.

"You said Ben left me a note?" I inquired, turning back to SAC Samuels while downing the last sip.

"On the table," he replied. "He also left us some parting gifts: two branding irons."

"Let me guess; the number 2 used on this poor guy, and the number 1."

"Yup."

I brushed by Samuels on my way to look at Ben's note. "This is where he'd been all along," I said, looking at the streaks of blood spatter along the concrete. "Detective Stull had been fielding calls from the landlord, Mr. Baldino. He was complaining about having squatters down here. It was Ben. Down here is where he must have killed and branded them all. But now, the location has been compromised. He won't be back. The irons are no longer of use to him. And.., Shit!" I instinctively reached for my hip. "He has my gun!"

"What? That's just great, Dooley," SAC Samuels barked. "Now he's got a gun to add to his repertoire of ways to kill. He's going to go on a goddamn shooting spree."

"No, he won't."

"What makes you think that?"

"He could have killed *me*," I returned. "He didn't. I wasn't part of his plan. I wasn't his number 1. He'll be going after one more, and then Vivian. And then, it will finally be over."

"It'll be over, huh?" Samuels griped. "Then what do you make of that?" He pointed down at the note.

I turned my attention to it and read the words aloud.

I told you before, Mick. Numbers go on forever. Beware. Infinity can be a real bitch.

I gasped, shaking my head. "I...I don't know. He's made it clear he's been counting down."

"Maybe he plans to start again when he's through," Vera's voice chimed in from behind us, obviously having heard me read Ben's words. "I wouldn't put it past the little shit. He's a real fruit loop if I've ever seen one."

"That won't happen," I said, turning to Vera. "We're going to stop him."

"It's about time you got here, Ms. Snell," Samuels scolded.

She threw her thumb over her shoulder toward her sidekick. "Danny gets motion sickness as a passenger. I had to stop twice to let him barf. Isn't that right, Danny?"

He gave an annoyed look and grumbled under his breath. "Only from *your* driving."

"Don't listen to him," she said. "He's still woozy. Anyway.., I hope you guys haven't disturbed anything in my crime scene."

"That's right, gentlemen," Barry piped in. "Vera prides herself on being the only thing disturbed at a crime scene."

"I'm gonna let that go because I know it was said out of love, Gingerale," she retorted.

"What the hell is going on right now," SAC Samuels snapped, looking at both of them.

"It's kinda their thing," I answered. "Better not to ask."

"Can we just get on with the investigation, please? Barry, what can you tell us?"

"The man's only been dead for about an hour. Maybe an hour and a half. The slice across his neck did it. It's deep. The killer was in a rush. His trachea and left carotid were severed. He would have choked on his own blood if he hadn't already bled out. He has an orbital fracture over his left eye. He was either struck repeatedly or hit really hard. And, of course, no death is complete without the number 2 burned into one's chest. Other than that, he's pretty clean."

"I think I startled him when I called down from the basement door," I stated. "I'm sure he had more planned."

"Do we know who he is?" Samuels asked.

We all shrugged while Vera stared intently at the man's face.

"Holy Fuck!" she shouted. "I know him. I mean, I don't *know* him, but I recognize him. I slept with him about six months ago. Although, if I remember correctly, there wasn't much sleeping going on."

She winked and nudged my left arm, causing me to reel in pain.

"You're a sensitive one," she remarked.

"His wrist is broken," the paramedic jumped in.

"Oh, fuck. Sorry, Mick."

"Enough, Ms. Snell," SAC Samuels raised his voice. "Can you tell us who he is?"

"Beats me," she replied. "It's not like I ask for their names before shagging sessions. Christ, I'd have to keep a three-ring binder to keep track of everybody. But he's a bartender over there at .22 CaliBar. You know, like .22 caliber, but it's a bar, so .22 Cali*Bar*."

"22?" I questioned. I pulled out my phone again and scrolled through my recent pictures. "And there it is," I announced. "The numbers on the brothers' wall. 9, 7, 2, 4. They add up to 22. Shit! That's where Ben was planning on dumping the body."

"No numbers this time, I'm afraid," Barry announced.

"That means we won't have the opportunity to figure out his next move," Samuels stated.

"Not that knowing the numbers had done us any good, anyway," I said.

"Are you boys done here?" Vera questioned. "Danny and I have a lot of cleaning up to do."

SAC Samuels exhaled heavily, staring down at the body of the man still tied to the chair. "We're done here."

"I've got to get to the hospital," I added.

"We're ready when you are," the paramedic stepped forward.

"Thanks, but I can drive myself. I still have one good arm. Him, on the other hand." I pointed to the deceased man. "He's not in any shape to drive himself to the morgue."

"Barry, did you come in the van?" Samuels asked.

"I did," he replied. "So, if the paramedics wouldn't mind hanging around a few minutes longer, perhaps they could help me get Mr. Number 2 up the stairs and into the vehicle."

"You heard the man," he looked to the paramedic. "You good?"

She and her partner nodded their reply.

"And you, Dooley. Get that wrist taken care of. I'm recommending Chief Copelli remand you to desk duty."

"The hell he will," I argued. "Ben threatened me. He threatened my family. He was here. I had a chance. Cast or no cast, I'm not going to sit behind a desk on this. Ben likes to play with numbers? Well, I can play, too. And you can quote me on this. I'm gonna put an end to that little fucker's numbers streak."

Chapter 35

A Necessary Lie

Hospitals weren't my thing. Were they anybody's? I didn't mind visiting, but I didn't like being a patient. My experience with broken bones was limited. I broke my pinky toe once when I stubbed it on the foot of the couch, but that's about it. You would have thought at thirty-eight, I would have had more. Up 'til now, I'd been pretty lucky.

I looked down at my arm in a cast resting on my thigh and thought, for a break, it wasn't so bad. I could still use my fingers. The cast was lighter than I thought it would be. That was a good thing. I'd be wearing it for the next six weeks.

I hopped off the padded table and grabbed my jacket that hung from the metal hook on the back of the door. The orthopedic surgeon wasted no time exiting after his job was through. If it wasn't for the physician's assistant coming in, telling me I was all set to go, who knows how long I would have sat there waiting for him to come back.

I folded my jacket over my casted arm, opened the door, and walked down the hallway until a familiar face standing at the nurses' station eased the tension I felt in my shoulders. Gina had arrived, looking worried. She looked ready to strangle the nurse aiding her before she happened to glance up and notice me walking toward her. She immediately dropped her arms from the counter and charged at me with concern on her face.

"Mick, what happened," she asked.

I had no intention of telling her Ben broke my wrist with a branding iron and that he'd put a gun – *my gun* – to my head.

"It's no big deal," I answered. "Broken wrist. I'll be in a cast for six weeks."

"But what happened, baby?" she said in her tender, sympathetic voice.

"I was responding to a call about some squatters in the basement of an apartment building, and when I went to check it out, I tripped on one of the stairs and tumbled down. You know how much of a klutz I can be."

"You had me worried, Mick. You can't text me 'I'm at the hospital' and not tell me anything. Why didn't you respond to my texts or answer your phone when I called?"

"You called?"

I patted my pants in search of my phone. When I didn't feel anything, a twinge of panic set in.

"Shit! Where's my phone?"

I slapped my shirt pocket instinctively while I turned to look behind me as if I'd possibly dropped it on the floor without noticing.

"Shit! Where is it?" I mumbled to myself. "Did I drop it in the room?"

"Is it in your jacket?" Gina offered, pointing at my arm.

I looked down at the jacket folded over my cast, forgetting I'd placed it there moments before.

"Right, my jacket," I said, as if I'd known it was there all along. I squeezed the pocket area and felt my mind relax as my fingers slid against the phone. I pulled it out and looked at the seven messages and the two missed calls.

"Yup, you called," I said, flashing her the screen while displaying my best *"oops"* smile. "I'm so sorry, hon. I didn't..,"

"Detective Dooley," a woman's voice interrupted me.

Gina turned while I looked over her shoulder to see Special Agent Hayes striding toward us.

"I came as soon as I heard the news," Hayes said. She smiled at Gina. "Hello, Mrs. Dooley. It's been a while." She presented her hand. Gina obliged.

"Hello, Special Agent Hayes."

Hayes turned her stare back to me. "So, what's the damage?"

I raised my left arm. "Broken wrist."

"So you saw him? It was him?" she questioned before I could feed her my fake story. "Ben did that to you?"

I noticed Gina's chin snap upright. "Wait, what?" she immediately questioned, turning an icy stare in my direction. "Ben did this? You told me you fell down the stairs."

"Gina, I..,"

"I'm so sorry," Hayes interrupted again. "Mrs. Dooley, I thought.., I mean, I didn't realize..,"

"It's okay, Special Agent Hayes," Gina replied, still staring at me. "It's not your fault my husband's a jackass. A lying jackass, at that."

"Mick, I..,"

"You've said enough, Agent Hayes," I said, glaring at her. She pursed her lips and stepped back a step to give us room. I looked back at Gina. "Honey..,"

"Don't," she snarled, putting her hand up in front of my face. "We talked about this, Mick. You said you'd be honest with me."

"Gina, you don't understand."

"I understand you lied to me. You can't keep doing this. I can't live like that, always wondering if you're telling me the truth."

"I can't always tell you everything," I responded defensively, my voice raised.

"Lying to me is different," she said. "You know that, Mick."

"I know, but it's not about that."

"Then what's it about?"

"I..,"

"Tell me!"

"He put a gun to my head, all right?" I blurted. "Ben put a gun to my head and said he was going to kill me. Then he said he was going to go after you and Stella. That's why I couldn't tell you. I didn't want you to worry. That's why I had you stay with your sister. Because *I* didn't want to worry. He's completely lost it, Gina. I don't know what he'll do; I only know what he's capable of."

"I get it, Mick," Gina said. "You *still* should have told me. I can handle whatever it is. The lies have got to stop."

I dropped my head in regret. I knew I was right, but I also knew I was wrong. It was a battle I couldn't win.

"When you figure it out, I'll be at Rosa's."

Gina walked away disappointed. I always seemed to be the one causing that disappointment. I didn't know what to do. I exhaled and shifted my eyes to Agent Hayes.

"Thanks a lot," I said, placing blame where it didn't belong.

She raised her shoulders and rolled her palms up in front of her. "Sorry."

I began walking forward toward the exit, hating myself and feeling sorry for myself at the same time. Hayes accompanied me.

"So it was definitely him then?" she questioned.

"It was him," I replied.

"Vivian is all squared away in her apartment. Chief Copelli has a plain-clothes officer parked out front, watching the entrance. I hope your run-in with Ben hasn't disrupted his plan to go after her."

"It hasn't."

"How do you know?"

"When I thought he was going to kill me, he told me the plan remained. He said he was going to finish what he started."

"Then we'll get him," Hayes said confidently.

"Yeah, we'll get him. I'm not worried about that."

"Then why the troubled tone? Is it your wife? You've gotta give it some time, Mick. She'll understand why a lie is sometimes necessary."

"It's not that."

"Then, what is it?"

"It's Ben. We took his kill spot away from him. He won't be happy about that. After today, I'm worried about what he'll do next."

Chapter 36

The Burden

Sleep was overrated. Between the cold sweat, the aching wrist, and the visions of Ben putting the gun to my head every time I closed my eyes, I couldn't catch a break. It was still dark out. The moon's bright glow flashed a beam of light across my blanket. I glanced at the clock on my nightstand for the fifth time in the last two hours. 4:06. It was clear that sleep wasn't happening. As much as my body desperately needed it, my haunted brain wouldn't allow it.

I let out a frustrated breath and wiped my hand across my face to remove the clammy dampness. I rolled my eyes, then rolled myself to the edge of the bed. I threw the covers off me and swung my feet to the floor. I didn't want to move. I knew if I stood, I'd get dressed and go to work. Would that be such a bad thing? I looked at the clock again and shook my head.

"Fuck it."

I grabbed the clock and tipped it over, face down, so I didn't have to see the numbers anymore. I slapped my outer thighs enthusiastically and stood. Work it was.

* * *

I arrived at the Detective Bureau, expecting to be the first, but when I got to the top step, a light was on in Lieutenant Garrett's office. I wondered if it was left on overnight or if Agent Samuels couldn't sleep either. I approached the door, only to find it wasn't Agent Samuels at all.

"Frank? I mean.., Lieutenant Garrett? What are you doing here?"

Lieu's eyes shifted from his monitor. "Dooley, what the fuc…" he froze, tilted his head down to his keyboard, and then looked back up at me. Clearing his throat, he started over in a much calmer voice. "Ahem, why are you here so early, Dooley?"

"I couldn't sleep," I replied. "I have things I've gotta catch up on."

"Like reporting your gun stolen to the NCIC?" he questioned.

"How did you..?"

"Chief Copelli has been keeping me in the loop." He pointed to my cast. "Ben's doing, right?"

"Yeah, he came out of nowhere and hit me with one of the branding irons."

"You're lucky you're still alive," Lieu said.

"Yeah, um.., you too," I responded uncomfortably. "How's things going? I mean, how are you feeling?" I tapped my chest over my heart to let him know what I was referring to. "Are you even supposed to be working?"

He grumbled. "Humph. You've never had to spend every waking hour with my wife. That woman dotes on me night and day like I'm an invalid. I keep telling her I'm fine, but she doesn't give me a moment's peace. She stresses me to no end. Trust me, it's healthier for my heart to come in here and deal with scumbags and serial killers. Besides, my doctor said I could return to work as long as I take it easy and don't get myself worked up."

"Is that why you refrained from swearing a moment ago?" I asked, smirking.

"No, that was my wife, nagging me in my ear. She says I swear too much and wants me to make a concerted effort to stop. Or, at least, reduce the amount I do. I'm practicing."

"That's probably not a bad idea, Lieu."

"You better not tell my wife you agree with her. Christ, I'll never live it down."

"You got it, Lieu. Either way, it's good to have you back." I threw my thumb over my shoulder, "I should probably get to it. The paperwork's not going to write itself."

He nodded. "Mmm," then went back to staring at his screen. He managed to shout out one last demand before I got my foot out the door. "Make sure the missing gun gets reported. As it is, it's late. If I get chewed out, you can count on getting it worse."

"I'm on it." Good ol' Lieu.

I sauntered sluggishly to my desk, questioning my sanity. Why was I here before the sun was up? That was something Jim would do when he was still with the force. Shit. Was I turning into Jim? No. The job was everything to him. I sometimes think he cared more for the badge than he did his family. That wasn't me. That would *never* be me. I loved Gina and Stella Mae more than anything. I just had an awful way of showing it. But the sooner we solve this case, the sooner they can come home.

I hated lying to Gina. And her finding out made it that much worse. When was I going to learn? The thing was, how could I tell her her husband was a coward? When Ben put that gun to my head, I just gave up. I was ready to go, to leave this world, and to leave my family alone. That scared me more than dying - that I would be abandoning them without putting up a fight. I should have done something. I should have grabbed for my gun. Maybe I could have wrested it from him. Something. Sure. Or maybe he would have shot me in the face. *Stop dwelling on it, Mick. You're alive, and you can still stop his madness.*

I sat down and rummaged through some paperwork. I had detailed reports on all of Ben's victims, but we still had no idea why he was doing this. Did he even have a reason? Maybe he was just so damaged that he couldn't stop himself. Hayes thought she might have been the catalyst for his behavior, but Ben seemed more interested in Vivian. Why? He could have killed her when he had her. Instead, he let her go. It makes no sense. And why did he burn her twice? None of the other victims were branded more than once. What was so special about "Victim Ø"? What was Ben trying to prove? Whatever it was, he was making us all look like a bunch of clowns. What were we missing? More importantly, would we stop him before his countdown reached zero?

I had to stop thinking negatively. We were going to take Ben down, one way or another. I was becoming anxious for it to be over. I turned on my computer and stared at my cast while I waited for the machine to fire up. I could feel the aching in my wrist. Ben did that to me. I'd relived the moment over and over in my head. Anger boiled up inside me. Agent Samuels was right to lecture me. Why didn't I call for backup? How could I have been so stupid? I knew what I was expecting when I went to the Springdale Apartments. As soon as I heard about Mrs. Bonderman's complaint of a burnt flesh smell, I knew the possibility was there. Was I trying to be a goddamn hero? Yeah, now look at me. Some hero I turned out to be. The only thing I proved was how underprepared we've been. Especially me. I'm lucky to still be on the case.

The morning hours flew by after others arrived. Everyone welcomed Lieutenant Garrett back with warm smiles and fervent handshakes. Chief Copelli issued me a new gun. Agents Samuels, Hayes, and Deitrich had their morning conference with the state police. I continued looking through the reports and evidence we'd gathered, hoping to find something useful. And through it all, Detective Stull kept looking up from his desk and shaking his head at me in disappointment. I didn't blame him. I could have involved him when I suspected Ben might be at the Springdale Apartments. Stull was enjoying shaming me. So, I had that going for me.

By 12:30, I was going out of my mind, looking through all the files on my desk. I went out to pick up some lunch and to pop a few more Ibuprofen.

By 1:00, I was back at my desk, unwrapping a juicy Deluxe Burger from the Burger Bistro down the street. I'd taken one bite of delicious heaven when Officer Riley charged up the stairs, out of breath and in a frenzy.

"We just got a call, Mick!" He said excitedly.

At that moment, Chief Copelli rounded the corner from his office and rapped loudly on the briefing room door before barging in on the three agents. Lieutenant Garrett stormed from his office to join them.

I looked at Officer Riley for answers.

"What the hell is going on, Riley?" I asked, plopping my burger down on its wrapper.

"It's Ben!" he replied.

Before I could question him further, Lieutenant Garrett charged out of the briefing room, along with SAC Samuels and Special Agent Hayes.

As they quickly strode past me, Hayes turned in my direction. "Lunch is over, Detective Dooley. Grab your jacket."

I wiped my mouth and threw the napkin down beside the best-tasting burger I wouldn't get to eat. I grabbed my jacket from over the back of my chair and hustled to Agent Hayes' side.

"What's going on?" I asked.

"Remember when you said you were worried about what Ben would do next? Well, we're about to find out."

Chapter 37

What He'll Do Next

"Can't you see? It wasn't my fault. It wasn't supposed to be like this. All of this is on them. They did this to you. Everything would have been cleaner. You would have seen."

Stop looking at me.

"They couldn't leave well enough alone. They took from me. They took everything. That's what they do. They take, and they take, and they take. They don't care who they hurt. And now they've hurt you."

I said stop looking at me.

I close my eyes like a child playing peek-a-boo. If I can't see her, she can't see me. I rub my forehead with the back of my sleeve and feel the warm wetness wash across it. I breathe heavily, in and out, trying to calm my thoughts. I must keep control. She mustn't see me like this. I slowly open my eyes.

Why are you still staring at me?

In my anger, I kick the nearest object. It's an old tire rim that barely moves. But my toes feel the effects. That

246

wasn't the brightest idea. I'm in a little bit of pain. I may have broken one of the little piggies. Stupid. Stupid. Stupid. I grit my teeth and display no emotion. I won't let her see the hurt on my face. She won't see any of it. Instead, I smile. The pain in my foot helps refocus my brain.

Is that what you are looking for, bitch?

I walk to the nearest wall and rest my head against the rough wood. "Why did they make me do this?" I liked the seclusion of my heated basement. I kept things clean. Well, as clean as possible. Blood absorbs into concrete too quickly. I washed up after myself so the landlord wouldn't suspect what was going on. But this? How do I clean this?

I look back in her direction, and she still has her eyes on me. She wonders why I do these things. The look in her stare begs me for an answer.

Don't judge me.

"You haunt me with that pretty face, your perfect complexion, that wild blonde hair. But you look up at me and see everything you despise. You don't see me for anything other than the monster you decide I am. I could have been something more. I could have been good. But it wasn't meant to be. They made sure of that. *You* made sure of that. You and everyone else. You are all to blame. So, go ahead and look at me with such hatred. Burn a hole through my chest. Shoot daggers at me. It changes nothing. I am here, and you are where you are."

Just stop looking at me like that.

I close my eyes and sigh. *Get a hold of yourself.* I open them and squat beside her, wondering what is going on in that head of hers. I rub my hand across her bare knee, the tight skirt she wore is no longer a hindrance.

She doesn't tremble under my touch. She isn't afraid of me. I trace my finger across her flesh, her pale skin the milky backdrop for the vibrant red taking shape under my artistry. "I won't get to burn you, my sweet, tender prey, but you are marked just the same. They will know who did this to you." I shift my eyes to her face.

Stop fucking looking at me!

I stand in aggravation and tug at my hair. "Why, why, why don't you understand? It's how it has to be." I squeeze my eyes shut as tight as I can. Images of my dad come to me in waves. He drops to his knees and smiles at me. He understands me. Even as he collapses on that rooftop, he gets it. He knows...,

My eyes thrust open at the sound. What was that? Did I hear a door? No, no, no. Not yet. It's too soon. Not like this; I'm not ready. I hear rumblings. Someone is coming.

I drop the crimson-stained machete to the floor and look at my wet, red hands. It wasn't supposed to be like this. It could have been cleaner. It's all their fault. I look at the blonde before me, and still, she stares at me, unafraid. She mocks me. She laughs at me.

I want you to stop looking at me.

"Who's in there?" a man's voice cries out.

It's over. It's done. I've been found too quickly. I'm sorry, my dear; we must part ways. I bend down and tenderly slide my thumb and finger over her eyelids to close them. She will no longer look at me. I stand up just as the door opens. Like a caged animal, I pounce at the man, knocking him down. He is not part of my plan. He will live. But I cannot allow him to stop me. I kick him in the face, and I run off. This part of my game has ended.

Someone else awaits me.

Chapter 38

...1

Flashing blue lights filled the street in front of Rajesh Patel's house. He sat on his top step holding a damp cloth to his bruised cheek, his wife beside him with tears in her eyes, consoling him. Rajesh was assaulted - attacked when he investigated strange noises coming from his shed. The noises were different now. A dozen strangers invaded his property, drawing neighbors' attention to the gruesome crime committed under his nose. Rajesh's unwanted fifteen minutes of fame had begun with the unfortunate murder of Piper Wells, a news correspondent from Channel 26.

"Jesus," Lieu commented, swiping his hand across his lips. "Is that who I think it is?"

"Yeah," I replied. "I liked Piper. She connected with the people."

"This is a goddamn mess," he said, pulling a cigarette from a fresh pack and slipping it between his lips.

"It sure is." I reached over and plucked the cigarette from his mouth, tossing it to the ground.

"Goddammit, Dooley; you're as bad as my wife."

"You mean, as smart as," I responded.

"No, I mean smart *ass*! If you pull another stunt like that, you'll have *two* broken wrists."

"Come on, Lieu, you just had a heart attack. I'm pretty sure you're not supposed to be smoking. For crying out loud, you shouldn't even be here. And you're supposed to be watching your swearing, remember?"

"Don't lecture me, Dooley. I get enough of that at home. Heart attack or not, I'm still a cop. I'm going to do cop things. Last I checked, you work for me. You don't tell me what I can or can't do. I know what I can handle, and I can handle this fucking mess."

I shook my head and rolled my eyes. There was no arguing with the stubborn, old coot. But he was right about this being a mess. Actually, "mess" didn't begin to describe what we were looking at. I was thankful I didn't get a chance to finish my burger. It would have only ended up at my feet.

Agent Hayes stepped away from the shed and huddled with us a few feet away.

"We knew this was coming," she said. "I don't think Ben likes that you took away his basement."

"No shit," Lieu grumbled.

"No shit is right," I reiterated. "But this? Are we sure it was him? Mr. Patel said he didn't get a good look at the person who jumped him."

"He painted a number 1 on the woman's thigh using her blood. Is that enough to convince you? You're welcome to take a look for yourself."

I put my head down and exhaled. Both Hayes and SAC Samuels made it clear this was the FBI's case, but I couldn't wash my hands of it. Ben called me out from the start when he addressed his first letter to me. Then, he made it personal when he put a gun to my head and threatened my family. I had more stake in wanting to take Ben down than the FBI did. I took Agent Hayes' words under advisement and stepped toward the open shed. I made it three steps before realizing Lieutenant Garrett hadn't budged.

"Aren't you coming, Lieu?"

"F no," he replied, restrained enough to keep from cursing. "I told you I know what I can handle. Right now, I can't handle..," he waved his hands in front of him, "...*whatever* that is in there."

I couldn't blame him. I didn't know if *I* could handle it either. I turned back to the open door. My curiosity and need to know overtook me. I drew in a deep breath and stepped into the opening.

There was blood everywhere. Most of it had pooled on the floor and had since seeped into the plywood, but there was spatter in all directions, staining the walls and the various items cluttered about. Barry stood over the body, clad in a full white bodysuit, shaking his head. SAC Samuels was fixed in the doorway beside me, not wanting to disrupt the crime scene.

I forced down some saliva that had built up at the back of my throat. "Barry?"

Pulled from his thoughts, Barry whipped his head toward us.

"Hmm? What's that Detective?"

I spread my arms downward in front of me to encompass what we were looking at.

"What the Fuck is this?" Lieu had to refrain from swearing; I had no such reservations.

"Oh," Barry responded, snapping out of wherever his thoughts had taken him. "Well, there's no mystery here, gentlemen. Dead body: check. Murder weapon: check. We have a bloody machete with bloody fingerprints all over the handle. I'm sure it will be easy to determine whose prints they are. Anyone care to guess? And, of course, the ah..," he choked up a little, "the body. Though, I suppose we can't really call it that anymore. It's just body *parts* at this point."

Barry wasn't joking about that. Ben, *assuming this was Ben*, completely dismembered Ms. Wells. Her limbs were severed from her torso and kicked aside. Ben used the machete to hack away at her stomach and chest like he was splitting wood. Her head lay face-up several feet from the torso. It was a gruesome, disturbing sight. No wonder Barry seemed a little shaken.

I mustered up the stomach to speak. "Have you found any numbers besides the one on her leg?" I asked.

"Not with my cursory inspection," Barry replied.

"Of course not. Fuck! Where do we go from here?" It was a rhetorical question, but Barry offered a response.

"I can't say for sure, Detective, but the countdown suggests Ø is where our killer would go next."

"Right. Thanks for that bit of insight," I returned, somewhat snippy. "I'd better check on Special Agent Hayes. I'm sure that same thought has crossed her mind."

I stepped from the doorway, leaving Samuels behind to admire the sight. He now understood the kind of individual with whom we were dealing. Some of us had seen it all before. The Alphabet Killer, The Letter Man, now Ben again – it's all the same. It's just another homicidal lunatic piece of garbage for Southbridge to take down.

I approached Hayes from behind, who was in the middle of a conversation with Lieutenant Garrett. She heard my heavy steps and turned to acknowledge me.

"It's not a pretty sight, is it, Detective?" Hayes asked.

"No. No, it's not." I looked at Lieu, "You were right to stay behind."

"I can see enough from my vantage point out here," Lieu attested. "Maybe too much."

Hayes bounced back in. "Mr. Patel stated he heard a man's voice coming from the shed. He said it sounded like he was talking to someone. He heard the man speaking right up until he opened the door and surprised him."

"Piper would have been dead long before that," I stated.

"Exactly," Lieu belted out. "Ben has gone full-on crazy. He's talking to himself; he's talking to dead bodies. He's probably hearing voices in that goddamn head of his."

"And we know where he's headed," Agent Hayes said. "Vivian will be next. I've got to get over there."

"Let me send a few units to her place as backup," Lieu said.

"No!" Hayes demanded. "No police presence. That will only scare Ben off. We need him to think we don't know his plan. There's already a plain-clothes officer outside watching the building. I'll be there with her; I won't let that son of a bitch get to her. Besides, I have an Ace up my sleeve."

"And what is that?" Lieu asked.

"Sorry, Frank. That's FBI intel I can't fill you in on. I've got to get going. There's no telling when Ben will make his move."

"It could be days," Lieu shouted at her back as she walked away.

"Then I'll be there for days," she replied over her shoulder.

"What the hell is that woman up to?" Lieu questioned.

"I don't know," *(I think I know),* "but she seems pretty confident."

"Or reckless," he added. "Jim used to be like that, and it got him killed."

I felt my heart leap into my throat, and a chill raced down my spine.

"Hayes knows what she's doing. Plus, we'll be in constant contact with her."

"Sure, Hayes knows what *she's* doing, but none of us know what *Ben* is doing. And that is what scares the fuck out of me."

"Language, Lieu, or I'm calling your wife."

Chapter 39

Old Haunts

They think they know me. They only know what I want them to know. They think I *don't* know them. Their arrogance amazes me. Have they forgotten my dad was a cop? I know their routines. They have rules that guide them along. They have protocols they must follow like good little sheep. Now, it's time to let the wolf out. All the little sheep are helpless. I've led them straight to the slaughter. I'm going to enjoy this.

The night air is cool. I close my eyes and breathe it in. It calms me. The street is quiet. Empty. Well, almost. I see you, Mr. Officer, sitting in that car, wearing those plain clothes, parked across the street from the building's entrance. Did you think I wouldn't notice? I can smell you from here. But you..,

You don't notice me. The darkness hides me well. But you will notice me when I'm ready. Under cover of night, I hide in plain sight. Chester Greene made sure of that. He was just my size. I knew he wouldn't miss the black jeans and black hoodie I took from his closet. I'm putting them to good use. He'd be happy.

My eyes drift upward to the third-story window. The light is on. Hello, Vivian. You're home, aren't you? But you're not alone. No, that would be foolish, wouldn't it? It's okay; that will make things more fun. And who wants to play a game that isn't fun? Not me. And I think.., not you.

My ears perk up. The sound of music echoes off the exterior face of the nearby buildings. A car with its radio blasting turns onto the street and pulls up by the front entrance, gaining the officer's attention. It is the perfect distraction. A young lady, maybe sixteen, hops out of the passenger side onto the sidewalk. She leans into the open window and blows the driver a kiss.

The officer intently watches the scene unfold. He pays no attention to his side of the road, where the shadows conceal me. His intrigue with the young couple will be his undoing. It is time. Shall we begin?

I don't blame the officer for not noticing what transpires out of his front windshield. The loud music and the girl hold his attention more than they should as he gazes out his passenger window. The car drives off, leaving the girl waving goodbye. As she stands under the street light, her body becomes visible. I notice the officer lick his lips. She wears a black leather mini-skirt, calf-high black leather boots, and a tight red halter top tied around her neck. She turns and makes her way to the apartment building door. Her appearance is stimulating enough to keep the officer's eyes entertained. He is probably fantasizing about the girl doing things to him to make the boring stakeout more enjoyable. The perv won't have those thoughts much longer. She enters the building as the car's music fades into the distance. It is now my turn.

I curl into a fetal position in the street in front of the officer's car. I wrap my arms around my stomach and begin to moan loudly. Officer Plain-clothes stares forward, curious about the noise. My disguise is too good. I blend into the darkness. He doesn't notice me. I groan louder. He turns his lights on to get a better look. I hear his door swing open and his voice ring out.

"What the hell? Where did you come from?" he mumbles to himself.

I rock back and forth on the ground, holding my stomach and moaning like I'm in pain. His footsteps hasten.

"Are you all right, buddy?" he asks as he bends over to check on me. Like a cobra, I strike.

I thrust my hand forward to his chest and deliver an electric shock from a Taser, courtesy of one Piper Wells. It was a fortuitous find in her purse. I didn't want to have to shoot the man. The shot would have alerted people who I had no interest in alerting. The Taser was the better option.

The officer stiffens and falls to his knees. I keep the current flowing a few moments longer. I wouldn't want him waking up before the game is through. He falls onto his back in a heap. I stand and take a moment. He'll be a tough one to move, but I can't leave him in the street for somebody to find. I stuff the Taser back into the hoodie's front pouch and squat behind the officer's head. I look down at my torn, scarred hands. They're not in the best shape, and the officer won't be as easy to drag as Piper was. I shake my head and exhale. Nothing worth it is ever easy. And my cause is most assuredly worth it.

I grab under the officer's shoulders and drag him first to the side of the street, where I drop him and take a breath. From there, I continue the struggle and drag him to his open driver's side door. Before I continue, I confiscate his sidearm tucked under his jacket. I don't need it, but he can't have it. That would make things messy if he regained consciousness. I place it on the ground by my feet and heft the officer into the front seat. He flops over the center console. I fumble around for his keys and cuff his left wrist to the steering wheel. I then take his phone, which is in a holder mounted on his dash, and I shut the door. If anyone should pass by and notice him, he's just a drunk who passed out on the side of the road. They're a dime a dozen in this city. He'll fit right in.

I throw both the keys and the phone into the darkness behind me. I pick up the gun at my feet and walk it over to the dumpster on the side of the apartment complex. I remove the clip and toss it in. I wouldn't want some kid finding it and accidentally shooting himself. No matter what they label me, I have principles. I tap my waistline and feel that my gun, well, *Mick's* gun, is still tucked away nicely. I slide the officer's clip into my sweatshirt pouch and feel the Taser within. I drop my head. I'd forgotten about it. I should toss *it*, too, but maybe I'll find a way to put it to good use. I glance back up at the lit window and smile. Things are about to get.., *fun*!

I enter the apartment building and see the stairs leading up to the higher floors. I feel relaxed as I navigate the stairs to the third floor, whistling Taps along the way. It feels appropriate. I place my palm on the top of the banister post at the third-floor landing and feel the excitement wash over me as I pull myself up the last tread. Door 3A to the left of me is of no consequence. Door 3B to my right is where my prize resides. I wonder if she knows what's coming. Does she know it will all be over soon?

I reach for my waist and retrieve the gun. I let my hand drop to my side while I take a deep breath. I am ready. Just then, a door on the second floor at the base of the stairs opens, and a haunting voice calls out.

"Ben."

I whip around, gun extended, to face the voice I'd almost forgotten but longed to hear once more.

"D-Dad?"

"It's me, son," he says, his own gun extended toward me.

I lower my arm to my side, struggling to understand what is happening and to whom I am staring.

"It's over," he says. "It's all over. Put the gun down and slowly get on your knees."

"But.., but how?" I mumble, confused. Am I speaking with a ghost? Has my father come back as a spirit to haunt me – to punish me for my sins? "Y-you're dead."

"I'm not dead, Ben." He says. "It's me. I'm here in the flesh. I *did* die that day on the rooftop, but they managed to bring me back."

"But they said you were dead," I respond, still unsure if this is an elaborate hoax. "They all told me..,"

"I *am* dead," he cuts me off. "At least, that's what everyone believes. It was easier that way. It was easier if I stayed dead. It was the only way I could get past everything that had turned to shit in my life."

"Y-you could have visited me in prison."

"I couldn't."

"You couldn't? Or you wouldn't?" I state louder.

"You need to understand, Ben. What I did wasn't only for me; it was for you, too."

"How the hell was it for me? When I needed you most, you abandoned me. I sat in that cell, grieving you, wishing I could see you one last time – to say goodbye to you. To tell you I love you. I thought you were gone."

"Ben.., son, I needed you to believe I was dead. I needed you to see that what you did was wrong. I needed you to learn that doing the things you did had consequences, and one of those consequences was getting your old man killed. I wasn't the savior of this city. I wasn't a hero to those people. I wasn't.., I wasn't the hero I should have been to you."

"Shut up!" I yell. "You were the greatest detective this city had ever seen."

"I wasn't, Ben," he replies. "Maybe, in your mind, I was this great, fantastic detective. But the truth is, I was just a second-rate detective barely standing on my own. I was a failure in your life, Ben. I had to believe you were better off without me in it."

"Is that what she made you believe?" I question.

"Who?" he answers.

"That Agent woman. Marion Hayes. It was all her idea, wasn't it?"

"No, it was mine. Right or wrong. Now, come on; put the gun down. Come down here with me. We can go inside and have a drink."

"She's gotten in your head. She did this to you – to *us*. It's all her fault."

"Ben, you need to stop this!" he shouts. "It's time for you to grow up and accept responsibility – like *I'm* trying to do now. Drop the gun and get on your knees."

I look down at my dangling arm and feel anger boil up inside me. "You mean this gun?" I swing my arm up and point it at the imposter before me.

"Ben, drop it! Don't make me do this."

"*You* drop it!" I shout back.

"This has gone on too long, Ben. I can't let anyone else..,"

His words are interrupted as the door to apartment 3A opens, and the girl with the red halter top steps out. Before she realizes what she's stepped into, I grab her arm and pull her in front of me. She lets out a screech as I squeeze her back against my chest and bring the gun to her head.

"Don't make me do this," I say. "I'm not here for this one. Now drop the gun and back the fuck away."

"I can't do that, son," he says, trying to trick me.

"I'm not your son. I don't know who you are, but you're not my father."

"Ben, I *am* your father, and I want you to put the gun down now!"

"My father is dead!" I yell.

"It doesn't have to be this way. Let the girl go. Put the gun down and get on your knees. Now!"

I clench my teeth. "I've lived on my knees for too long.., '*Dad*.' I won't do it anymore." Keeping the girl within my grip, I remove the gun from her head and point it at this man claiming to be my father.

And then..,

Chapter 40

Before Your Eyes

I rested my casted arm on my desk, letting my fingers tap dance on the hard surface. Why was I still here? Everyone on the second floor had already left for the evening. Well, not quite everyone. I glanced over at Lieutenant Garrett's office and saw his light on. That meant there were two of us who currently had no life outside of work. The difference was, without Gina or Stella at the house, I had no reason to go home. That would change once this case was over. Lieu, on the other hand, would have to figure out his home situation on his own.

I stared at the paperwork in front of me, looking over the evidence Vera had collected from the last two crime scenes. The bloody fingerprints on the machete came back as a positive match. As we suspected, it was Ben. He'd never done anything like that before. We really pissed him off. Piper's purse was recovered on the side of the shed, its contents emptied onto the grass. Either she was looking for something, or Ben was.

From the Springdale Apartments' basement, a gold wedding band was recovered from under the furnace. It wasn't difficult to determine who it belonged to. Even if it didn't have the inscription, *"To my Bernie, forever"* etched on the inside of the band, we could have guessed correctly. Bernard Tussle's ring finger had been cut from his hand; it made sense it was his. Judith Bentley's ring was missing from her finger, too. Was Ben targeting the items? Is that how he financed the branding irons? He didn't get Bernard's ring, though. I bet that ticked him off. My thoughts shifted back to Piper's purse. It had to be Ben who was looking for something. *What did you get from there, you little shit?*

Also found in the apartment building's basement was a loaded duffle bag with six additional branding irons to complete the set, a hammer, a box of 3-1/2 inch long framing nails, a bloody pair of pliers, a bloody knife, cord rope, and a damp rag. He used the basement as a goddamn torture chamber.

I thought of Vivian and what she must have gone through. Some people would consider her lucky to be alive, but I doubt she felt that way. All that pain. All the suffering she endured. Seeing what was confiscated from the scene and knowing what happened to some of the other victims, she wasn't lucky. She now had to live with the fear and emotional scars for the rest of her life. And with those thoughts of Vivian, I wondered how things were going with her and Hayes.

The entire precinct was on high alert, ready to respond to any call from Vivian's apartment building or nearby vicinity. A couple of cruisers were parked three blocks away, keeping their distance as instructed but close enough to arrive in minutes if something should go wrong. The officer stationed in front of the building reported every hour with an update. Even Hayes had called SAC Samuels with a status report a couple of hours ago. Everything seemed fine. Still, I would have felt better if I heard from her myself.

I picked up the phone and rang her. A moment later, she picked up.

"Hey, it's Mick," I began. "Anything happening over there? What was that? You're breaking up. No, they're blocks away. How's Vivian handling things? Good. You know.., the lieutenant was right; you could be there for days. We are; I can feel it. It's not a matter of if; it's a matter of *when*. Say again, I didn't catch that. You're fading in and out, Agent Hayes. No, no, I was just checking in. I'm going to let you go. I can barely hear you. Yeah, it's an awful connection. All right. Take it easy."

That was almost painful. I didn't know what was worse, the static or the glitchy service, with Hayes cutting out. Well, at least things were quiet on her end. As much as I wanted to catch Ben, I wouldn't mind if he never showed up. Anywhere. Ever. But then, he would never see justice. The families of the victims would never find closure. They deserved that much. And my family.., they needed closure too. Gina needed her husband back. Stella Mae needed her father back. And I.., I needed them both more than they would know. I couldn't wait to show them how much.

I grabbed my cell and dialed Gina. I needed to hear her voice. She was still upset with me about lying to her. I'd smoothed things over a bit, but I knew it still stung. I promised I'd be better. I would.

She picked up.

"Hey, Gina. How are you doing? I'm.., well, if I'm being honest, I'm afraid. But I'm also pissed off. No, no, not at you. Ben. He killed again. I can't, hon; you know that. I'm sure you'll hear about it soon enough. We believe we know his next move, though. If we're right, this will all be over soon. We can finally put it behind us. You and Stella can come back home. I miss you two so much. How is Stella doing? Oh, she's taking a nap? I was hoping to hear her. No, it's okay. I'll check back later. Listen, I wanted to tell you..,"

My desk phone rang, distracting me. The caller ID showed it was Vera calling from the lab. Make that three of us who had no personal lives.

"I wanted to say I was sorry."

The phone rang again, drawing my eyes to it.

"I won't lie to you again. I promise."

A third ring chimed.

"I've gotta go, Gina. I'll talk to you tonight."

It wasn't until after I ended the call that I realized I hadn't said "I love you." *Do better, Mick*, my brain yelled.

I swiped the receiver from my desk phone. "Vera, what the hell are you still doing here?" I said with attitude, taking my frustration out on her. "Yeah, sorry about that. What do you got? What about the rag? Sevo.., what? Sevoflurane? What is that? Well, that would explain how Ben was subduing his victims. Where would I get the stuff? What? Are you sure?"

I began frantically fumbling through the folders on my desk until I came to the one I was searching for. Vera had continued talking, but I wasn't giving her my full attention. I opened the cover and began skimming down the first page. When I found what I thought I'd recalled, a chill ran through me.

"Vera, I gotta go. Thanks."

I hung up without saying goodbye. That was something Lieu would have done. I think I finally understood his reasoning. There were more pressing matters on which to focus one's attention. I dug deeper into the folder, studying the documents. The more I dug, the more I disliked where my head was going. Shit! Maybe I was reading too much into it. Still…,

With my heart pounding, I grabbed my phone and dialed Agent Hayes. There was no ring, only a clicking sound that I thought would bring me to voicemail, but then.., nothing. Shit! Shit!

I looked over at Lieu's office and called out. "Hey, Lieu – you in there?"

I heard the back of his chair slam into the wall behind him as it often did when he'd get up from his desk. I couldn't understand why, after all these years, he hadn't moved his desk forward another six inches to avoid that from happening. He appeared in his doorway.

"Jesus Christ, Mick. Why don't you go home?"

"Soon, Lieu; I was just going over some things."

"Well, what did you call me for?"

"Who's got watch right now over there at Vivian's apartment?"

"It's Officer Tout until 9:00," he replied.

I looked at the time. 8:15. "Did Officer Tout check in?" I asked.

"Yeah, about fifteen minutes ago. Everything was quiet."

"Okay, thanks, Lieu."

"Yeah," he grumbled, disappearing back into his office.

I keyed in Officer Tout's number and waited for him to answer. It rang five times before bouncing me to voicemail. Shit! What the hell was going on? I had a bad feeling building up in my stomach. The gut didn't lie. Fuck!

I grabbed my jacket and yelled to Lieu again. "Lieu!"

"Goddamn it!" he barked, followed by the chair crashing against the wall. "What is it, Dooley?"

"I'm not sure," I replied. "Maybe it's nothing, but I can't get ahold of Hayes or Officer Tout. I don't like it. I'm gonna go check things out. Can you maybe send one of the other cruisers that way to do a drive-by?"

"Are you thinking it's Ben?"

"I don't know, but something doesn't feel right."

"Let me get a unit over there," he said. "Hang on a minute, and I'll go with you."

I kept my fast-paced stride toward the exit. "I'm not waiting, Lieu. Just make the call. You can meet me there. I'll call you and explain things on the way."

Chapter 41

A Day in the Life

Everything was disorienting. The flashing lights penetrating the spaces between the blinds, the panicked, jumbled voices in the hall, all beating down on my senses. My breathing lacked the vigor to keep up with my pounding heart. My chest tightened, and my legs gave out. I dropped to one knee as one of the paramedics on the scene brushed by my crumpled frame to rush to Vivian's side.

Blood streamed onto the floor from the two bullet wounds in her abdomen while she clung to life, her lungs gasping for Oxygen. An officer placed his hand on my shoulder.

"Are you all right, Detective?"

Wasn't it obvious? Dumb question. I pushed his hand away. "Get out. Clear the scene."

He maintained his stance behind me and grabbed me under my arm. "Let me help you up."

I shrugged angrily, pulling free from his hand. "I said, get out! Help the others in the hall. Keep the other tenants away."

They didn't need to see this. *I* didn't need to see this. I swiveled my head, surveying the room and the ugly scene in the hallway through the open door. It was all fucked up. I turned back and looked at Agent Hayes, a look of dread frozen on her face.

"It's over," I said.

I heard the loud clopping up the staircase and pushed myself back to my feet just as Lieutenant Garrett entered.

"Jesus Christ! Fuck!" he bellowed, his refraining from swearing gone by the wayside.

"I count three guns," I said. "One out in the hall, two in here. Four gunshot wounds. Ballistics is going to have a field day with this."

Lieu nodded his head forward, signaling near the paramedic's boot. "And the knife?" He questioned.

I exhaled. "Yeah.., the knife."

"What the hell happened here? How the fuck did this happen?"

Lieu's words echoed in my brain. *"What the hell happened here? What the hell happened here? What the hell happened..,?"*

Marion

Vivian sat in a cushioned chair across from the couch, silent, brooding, biting her nails. She tried to be strong, but fear gripped her tighter than she cared to let on. I poured hot water over the teabag, the soothing aroma of mint and orange peel washing over me. I hoped it would do the same for Viv.

I delivered the hot cup to her side, placing it on the small table beside the chair.

"This should relax you a bit," I assured her. "You have nothing to worry about, Viv. You're safe here. I won't let anything happen to you. Ben can't get to you here. There's an officer outside watching the building; there's a couple more down the street. We're all looking out for you." I gently touched her arm, "You're safe."

She removed her finger from her mouth and bit down on her lower lip. She nodded as if she desperately wanted to believe me. She grabbed the cup of tea and took a sip. I displayed a hopeful smile. I backed up and sat on the couch, giving my attention to the frightened woman.

"Now, Viv, why don't you tell me..,"

The vibrating phone in my pocket distracted me from my thoughts. I pulled it from my pocket and saw that it was Mick. I put up my index finger to let Vivian know I'd only be a moment. I stood and made my way to the kitchen.

"This is Hayes," I answered. "No, it's pretty quiet here. Hello? Did I lose you? I said it's quiet. The other units haven't made any moves, have they? She's good. Well, you know.., considering everything she's been through. I know. And if that's what it takes to catch Ben, then so be it. I still wonder if we're doing the right thing. We'll know for sure if we catch him. It's sad to say, but I almost *want* him to try something so we could finally get this over with. Mick? Hello? Are you still there? Okay, you're back. So, did you need something, Mick? I know. It's this damn building. There's barely any service. It should make for a quiet evening. I'll check in with you later. Bye."

I ended the call and noticed Vivian had made her way to the window. It wasn't the safest idea, but I didn't want her to feel like a prisoner in her own place. I placed my phone on the counter and walked over to join her.

I stood beside her, my broken reflection through the blinds staring back at us from over her shoulder. I peeled a few of the blinds apart with my fingers and pointed.

"See that car across the street?"

She nodded.

"That's an undercover officer. He'll keep an eye out for any unusual activity. Okay?"

Again, Vivian silently nodded.

"We shouldn't stand by the window," I said, placing my hand on her shoulder and urging her away. "Let's sit down so we can talk."

<u>Mick</u>

We waited in the hallway while Vera meticulously combed through the apartment. A few curious gawkers remained; they were politely commandeered back to their apartments. A distraught young woman from apartment 3A came forward. She stated she had information for us. Lieutenant Garrett and I followed her into her apartment to ask some questions.

The girl sat on a tan cloth sofa beside her mother, who had tears streaming down her cheeks. The mother pulled a black cardigan sweater over her daughter's shoulders, adjusting the front to cover the small, red halter top she wore.

"You said you know what happened out there?" I questioned the scared girl.

She quickly gave an affirmative nod.

"Did you see any of it?" Lieu jumped in.

"See any of it?" the mother shouted excitedly. "That man grabbed her. He had a gun to my baby's head." She pulled her daughter close and kissed the top of her head.

Before I could ask another question, an officer knocked on the open door.

"Excuse me. Detective Dooley, Officer Snell is asking for you."

"Thank you," I replied. I turned back to the mother and daughter. "I apologize..,"

"Go ahead, Detective," Lieu stated. "I'll stay here with these two."

"Thanks, Lieutenant."

I traveled across the hall to see what Vera was anxious about. She was holding a small wooden box in her right hand. Her left hand was extended toward me, a pair of latex gloves dangling from her fingers.

"What's that?" I questioned, snatching the gloves from her hand. "It looks like a jewelry box."

"You would think," Vera responded. "But there's no jewelry in this box. Take a look."

I snapped the second glove on and opened the cover.

"What the hell is this?"

Marion

I've tried to get Vivian to open up to me, but the scars Ben left her with are much deeper than the physical ones. I saw her looking in a jewelry box when I exited the bathroom. She looked happy, but when she realized I was back in the room, she quickly closed the lid and shuffled the box to the lower shelf of the end table.

"You looked content just then," I said, sitting back down. "Do you like jewelry?"

"It's just some knick-knacks," Viv replied. "They're nothing special."

"Oh, I'd love to see them. If you'd care to share."

"I...I..,"

Just then, a voice in the hall yelled, *"Shut up!"* I sat at attention, looking toward the door. It could have been just a noisy neighbor having a spat with his wife. I glanced at Vivian, her eyes wide with fear.

"It's okay," I said to calm her. "I'll check it out."

As I stood, I heard the words *"You drop it!"* ring out. I threw my palm forward toward Vivian to have her stay put. I put my index finger to my lips, telling her to remain quiet. Then, a girl's scream filled the hallway. Viv jumped from her seat, looking terrified. I drew my weapon and grabbed Vivian's sleeve.

"Get behind me!" I shouted. I slowly backed up toward the kitchen, where I had left my phone on the counter. Vivian moved in sync with me, shuffling backward into the kitchen space. I grabbed my phone, hearing her breaths quicken behind me. "It's going to be all right," I said for both of our sakes. My positivity quickly diminished when I couldn't get a signal on my cell. "Shit! Just stay behind me, Viv."

Then, I heard a second male voice, one most familiar to me. Jim had intercepted Ben in the hallway. I felt relief as much as worry. I wanted to run to his aid, but Vivian squeezed my arm in terror. I patted her hand.

"I'm here, Viv. I won't leave you. He won't get to you."

I felt her grip relax. My arms remained taught, my finger poised on the trigger. A gunshot echoed from beyond the door. Then another. Vivian screamed and began rummaging through a silverware drawer.

"Calm down, Brittany. I won't let anyone hurt you again. I'll keep you safe."

Mick

I couldn't believe what I was seeing. Letter after letter, I pulled each article from the box, and with each one, my heart sank further and further. I turned and looked at Agent Hayes and shook my head in disgust. Lieu came lumbering in, looking over my shoulder.

"The girl said another man was arguing with Ben in the hallway. He had a gun, too. It wasn't anybody she recognized from the building. She said when the first gun went off, she dove to the ground and covered her eyes and ears, then heard the second shot. She didn't know what had happened until the man checked on her to see if she was all right. I've got officers in the building and on the street looking for the other shooter now. What do you have going on in here?"

I held up one of the letters for him to read. When he was through, he looked at me with his brow furrowed.

"What the fuck is this?"

"It's exactly what you're thinking it is," I said.

"I don't know what I'm thinking," he responded. He shifted his gaze to Agent Hayes. "Do you think our mystery man did all this damage?"

<u>Marion</u>

I heard sirens in the distance and hoped it wasn't too late.

"Jim!" I called out, hoping, beyond hope, he was still alive. For an eternity, there was silence. "Jim!" I screamed louder, feeling tears well up in my eyes.

I heard Brittany.., I mean, Vivian, slide closer to me.

"Stay close," I said. "I won't let Roy get you again."

"Roy?" Viv questioned.

"*Ben,*" I restated. "I won't let *Ben* get you."

Someone jostled the locked doorknob, and my muscles tensed.

Then I heard him.

"Marion? It's me. Everything is okay."

It was Jim. My shoulders immediately relaxed, and I dropped my arms to my sides in relief. I took a step to unlock the door and felt an immediate burning sensation in my upper back. My legs stumbled, and my body jerked. When the second feeling came upon me, I realized what had happened. I coughed, spitting blood to the floor. After I felt the third sensation, my body crumpled to the ground. How could this have happened? Why? Struggling to breathe, I rolled onto my back and looked at the woman I promised to save. She held up the bloody kitchen knife and smirked. She took a step toward me, and that's when I knew I had to break my promise. There was no saving her.

I muttered three words, "I'm sorry, Brittany," and then squeezed the trigger twice. I watched her fall to her knees before I heard the door bust open. Jim cried out, "Marion!"

I felt his hand upon my face, and a tear rolled down my cheek.

"Don't do this," he cried, his voice getting quieter. "I need you, Marion."

Everything became blurry. I felt myself cough again, and liquid splashed across my face. I knew it was my own blood. I tried to speak, but nothing came out. Jim continued to caress me. I could no longer hear or see him, but I could feel his touch. I could feel his...

Mick

Special Agent in Charge Samuels charged into the apartment. He had a look of dread on his face. He looked over at Barry, who was examining Hayes' and Vivian's lifeless bodies.

"No, no, no. What the hell happened here? How could this have happened?"

"It was Ben," I said. "He played us; this was his plan all along."

I walked over to where Hayes and Vivian lay dead on the floor and stood over Vivian's body. She was on her side, her bent right arm had fallen in front of her, the branded Ø displaying prominently on her arm. Then I saw it.

"Son of a bitch," I let out. "It was there the whole time. That monster said it in his first letter to me. And then, in his most recent letter."

"What are you talking about, Detective?"

"*Numbers go on forever,*' I said, looking down at Vivian, whose shirt had bunched up, exposing her ribs. *'Infinity can be a real bitch.*' The countdown.., all of it. He laid it out for us, and we still didn't figure it out. They did it. Both of them. They led us to believe Vivian was Victim Ø."

"She's got a Ø right there," Samuels said, pointing to her arm.

"Yes, but she was burned twice," I responded. "I kept wondering why." I bent down and pointed out what I was seeing. "Now tell me what you see," I said.

Vivian's arm had fallen perfectly to her side so that the Ø on her arm was lined up with the Ø on her side to form..,

"That's an 8," Frank announced.

"Right where Ben started the countdown," I added. "Vivian wasn't Victim Ø; she was Victim 8. His next victim, Judith Bentley, was 7. Now, take a look at the brandings from here." I shifted to Vivian's posterior. "What do you see?"

"An infinity sign," Samuels acknowledged. *'Infinity can be a real bitch.'* he repeated.

"Ben and Vivian were in it together," I said. "Special Agent Hayes was their target. *She* was Victim Ø. I was on my way over to check on them."

"Check on them?" SAC Samuels asked. "You knew?"

"I didn't then. I do now. The letters confirmed my suspicion."

"What letters?" Samuels questioned.

Vera stepped forward and pressed the wooden box into his chest. "Have at it."

Samuels sifted through a few of the letters before looking back at me.

"You didn't know about these?" he questioned.

I shook my head.

"Then why were you on your way over? What made you suspicious?"

"My gut," I said. "The rag found in the basement with Victim 2. It was drenched with Sevoflurane - an anesthetic used to knock out patients before surgical procedures. That's what Ben used to incapacitate his victims. The thing is, that particular anesthetic is more common during children's procedures. Vivian is a.., *was* a pediatric anesthesiologist. She had easy access. She supplied Ben with all he needed."

"Son of a bitch," Samuels seethed.

"That explains some of this shit," Lieu barked, but what about our mystery shooter? Who the hell killed Ben and saved that kid?"

I shrugged my shoulders. "A good Samaritan, I guess."

I knew who it was, but I couldn't say. Jim was gone. With Ben and Hayes dead, he wouldn't be back. He must be devastated. He was in a hurry to get out of here. He must have heard the sirens and ran off. He left his gun behind. The prints would come back positive, leaving everyone to scratch their heads. Eyebrows would raise. It's not every day a dead man comes back to kill his son. Things would get shuffled away and forgotten, overshadowed by the bigger news. The terror of The Alphabet Killer was over. Ben was dead. His accomplice, Vivian Yarrows, was dead. And sadly, Special Agent Hayes was killed in the line of duty.

I thought when the case was over, things could become normal again. Now that the threat had ended, Gina and Stella Mae could move back home. We could be a family again. As I looked at the carnage left in Ben's wake, I wondered, would anything be normal again? Would I even recognize what normal looked like?

Chapter 42

Victim 8 (What Was Then)

"You know what I'm asking of you?"

"Yes," she returns.

"You can still change your mind," I remind her. She won't. She'll do what I ask of her. Such is true love.

"I want to do this.., for you," she replies.

Stupid bitch. She thinks I share her feelings. I care nothing for her, only what she can offer me.

"You must get close. I will lay the seeds; the rest is in your hands."

"I understand," she responds, staring straight ahead.

"You know why I've brought you here?" I ask her, wiping a cloth across her forehead to wipe away the sweat before it hits her eyes.

She shakes her head.

"You have to be convincing. That bitch must feel sympathy. We must make it so she feels compelled to protect you."

"How will I do that?" she asks. Her innocence disgusts me as much as her ignorance.

"I will take care of that," I answer her. "You worry about your part. You play a crucial role."

"And then we can be together?" She asks.

"After it is over," I reply. "But first, the hard part."

I pull out some tools from the bag I brought and place them in front of her on the table. I see the worry in her eyes.

"Don't be afraid," I tell her. "You can do this."

I reach into the darkness between the furnace and the wall and pull out a branding iron with the shape of a Ø at one end, the tool that will secure the Agent's downfall. Thank you, Google. If not for you, I would not have learned of Roy David Willmecki's treatment of the sister, Brittany Hayes. It's perfect. One sister's tragic death will lead to the other's.

I turn to see a look of doubt on Vivian's face as I place the branding iron into the flame.

"You are afraid?" I ask.

"I..,"

"Remember my letters to you; what I promised you? You know how I feel. I know you feel the same. Your letters were all that kept me alive while I was inside. That's why I held onto them, so I could give them back to you to show you what they mean to me - what *you* mean to me."

All lies. She doesn't need to know. She is damaged, so desperate to want someone to love her. I will do that for her if it gets me what I want.

"Just as I promised you, we are together. It's time for you to show me how much I mean to you. You can do that, can't you?"

She nods. "Yes."

"Good. If we are to make this work, everything must be believable. As much as it pains me, I must do nasty things to you."

She nods her acceptance. I kiss her, but only on the forehead. It's all I can stomach.

"I need you to play the victim. It must be perfect. Real. That is why I have bound your hands behind the chair. You must show me you are afraid. You must struggle as if your life depends on it. If you can't make me believe you, how do you expect them to? Especially her?"

"I can do it," she says. "I will be afraid. I can play the helpless victim. Blindfold me. I can pretend it isn't you."

"Not yet," I tell her. "Soon enough."

I am not heartless. I tie a cloth around her head and stick it in her mouth. I tell her to bite down on it to help reduce the pain I am about to inflict. She nods enthusiastically. I tell her not to scream. She nods again. She looks into my eyes, fully trusting of me. I wink. Then, I slam my right fist into her left cheekbone. Surprisingly, she doesn't make a sound. I pull the gag down from her mouth to check on her. Before I can say a word, she glares at me, and through a clenched smile, she says, "Hit me again!"

I grin. I knew I liked this one. I maneuver the cloth back into her mouth and lean forward, getting closer to her. I whisper in her ear, "There's going to be a lot more. You will cry for me; you will bleed for me. Be strong for both of us. Let me show you how much I love you."

Then we begin.

Epilogue

Letters

Dear Mr. Haddick,

    I watched your trial on television. I think it's a shame the way they treated you. It was a travesty of justice. Couldn't they see you were a victim, too? You even lost your father because of them. It's so devastating what they did to you. I can only imagine what you must be going through. I just wanted you to know that some of us know you are innocent, and we believe in you. Try to remain strong in there. If you ever feel you need to chat, I'll be here. I'd love to hear back from you.

Regards,
Alicia Bower

P.S. I thought you looked cute in court. I've even dreamt about you a few times since.

Dear Alicia,

Thank you so much for your kind letter. I appreciate the formality of addressing me as Mr. Haddick, but please, call me Ben if you should ever find it in your heart to write me again. Mr. Haddick was my father. Seeing it on paper only brings me sorrow.

I would like to express my sincerest gratitude. It helps to know there are people out there looking out for me. Your support means the world. I'm here for the long haul, but I will try to find a way to remain strong.

If not for me, then for you.

I will keep your words in my thoughts and hope to hear from you again.

Sincerely,
Ben

Dear Ben,

I was so excited to receive your letter. I wasn't sure if you'd write back, but I'm so happy you did. I'm sorry for stirring up memories of your father. I never meant to cause you sadness or sorrow. I never want to do that. I should have known better. I'm so stupid. I hope you can forgive me. I know how it feels; both of my parents died a few years ago. I have younger siblings I now have to take care of.

I have a confession to make. Alicia Bower isn't my real name. I know the mail gets screened, and I was nervous about people knowing who I was. I've always loved the name Alicia, so I figured I would use it. I want to tell you my real name, but I'm also scared you won't like it. Does that sound weird?

I am glad I could make you feel better about your situation. Your sentence was too strict. You should appeal. When the police figure out you're innocent, the judge will order your immediate release. That would be a great thing. I'm not religious, but I will pray for that to happen. When it does, I hope they have to publicly apologize to you. It would serve them right for the way they treated you.

If you want to write back, you don't have to worry about anyone outside the prison reading your letter but me. It goes to a post office box.

Your friend,
Alicia

Alicia,

It's so good to hear from you again. I was surprised to hear about your name. I thought about it for a while, and I think it's for the best. It's a beautiful name; you should continue to use it when you write to me. The guards don't need to know who you are.

I must admit, I felt a rush of excitement when I received your letter. It keeps me hopeful. There aren't many people who would offer their encouragement as you have. I typically receive letters from nosey people wanting details or angry people damning me. I sometimes receive them from church groups offering to save me. Crazy.

I have an appeal in three months. Maybe your prayers will work their magic. Even if they don't, to know you tried is enough for me.

Thank you for being there for me. You are a very special person.

Yours,
Ben

Ben,

OMG!! I thought receiving your first letter was just you being courteous. But now, I know. You truly are a decent person. I knew it. I could tell from the way you conducted yourself in court. There was one time the camera caught you in a smile, and it was then that I knew the person you were. You can't look as good as you do and be a bad person. I imagined that smile was just for me. I hope someday I'll get to see the real thing. I hope it doesn't upset you that I said that. I am blushing so much right now.

Your appeal is coming up in another month. If I don't hear from you before then, I wish you the best of luck. I will continue the prayers. I can't wait for your next letter.

Truly yours,
Alicia

P.S. Maybe I'll share some other thoughts I've had of you, too.

Dear Alicia,

Your letters bring me such enjoyment. I hope we can continue writing to each other. I've never had a friend like you. It feels good. I don't mind telling you that I have had some thoughts of my own - some very.., interesting thoughts. I didn't think I would feel such things again, but you have done that to me. Thank you.

My appeal is next week. If all goes well, maybe I'll be back in Southbridge soon. If that were to happen, I'd like to buy you a coffee to pay you back for all the prayers.

Fingers crossed.

Ben

Hi Ben,

I just heard about the decision. I'm so angry right now. How could they do that? It's like they weren't even listening. I read it was the FBI lady's testimony that played a part in the jury's decision. That makes me so mad. Why did she have to say those mean things about you? I don't think I like her.

I was looking forward to that cup of coffee and whatever might have come after. I was so sure they'd realize their mistake and let you go that I bought a new outfit for the occasion. I think I look pretty good in it. If you want to see it, I'll send a picture. Am I allowed to do that? I hope so.

I'm glad that you want to keep in touch. I would like that, too. I don't have many friends, but I consider you one of the special ones. I only wish others understood you as I do. Then you'd be free, and we could meet each other. I will keep hoping for that day.

Sincerely,
Alicia

My dear Alicia,

I had hoped our conversation could have been in person. They are trying to keep me down. If I may be so bold, they are trying to keep me from you. They screen all of our letters. They know the special bond we share. They may keep me locked up, but they can't keep my feelings locked away.

To answer your question about the picture, I would love one. I only have fake images of you that I make up in my head. If I could see you, then I feel I would know you. And I want to know you, Alicia - the real you. One day, I will. And you, my dear Alicia, will learn all about the real me.

Very truly yours,
Ben

My dearest Ben,

I hope you receive this. I know they aren't the best pictures. I took so many, trying to get the perfect ones for you. I hope you like them. I'd hate for you to be disappointed. I only want to make you as happy as you make me. I'd be so angry with myself if they didn't bring you some pleasure.

I cut out a picture of you from the paper. I keep it in a special box with all of your letters. Sometimes, when I'm feeling lonely, I pull it out and slide it under my pillow before I go to sleep. It gives me comfort to know you are there with me. Sometimes, I even.., do other things while looking at your picture. Oh my God, you make me blush so much.

I wish things could be different. I want so badly to talk to you face to face. Do you think I could visit you sometime? Am I asking too much? I already know so much about you from the trial and your letters, but it's not the same as seeing you.., as touching you.

You are right; we do share a special bond. It's incredible how close we are, even in such a short time. I think about you constantly, and I cherish every letter you send. I care about what we have together. It is amazing. You are so perfect. How did I get so lucky to have you in my life?

Love always,
Alicia

My lovely Alicia,

I received your pictures. You are even more beautiful than I imagined. I now have something I can keep close to my heart. Thank you.

As much as I would love to have you visit with me, I don't think It's a good idea. You shouldn't be around this. And others would stare at you and have evil thoughts. I wouldn't want that. I want it to be only us. We understand each other. But don't worry; there will be a time when I will see you. I have plans – plans for us. When it is time, I hope you will want to go on that journey with me. It will be a good time. I promise you. Until then, I hope my letters will fill the void in your heart.

Love,
Ben

My love, Ben,

I would love to go on any journey with you. Whatever it is, I will be there with you. I am yours. I would go anywhere and do anything for you. That is how much I love you. It means so much to me that you feel the same way. I didn't think it was possible, but here we are. It is like a dream come true. You are my soulmate. Whatever you want, I would love to give that to you. I will wait as long as I have to. I know we will be together. It will be magical.

Love,
Alicia

Alicia, my love,

It is hard to believe it has been two years since I received your first letter. I am thankful every day for that miracle. You have given me such hope. You have given me a purpose to live. I have been doing a lot of thinking over the past several months. I am so happy and fortunate that you are willing to do whatever I need. That is what I love about you. And, as it happens, I have something perfect in mind – something you can do for me. But that is a discussion for a later date.

For now, I want you to know how much I love you. It is our love that will endure. But I must ask a favor of you, and I don't want you to hate me for this. I must ask that we stop communicating. But only for a little while. I have some things to attend to. If all goes well, I think you will be pleasantly surprised. You may respond to this letter, but make it the last time until you hear from me again. And you *will* hear from me. It may take some time, but nothing will keep me from you. I have great things in store for us. One day, we will be together. You will learn of those great things. And when you do, you will make me a happy man.

All my love,
Ben

My love,

    I will honor your wish. This will be my last letter until I hear from you. I hope the silence isn't too long. I will wait as long as you need me to. I love you. I promised I would do anything you wanted, and I meant it. Please, please, come back to me when you can. I love it when you say we will be together. It feels so real. I know it will happen. That is how much I trust your word. I believe in you. I believe in us. And I can't wait until that day comes. And when it does, I will show you that you can trust me, too. Ask for anything, and I will do it. Nothing can stop us. Nothing can keep us apart. You are mine, and I am forever yours wholeheartedly.

Yours forever,
Alicia
Your true and only love

A LETTER FROM THE AUTHOR

Dear readers,

I hope you loved *Killer by Number*, and if you did, I'd be very grateful if you'd consider writing a review. I love to hear what readers think, which helps me grow as an author, and it makes such a difference in helping new readers discover my books for the first time.

Check out my website at:

javo-publication.square.site

Where copies of all of my books (including signed copies) can be purchased. You can also find them on Amazon.

Thank you so much!

Jeff

Acknowledgments

I'd like to start by thanking my editor, Elizabeth Kelly. I don't know how she puts up with me, but she does, and I'm so very thankful. She notices the finer details that I might have otherwise missed and offers suggestions on how to clean them up. The result is a better story because of her meticulous editing.

I'd like to offer my appreciation to Police Chief, John Cartledge, for once again proofreading the book to ensure proper law-enforcement procedures were being described within. He was amazing with his feedback. Thank you.

I would like to thank the members of the Psychological Thriller Readers Club and Killer Thrillers on Facebook. Some notable members I must recognize: Brittany Hammes, Jamie Smith, Elaine Rainbolt, Matt Dudley, Andrew Baumgardner, Mark Jenkins, and Billie Jean Wiley. There are so many others, but only so much space in my brain to remember all of them.

I'd like to send my thanks to the WhipCity Wordsmiths for their valuable feedback on the chapters I read for them. They are always so honest and helpful.

And to my wife, Elena – thanks for sticking it out with me during my anxious moments when it gets close to release time. I know I can be a handful.

WHO CAN YOU TRUST?

SECRETS NEVER STAY HIDDEN

Just
Listen
No secret stays safe forever
Jeff VanOudenhove
Author of The Alphabet Killer

TALES TO SHOCK YOU

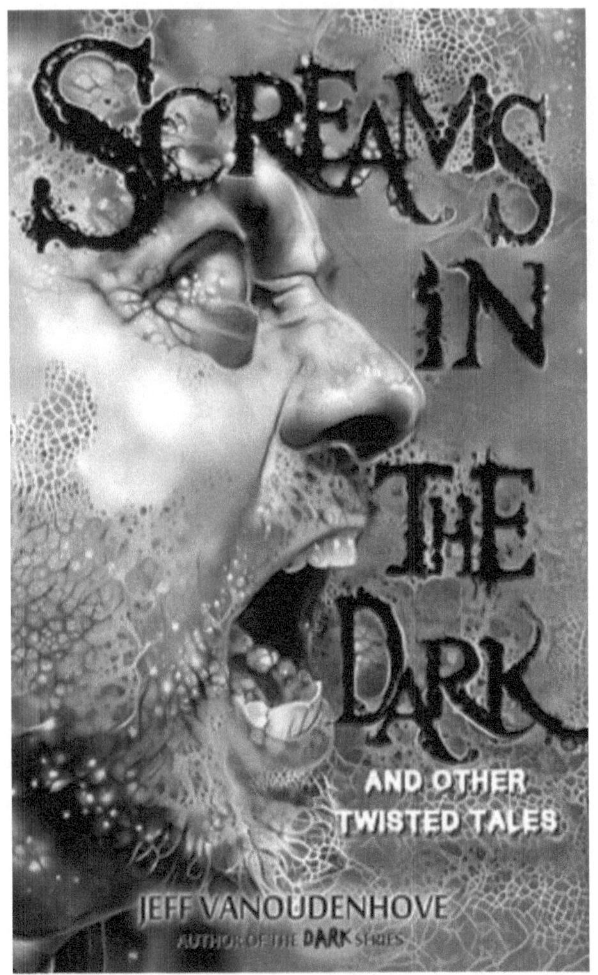

THE DARK SERIES

Jeff VanOudenhove has written several novels in the genre of dark fiction, including the **Dark Series,** a psychological thriller with supernatural elements, crime thrillers **The Alphabet Killer** and **The Letter Man**, the psychological suspense thrillers **Just Listen** and **Emma**, and a book of truly twisted short stories, **Screams in the Dark and Other Twisted Tales**. His talent for storytelling combines unforgettable characters and dire situations, mixed with astonishing plot twists. **Killer By Number** is Jeff's eleventh book. He lives in Western Massachusetts with his wife, Elena.

www.ingramcontent.com/pod-product-compliance
Lightning Source LLC
Chambersburg PA
CBHW032346310726
48973CB00007B/1880